HE DOES HER WRONG . . .

Matt reached out one shaking hand to take a wisp of Lacy's hair around his forefinger. "I watched a hundred men gaze at you tonight with longing."

"I saw no such men." Lacy knew she had eyes only for him. "Other ladies revealed more virtues, sir, than I."

He cupped her cheek and whispered, "None of them shines with the glory of you. Every man there went blind at your brilliance."

His eloquence brought t[illegible]s to her eyes. "Why, oh why are you so sw[illegible] my husband?"

"I cannot help my[illegible]w her flush to his chest. "I never knew yo[illegible] so lovely, in soul and body." She shudder[illegible] he placed little kisses on her eyes and across her cheek to her ear. "My Lacy. My delicate, delicious Lacy. I want to leave you to your own desires and find I cannot leave behind my own. I care for you," he admitted, and trailed hot lips down her throat.

Her world reeled. She grabbed at his shoulders. "My lord, you do me wrong to kiss me so and tell me such endearments. I cannot endure this maelstrom of emotions."

He paused, his face buried in her neck. "Aye, my love. I do you wrong. Again."

YOU AND NO OTHER

JO-ANN POWER

POCKET BOOKS
New York London Toronto Sydney Tokyo Singapore

An *Original* Publication of POCKET BOOKS

POCKET BOOKS, a division of Simon & Schuster Inc.
1230 Avenue of the Americas, New York, NY 10020

ISBN: 0-671-89704-7

First Pocket Books printing November 1994

10 9 8 7 6 5 4 3 2 1

Cover art by Lina Levy

Printed in the U.S.A.

This book is for the marvelous people who make my days a joy:

For my husband, Steve, who believes when I think I cannot, who endures when I falter, and who understands when I do not.

For a wonderful group of writers and stout-hearted friends who helped me learn so much and who still stand by me when times are good and bad—my critique group: Sandra Bregman, Barbara Cummings, Linda Janus-Napier, Joyce McClay, Bette McNicholas, Cynthia Richey, Ruth Schmidt, and Marolyn Caldwell.

Finally, for two people with whom I have the honor to work: my editor, Caroline Tolley, who not only gave me the opportunity to write a book whose characters thrilled me to my curling toes but also taught me wonderful intricacies with her special charm; and for my agent, Alice Orr, whose unfailing support and marvelous verve and wit color my business days with delight.

CHAPTER 1

The Midlands, England
August 24, 1485

ONE MAN WOULD DO.

One, alone.

Lacy thrilled at her resolve, then wiggled in her scratchy, leaden layers of clothing as two fat trickles of perspiration beaded down her back. Her faithful mount, unused to the added mass of her gargantuan clothing and her resulting clumsiness in the new sidesaddle, whickered at her as he walked toward the open gates of Renwick Castle. Lacy swiped at her burning cheeks beneath the translucent veils. The gathered gauzy stuff caught at the inscription on the golden ring of her left hand—the ring that symbolized all her problems, all the unfulfilled promises she'd ever been rendered.

There seemed no relief from them. Just as there seemed no relief from this infernal August heat, her boiling nausea, or her torrid fear. She swallowed hard against all three. Replacing the two layers of veiling as her shield in her battle, Lacy trained her mind on her day's only goal.

Ring or not, she needed a man.

And by nightfall, she meant to have one. Another one. One *willing* one. One who wanted her. One who adored her. One who would fight for her. Yes, by eventide, she must be free of the one who did not, could not, would not, *had never* done any of those things. She must be free of him, free to choose the other one who waited for her—or lose everything she valued in this world.

Another hot trail of perspiration circled one breast and dribbled from her ribs to her queasy stomach. Writhing, she surreptitiously pressed the back of her hand to her chest to stanch the wicked flow and moaned when the multitudinous layers prohibited any relief from the torture of the garments and the stifling heat of noon.

"Milady, fare you well?"

Lacy shot a glance at her kindly handservant. Through her two layers of creamy veiling, Lacy could see only the endearing vigilance that implied Anna's ever-solicitous concern for her welfare. Especially today. Especially on this particular journey, so daring, so outrageous as it was.

"Aye, Anna. But the heat does wear on me."

Anna, one year older and sometimes ages bolder because of her lesser station and riper necessity for self-preservation, covered her mouth to quell a chuckle so that their paid companion, the carrier, could not hear. "Milady, we both know what *wears* on you is not the heat so much as the bulk you carry."

Though Lacy knew Anna meant to lighten her burdens with laughter, Lacy could summon no hilarity. While Lacy prayed she might one day chuckle with Anna about today's adventures, her urge now was more to slide from this ridiculous sidesaddle and sink into a puddle of her own sweat here—right here by the side of the village road and the farrier's simple cottage—before they entered the gates of Renwick Castle. Because once inside Renwick, once committed in voice and body and heart to this ruse she'd devised, Lacy would not be able to turn back.

Luckily, the carrier did not deign to look over at them. He sat upon his rough-hewn seat in his rickety cart and stared straight ahead at the entrance to the gray stone Norman monolith, which today flew from its tower the giant green-and-white standard of England's newly proclaimed ruler, Henry Tudor.

Lacy smarted as something bit her—in a most indelicate place. She shifted in the uncomfortable saddle, attempting furtively to relieve the piercing itch the creature had left her to endure. She succeeded only in finding herself slipping toward the ditch. She grabbed for the pommel and struggled back into the rightful position of this most unrighteous saddle. The bug bite burned more viciously as Lacy muttered a decidedly unladylike oath. "I do know, Anna, my troubles would be fewer—if not my burden lighter—had I never ordered the saddler to craft this silly seat."

"Mayhaps, milady." Anna's pert mouth flirted with a smile. "But then we would contend with more problems than we need."

"Aye, I will not have rough words run to Henry Tudor to influence him in any way before I personally explain my case to him."

That made the carrier's bald pate rise up. Through her thick veils, Lacy could see his pale eyes grow wide in the blazing midday sun. He gaped at her, his first expression of emotion since she had hired him last night at the White Swan Inn.

"Marchioness, ye go to see the new king?"

Lacy nodded, a natural response that sent her coned hat's great bulk sliding toward her nose. She clutched at the offending horn as it dipped over her forehead, threatening to disabuse her of her voluminous disguise.

"Yes, Carter." She tucked her hair, escaping here and there from the restraining wire caul, back up under the hat she began to hate. In the process, the ring snagged on the veils so that she had her hands full of hair or hat or cream linen tissue, all in one vast tangle.

Lacy muttered in frustration as she felt Anna edge her horse closer and then push aside Lacy's trailing fur-lined sleeves to adjust the irritating hat and arrange the veils about her high collar.

"There, my lady. You are once more secure against all prying eyes."

As Lacy offered her thanks, she noted how the wayfarer had never registered the women's distress. He had frozen the moment Lacy confessed she sought England's newest monarch. Clearly impressed, his mouth dropped to his crinkled rooster's neck. "Ye *know* His Majesty?"

"Well, no." Lacy demurred at ever telling a lie. "But I have business with him."

"Will ye tell him who escorted ye into town? Will ye?" The carrier's round red face took on the taut eagerness of a man half his age receiving New Year's gifts. "I would like a royal commission, I would. If ye know him, ye could tell him how I protected ye along the road. How I am fast with my load." He cast out a hand toward his tiny two-wheeled wooden cart filled with bolts of cloth and countless smaller packages. All had been entrusted to him by nobles or farmers or merchants to transport across the robber-riddled, pockmarked roads of England to their proper destination.

In gratitude for how he had protected her and Anna on their journey, Lacy smiled broadly at him. And since she knew he could not glimpse the flash of her teeth beneath the linen layers, she let her voice convey what sight could never reveal. "Yes, Carter. Should I have the opportunity to express my satisfaction with your respect and your care of me and my handmaiden, I will do so."

"Ah, I thank ye, milady." He seemed to swell in his coarse russet tunic. "My horse here must needs be let to pasture. She's old, and I cannot retire her until I have the means to barter for a younger one. Surely ye understand, a man of my station . . ."

Lacy nodded once more and caught the elusive hennin before it dislodged yet more of her willful curls. "I do, indeed, Carter. A person never relinquishes that which they possess, no matter its condition, until he or she has another to replace it."

Anna tucked her chin into her neck and arched one knowing brow at her mistress.

This time, Lacy couldn't help but smile at Anna's continual ability to detect and mark all the comic puns of life. She knew as well as her cousin that her statement applied not simply to horseflesh but also to human flesh. Male flesh. *Supposedly*—she grimaced—*flesh of my flesh.*

Yet never had that been so.

And now, if she were successful in her suit this day,

never would it be so. Her husband, who never had truly been such, would be no more. And she could take another.

The *one* other she chose. She grinned and threw back her head to laugh at what freedom she'd garner. Yet again, the weighty steeple toppled from its silken pediment, and she grabbed at the tumbling tower with both hands. The veiling caught at the ring, once more sweeping up the layers that had separated Lacy from the glaring realities of the day. She squinted, blinded by the August sun. Suddenly, between the folds of her enormous fur-lined sleeves, she found herself staring straight at the stunned carrier.

"Milady!" He gasped, blinked, dropped his reins, and worked at words like a groping fish. "Yer not—not—"

"No, Carter." Lacy whipped the veiling down around her face and in the process ripped a long gash in one layer of crimped gauze. Silently muttering about her fate, Lacy rearranged the torn tissue firmly around her sapphire satin cloak collar. "I am not what I seem."

"Nay, Marchioness. Not at all!" He frowned, clamped his jaws shut, and narrowed his eyes at her now. "But . . . but ye *are* the marchioness De Vere?"

His eyes traveled to her white horse's azure livery. He had helped the women drape the satin colors over the horse this morning at the inn. Her livery displayed her heritage from two famous families—the De Vere glass bottle and the De Lacy embellished Maltese cross. Clearly, the man wondered if she had fooled him about her ability to pay as well as her rather obtuse appearance. This time, her cousin Anna sought to allay his fear.

"Aye, Carter. This is truly the marchioness De Vere Fletcher." Anna cast a wickedly amused glance at her nobleborn kinswoman. "Though soon she may not claim the Fletcher name, she retains all else. Money, lands, rents, tariffs. You shall be paid, Carter. And in the total sum my lady offered you. Simply accompany us to the inside courtyard as you promised last night, my dear man, and the marchioness will show you her immense gratitude." For Lacy's ears, Anna leaned over to add in a whisper, "She has shown you her immense form, why not her purse?"

Lacy shook her head at her irrepressible servant. To the carrier's ears, she offered more. "Carter, I hope that as we pass this gate, you might render me yet another vital service." She sought to fill herself up with the so-called importance of her rank and her combined families' three hundred years of hegemony in this land. As the three of them passed through the huge iron and wooden gates of Renwick Castle, Lacy spitted her courage on the legendary rod of her family's power—and turned to the congenial carrier.

He awaited her pleasure—or, from the morbid state of him, her displeasure. "Aye, milady. Whate'er ye need, I can assist ye. Ye have but to name it."

"I need your silence about my true appearance, Carter. What you have seen and what you have heard must remain with you alone, lest I lose all I treasure in this world. And as you see me now, except for my good cousin and servant Anna, I am alone. I beseech you, Carter, to help me." They came to a halt as the crowd inside Henry Tudor's temporary residence milled and pushed at them. "Will you keep my secret, Carter?"

"Oh, aye, milady!" His head bobbed like a bird

tugging at a struggling worm. "I'll say naught a word of such beauty as I have seen this day. How could I? Nary a soul'd dare believe me."

"You are kind, Carter. I shall remember it." Lacy flipped open her purse at her thickly padded waist, dug four shillings from the leather receptacle's crowded depths, and handed them to Anna to pay him.

"Ah, milady, ye're generous. This day's events go with me to the grave. May all the saints witness my vow."

"Vows . . ." Lacy inhaled, struggling with her greatest sorrow. "I like vows and men who keep them." She deposited an extra coin in Anna's hand.

"God does bless ye, milady," Carter murmured as he counted the five coins over and over in mute wonder. "If ye ever need a regular carrier—"

"Aye, Carter. I will send for you." She would have inclined her head to bid him adieu but remembered the wobbly state of her hat and what terrors its escape could cause. "Good day, Carter." She watched him go, then reined her horse toward the castle's inner door and murmured to Anna, "I hope to heaven the man keeps his word. If he spreads any rumors of my true looks before I disentangle myself from my husband and the man decides he suddenly wants me, my cause is lost. Worse, if he tells tales of my presence here at Renwick before I win my case with King Henry, I might as well invite all suitors and intruders in my front door and depart through the back one."

"Now, now, milady." Anna waved the carrier off with one of her winning smiles. "We need concern ourselves with only one gentle suitor, Viscount Wentworth, and—"

"And a pack of wolves named Arnold. If they learn

I have left home to plead with Henry Tudor, God knows what they will try to plunder whilst I am gone." Lacy suppressed a violent shudder at the hideous memory of what priceless commodity young William Arnold had attempted to divest her of last month. "I wish I could buy compliance from King Henry with as much ease as I can from Carter."

"Mayhaps you can, milady. Fear not."

"I do fear greatly at every turn. I did not devise this plan to misstep in any bog. Although I must say"—Lacy rubbed her nether parts against the hot, slick saddle—"what vermin live in these layers certainly feel as though they came from a teeming, fetid marsh."

"I did clean and air them as best I could, milady. But what could I do when you wished to be off so quickly? The quilted arming doublet from Sir Humphrey I stripped practically from his back, and he not one day from the battle at Bosworth field. I wager he wore the fabric for months while in the saddle. I cannot vouch for its history. If I thought your slender form could have supported them, I would have charmed from Sir Humphrey his thick chain mail and brigandine, as well as his padding. What better to do than ask a soldier for his best three protections, next to his armor?"

"If I could assure success, I swear I would don full seventy-pound Augsburg plate harness itself!"

Anna almost lost her own horned hat with her laughter. "Milady, much more and you would have fainted. Two kirtles, one cote-hardie atop Sir Humphrey's quilt, plus the fur-lined sleeves are more than sufficient. Rest easy. You make quite a picture. No man could desire the overblown creature I see."

"Thank God for that, Anna. I seek only to have this

farce ended so that I might save us all from ruin. Forgive my complaints. You did very well. Though I fear now the fleas"—Lacy rose up in the saddle at one insect's incessant nibbling—"may defeat me before I begin."

"Your cause is right, milady. Fix your courage. Here approaches the first of our tests."

Lacy stopped her mount at the advance of one of Henry's guards. She wondered which clanked louder—the man's leg armor as he strode forward or her knees that knocked in rhythm with her clashing heartbeat.

A bull-faced man peered up at her. "How say you, my lady?" Dressed in a Tudor green-and-white tabard, the man examined her with bleak black eyes. But evidently unable to see or believe quite all of her, he pushed his sallet back from his forehead and cocked a bushy brow at her.

"I seek entrance, good sir."

"No one enters here, save those invited."

At his stubbornness, Lacy sat amazed that she found her voice. "I have business with King Henry."

"I repeat, Henry sees no one he has not invited, milady."

"He will see me," Lacy chanced with a chilly hauteur, hoping that her tone through the layered veils numbed his determination.

"I have orders."

She froze. Her horse snorted, understanding what this man of war did not. In her next breath, she unfurled an infrequent but famous fury. "And I, sir, have gold to pay you and your cohorts their bounty. Fail to admit me and your good sovereign will have no means to compensate you and your friends for your recent labors of love."

Stunned by her adamance—and lured by her bait—the guard fell back a pace as Lacy allowed her mount a step forward. "Milady, I still must learn who seeks—"

"I am the marchioness Catherine Lacy De Vere Fletcher. And I require an audience with His Majesty now."

He ran as if her fleas harassed his hide.

Lacy coughed back the urge to laugh.

To suppress her own chuckles, Anna took to clearing her throat. "That surely inspired him. He's off to tell his commander what a spectacular lumpy pudding stands outside his door. Little can he imagine . . ."

The man emerged scant minutes later, trailing two men. His first companion, dressed also in green tabard and silver leg armor, scowled at Lacy and then her maid. But the other appeared, took one glance, and halted, framed in the sawtoothed Norman archway like Atlas supporting heaven and earth.

His power, his presence pervaded the courtyard. People paused. Some whispered.

Lacy stared.

Fists curled on his hips; long, muscular legs astride; massive chest rising and falling with measured beat; this black-haired Titan could surely heft any burden, fight any battle, seize any objective, and win at the meager glower of his magnificent dark gaze.

He stole her breath away. At once, she knew the theft occurred not from fear. No, never that. But totally from sheer admiration.

Because *this*—aye, *this* was a man's man. A woman's man. She surveyed his godlike visage, cursing her veils' shrouding his finer features. Then she admitted to her pounding heart, despite what details were left to her imagination, that a man such as this could easily hold back the night from the day, the seas from the land, and all of hell's wrath from God's good earth. Truly, a man such as this could quickly secure one woman her birthright, her land, her vassals, her freedom from fear.

Her heart lurched with sadness for her lifelong lack of such a man. What she would not give to gain one glorious man such as this! If only for some small space of time, she might then enjoy the virile protection and decisiveness of one such man. She might gain companionship and dare to renew her hope to share some affection. Even love. And God willing, she would soon have a man. Perhaps, not one so bold as he, but a kind and good man.

"Merciful Mother of God," squeaked Anna. *"Who* is *he?"*

As if he heard her, he dropped his arms and strode forward. The earth trembled at his footfall, down the stone steps, across the cobbles, his leg armor jangling, his square jaw flexing, his eyes—oh, Lord above—his eyes flashing some fierce, bright light that Lacy could not discern for color. He gazed up at her, so tall his lightning eyes nearly leveled with her own.

Beneath the veils, she smiled at his swarthy, mythic handsomeness. His jaw was angular, his beard heavy stubble even at noon, his mouth molded granite, his cheekbones high Norman, and his snapping eyes some fabled shade of lavender. He was a man any woman would itch to touch, swoon to kiss, die to caress. He was a man a woman could cherish. That is, of course, if he ever unwrinkled his broad brow and dared to set the world spinning with a smile.

He narrowed his lushly lashed eyes at her. "My man tells me you demand an audience with King Henry."

His voice boomed at her like ignited gunpowder.

Hers had deserted her, lost in the maze of her daydreams of how his ripe lips might feel beneath her fingertips. Lacy shivered, then straightened in her saddle, her hand gripping the pommel against such raw temptation and all the disastrous possibilities of losing her head—and her seat.

"Aye, good sir. I have business with him."

He dipped his perfect blue-black satin head, and his curious, incomparable eyes sought—amid the copious folds of cloak and tippets and other garments he could not fathom—her purse, tied at her wide waist with a sash. So, then, his soldier had revealed the fact that she came with money for Henry Tudor's hired army.

She smiled once more, yet embroidered her guise as the disgruntled yet polite noblewoman. "If you tell King Henry I am here, I am certain he will not become angry. I ask of you, do not turn me away, for our sovereign's sake as well as your own—and mine, too. I have traveled two days to Renwick over rough roads with only my servant and a carrier whom I engaged to protect us last eve. If I were not so overjoyed to know my Henry had won against the scurrilous King Richard, I assure you I would not have left my home." *That* she would swear on a Bible. "As it is, I wish to see him firmly upon the throne in Westminster and know he will require the gold I promised him so that he might sit there with clear conscience and all due homage from those men who offered their lives that he might rule."

The man acquired an even more avid curiosity, his extraordinary pale eyes traveling over her hat, her veil, her torso like a man encountering the burning bush or the Holy Grail. He trailed his tongue languidly over his lower lip, while his eyes grew roundly suspicious. "King Henry's supporters include few women, milady."

"Aye, save for his blessed mother, who would scour heaven to find supporters and money for his cause, no women whom I know have rallied to King Henry's banner. Save myself."

He stood stock still, his eyes now wide with lavender surprise as he gazed upon her livery. His mouth worked. "And you are—?"

She sighed. "I am the marchioness Lacy De Vere Fletcher." She stretched out her arms, put her hands on the breadth of those two endless shoulders, and leaned forward. The need to save her hat and her disguise receded in importance next to the quaking need to feel this man's wonders within her grasp. Slowly, gently, she moved toward his embrace. "Won't you please help me down from my horse?"

As if commanding himself to her plea, his arms jerked up to her padded waist. She fought down despair that she could not discern the full power of those big hands, caring for her, protecting her. He clutched her, though, grabbing at the girth of her, and then bracing his legs for her mighty descent. In that fleeting second when she surrendered herself to his support, she knew she had been right about him moments before. He was every luscious inch of solid muscle, virile strength, unrivaled manliness. He was everything she could ask for and desire. But she had already chosen another, which required she be successful here with Henry.

On a wave of nausea, caused now as much by her remorse as her overheated condition, she rallied herself for her siege of her country's new monarch.

"Please lead us to King Henry, sir. I am eager to finish with my cause and return quickly to my home."

CHAPTER 2

"I CANNOT SEE THE MARCHIONESS NOW, MATTHEW!" HENry Tudor thrust down a sheaf of documents. "God's blood, what poor occasion is this! How came the woman here today of all days?"

"I did not ask, Sire."

Henry, who began to spin away, now halted. His gray eyes delved into Matthew's with that same relentlessness he'd shown him when first they'd met years ago. Matt gazed at his friend with an equanimity born of lifelong trust and mutual respect.

Still, Matt struggled with words suitable to the enormity of the situation. "She . . . she stops the mind . . . and the heart." *In many ways.*

Henry beamed and slapped his thigh. "Ha! Just as I always told you. She is the spawn of the De Veres and De Lacys, who create the most exquisite—and the most instantly fertile—women of English legend."

Matt focused his gaze somewhere over his king's shoulder, beyond Henry's eternal scrutiny.

"What say you, Matt? Am I not correct?"

"Sire, I grant you she is the stuff of legends."

"Well, then. Deal with her."

"She insists it must be you she sees. She implies that no money will transfer hands unless she gazes upon you—in the flesh."

Henry, who had won his crown by his decisiveness as much as his finesse, sighed at the need for the latter. "My future mother-in-law awaits me, Matthew. I must put the final conditions to my marriage settlement. Go to the marchioness. Assure her of my great devotion and gratitude. Apologize for my absence and quickly relieve her of her purse for me. Then, once done with my business, you have the stellar opportunity to take up yours!"

Matthew examined his monarch bleakly. "Sire, I question my desire to—"

Henry's patience snapped. "Why not?"

"She does not know it is I who escorted her inside, and I—"

"Well, tell her, man! What better chance? You have oft declared your intention to present yourself. Do it now."

Matt winced. "I think it might be a shocking disclosure, Sire." *For both of us.*

"Best to set it out in the open now, Matthew. She has been too long without you. If I miss my guess, she would be eager to know you are finally within reach."

Matt's hands flexed, remembering the fluid sensation of his wife beneath his fingers. She came into them easily for one so huge. More, her flesh seemed flabby, awkward, and . . .

"What ails you, Matt? You appear green. She is

merely a woman. And you, my friend, are the legendary Sure Arrow. You, of all men, know how to handle a woman."

Handling a woman—aye, handling *this* woman—made Matt's mind curl about the distinct memory of how it felt to handle her. Saggy, spongy, lumpy . . . Some element nagged at him about the girth of her—and the weight of her.

Henry came to face him. "For God's good sake, Matt, go to your lady wife and reveal your identity. She might then be so overjoyed, she will accept you as my sole emissary."

Matt inclined his head in a sign of obeisance he did not feel. "I will accomplish both objectives with as little detriment as possible to us both, my liege."

He backed himself from Henry's smiling presence and shut the door upon his king's demands.

Matt summoned a shaking breath. Easier to face the Yorkist foes than this one woman. Easier to fight the nameless knights who charged a battlefield than confront one woman who could claim you with a word and change your life forevermore. Easier, yes. But not prudent. Certainly not valiant. Not for a man who had spent his courage—aye, squandered it—for another's quest of crown and glory.

He pounded his fist into his palm.

Nothing would suffice then but that he meet this one woman on a battlefield neither had ordained. For she, God help her, had been but four when first they met outside a church door. And he himself had counted only ten more years than she when his father and his liege lord had placed them before a priest.

Matthew's heart was wrenched as much for her as for himself. They both had played pawns in his father's knightly ploys and his now-king's maneuver.

Always had his father and his new king benefited from their own game. Often so had Matt himself reaped the rewards of their cleverness. His lady wife's money had outfitted him in silken wools and fine velvets, the best forged Augsburg armors and unrivaled horseflesh. Of all those who had profited from the union of the lowly Fletcher lad to the highborn Lacy De Vere, the lady herself had gained only one compensation: protection from Yorkist meddling and trespassing. And while that had allowed her and her villeins to flourish during years of belligerent contest for control of the throne, political and economic power bought frail compensations to the soul. That he knew so well.

He would give her now what he could. Even if it were only courtesy.

Matthew beckoned one of the guards stationed outside Henry's chamber. "Lord Norwich, summon the king's councillors to the solar. Tell them His Majesty requires their presence to a very heavy matter. Arrange a table with ten—no, twelve chairs for the audience. I will also attend but will not sit, speak nor wish to partake in any way, as is my custom. Please convey this to them and notify me in the oriel when all is accomplished."

Young Thomas, ever compliant to his friend, looked at him oddly, but murmured his acquiescence and strode off. His cohort who had stood on the other side of the great oaken portal now stepped before it to guard Henry's inner sanctum.

Running two hands through his unruly hair, Matt inhaled and prayed for some clarity of mind. If he were to unmask himself, he would certainly need an objectivity that would overcome a woman's natural outrage at such an unexpected revelation. He straightened his green tabard and headed for the oriel where he had left his wife and her maid to their musings.

As he opened the door, Matt told himself he would be rational about this meeting. Yet, as he once more gazed upon the vision of his mate, his purpose fled.

The hulking woman before the narrow arrow-slit window turned to consider his approach. Despite her size, her movements spoke of grace. Such comportment came from boundless caring in the nursery and pampering in her youth. All those years when he had shared Henry's forced exile in Brittany, his orphaned child-wife had been cared for by his father's appointed guardian, a spinster noblewoman and friend of his mother's who tended her, taught her, and tempered her will. Though Lacy seemed to have learned Lady Margery's lessons of ladylike disposition, Lacy's will had obviously rampaged, leaving her with a vicious appetite that obscured whatever other beauties her station and wealth—and his protection—had afforded her.

He railed anew at his own cowardice of the past fifteen years: He had left Lacy to the care of Lady Margery Wentworth just as he had left Lacy's estates to the management of his agent, Robert Morris. Still, his conscience taunted him now, he could have gone to her and given her one person who cared enough for her to warn her from such intemperance. He could have visited. God knows, he had traveled to the edge of her estate many times when he was younger and more impulsive. If he had ever completed the journey, he might have met her, led her, advised her against such satiation, as was a husband's duty and right. At the least, he could have written. Sweet heaven, he had tried often. But just as often he had torn the letters to shreds. Always his better judgment had prevailed whilst he justified his actions or their lack by claiming that such proximity would jeopardize her life and his own sanity. But even after all those years of carefully sidestepping any chance for discourse, now the two of them had come to this unplanned meeting, unprepared for the holocaust of truths.

He swallowed hard against the pain such a confrontation would cause her and watched her leave her lithesome maid's side.

His wife glided forward, a huge cloud of impossible coned hat, yards of veiling, and bolts of brilliant sapphire satin. "Sir knight, you seem very sad. Why so? What says our king to my request?"

Matt sorrowed at the sound of her compassion and her fear. Then he frowned. Her voice skimmed over him like sheerest silk sliding over skin. Hardly the stentorian tones of cavernous lungs. She stopped, feet from him, as he narrowed his eyes at her. Damn the veiling! The material did its work too well, while the light—in the courtyard or in this room—did conspire to glance off the linen rather than pierce it for his benefit.

He closed the gap between them. Her voice did stroke the natural geyser of his good humor so that he smiled readily. "Please, my lady marchioness, rest easily. We will discuss your business with our new king presently." He turned out a cushioned high-backed chair. "Do sit for a few moments while we prepare to grant you your audience."

She stood for an untimed moment, as if assessing him for veracity. Then, she turned her back and, in one whoosh, compressed herself into the carved armed affair. At the movement of her body, he caught a whiff of the lavender scent he had barely registered in the courtyard. So, though she might not care for her person in apparent ways, she indulged herself with frivolities. Strangely, the thought warmed him, and all too soon he realized that it came wrapped in sympathy.

He rounded the chair and gazed down at her, his hands pressed to his thighs. He could with one bold stroke divest her of her veils and contemplate that which she hid so well. But to what end? To rob her of her dignity, her privacy, only to replace it with some other service to himself? Hadn't he, his king, and his father, robbed her of as much and more over the years, all in the name of politics and money?

She had raised her face to watch him, one delicate, long-fingered hand anchoring the ridiculous wobbly hat.

"Sir?" came the silk of her voice in ragged uncertainty. "Sir, I beg of you . . ." Her tone rose, patched now with noble rectitude. "Please tell me, how fares your lord, our king, today?"

Matthew blinked, his heart swelling with empathy for this woman who had endured so many years alone and yet recognized another person's every emotion. She was extraordinary. Not coy. Not self-possessed. Not weak-kneed. She had even traveled without a man's protection to reach her new sovereign. If what drove her was loyalty to their king, he commended her. Surely, few men would come so far to voluntarily relinquish coins to another's coffer. Unless, of course, they had other cause. Eager to know all of her causes, he was suddenly ravenous to learn all her cares, all her thoughts, all the thousand and one things he had deprived himself of knowing lo these fifteen years.

He pulled out a matching chair and sat before her. His hands draped over the ornate finials as he stretched his legs out. He smiled at her, wishing he could see her eyes crinkle with an answering pleasantry.

"Henry does quite well, milady. He is in increasingly good spirits these past two days since the final victory at Bosworth field." His eyes darted here and there, daring the cursed veils to yield their secrets. "He hastens to London. You might well imagine his desire to reach Westminster Abbey within days and arrange for the formal enthronement. Meanwhile, as he progresses south, he cares for his wounded and begins the organization of his new government. He particularly wishes to end many injustices as well as the strifes of the past decades." He leaned forward.

She shifted, then jumped as if bitten. He would wager she did so because his pose had the desired effect of disconcerting her. Nonetheless, years of self-reliance had her speaking in those sylphlike, courageous tones once more. "I wonder, sir, cares he well for women?"

Matthew chuckled, throwing his head back to let the room fill with his laughter. "You amaze me, milady," he blurted, finding himself at ease with this woman with whom he had passed scarce minutes fifteen years ago. "Is it your habit to probe a man's nature so quickly, so deeply?"

"Nay, my lord," her voice lilted, "I know few men." Her own amusement matched his, twining her voice's dulcet chords about his resolve.

His loins stirred within his tight hose. He marveled that with the slide of that gossamer voice his body would stir to its husbandly duties and ripe desire. His expression fell, as did his tone, from his own amusement to bald enchantment. "Yet you do not prevaricate. How came you to such practice?"

"I have lived alone most of my life, sir. My parents

died when I was two years of age." She squirmed in the chair, bearing down in it oddly—very oddly, as if she wished to scratch at her derriere. But presently she stopped, sighed, and continued. "I have no brothers nor sisters. My nurse, the Lady Margery Wentworth, died last summer. I have only two friends—my unrecognized cousin, Anna here, who assists me as my serving maid, and my distant cousin, the earl of Oxford, who visits me often to do what he can for me."

"I see," Matt murmured, her lack of citing a husband hitting him with the force of a battle-ax. "You have made your way in the world alone."

"Yes," she admitted, her head inclining to her elegantly entwined fingers, which she laid in her voluminous lap. Her horrid hat then did slide forward, and with a gasp she caught the wayward item, baring one slim forearm beneath the trailing tippet. The hat once more secured, she gulped. "When one is alone, sir, one learns the realities of everyday life quickly."

Her admission of her solitary condition acted like a sword gutting his enjoyment of her nature. Try as he might, he could not find voice.

She leaned forward and placed one hand on his wrist. "Oh, you must not sorrow for me, sir."

He stared at the fragile, creamy skin of her hand, her delicate comfort burning a hole in his own hand and his aching conscience. More, her understanding of him gored what was left of his objectivity. His eyes burned with some bittersweet emotion he had never allowed himself. "No? Why may I not sympathize with you, milady? One such as you deserves support and companionship."

"I thank you, sir. I would agree with you. But it has

not been possible for me. And in this life, one takes what one is handed and makes the best of it."

"Aye, my lady." He covered her warm hand with his own and felt his heart, rather than his eyes, flood with bursting sorrow. Beneath his grasp, her moist hand felt as silken as her voice and as soft as the rest of her.

A knock at the wooden door made them both jump and snatch their hands away. A moment later, Thomas Norwich stood at attention beside Matthew.

"Sir, I have accomplished your bidding."

"Thank you, Lord Norwich. We will follow you." Matthew stood and offered Lacy his courtliest gesture. He outstretched his arm. Courtesy bought him another touch of her hand, this time upon his forearm. His eyes trailed down to the delicate hand that claimed his sleeve and stirred his soul. His gaze fastened on the bright thing she wore—the ring of inscribed gold. The ring that, through all the lonely years, she had preserved. The ring that matched the one he wore upon a chain around his neck.

The shocking sight made him seek her eyes, which of course he could not view. He cursed to himself. Such delight in her wearing of his ring was pointless vanity. How could she value that which she had never possessed?

"Sir"—she moved inches closer—"fare you well?" Her lavender perfume swirled through his reeling senses. "You look quite odd."

"Aye." He smothered her hot little hand in his own. "'Tis an extremely torrid August."

"And you are not yet recovered from the rigors of the battle."

"Aye. You are perceptive beyond words."

He felt her smile as searingly as if the rays of

afternoon sun warmed his face. "Through my veils, I do detect a certain sad weariness in your eyes as well as your body. You are tired of many battles."

"Ah, yes. Far more than you know." His mind reverberated with the compliments she paid him by noticing emotions he had barely described to himself. "My lady Fletcher, you are unique. And I would see you gain that which you desire."

"Would you, sir? Thank you. You are a true knight after a lady's heart. I shall remember your sentiments in the next few minutes. I have not ever faced a king before, and I need to remember those who would support me."

He grinned broadly. "As a true knight after a lady's approval, I pledge you my support, my lady."

She pressed herself against his arm in affection. "Thank you, sir knight. I need as many friends as I might garner for my quest." She pivoted even more now, turning to her maid but into his body. Her copious bosom mashed against his chest.

His senses thrilled. His heart rejoiced, then questioned her sense of propriety. Did she touch men so carelessly? Or was she perhaps so large that she was insensitive to what and whom her body touched?

Whatever the cause, her action suddenly summoned two demons he had for so many years vowed to avoid. In a puff of smoke, his hated green dragon of jealousy appeared and snickered in ribald triumph. Over the green one's shoulder drooled his blood red brother—that fiend of anger—a similarly slimy creature who bared gold sardonic teeth. Both coiled their long tails about their slick bodies and stared at the man they had so long hunted. All too satisfied, they sneered.

Perspiration popped from Matt's forehead as he watched them hasten to his side, smacking their gums that this elusive prey finally writhed within their talons.

Meanwhile, his wife was smiling at her maid and saying, "Come, Anna. I would have you beside me as I seek King Henry's favor. Lead on, good sir. I am ready."

I am far from ready, Lacy agonized as she walked beside her noble knight along the endless corridors of Renwick Castle. She would have preferred to stay in the oriel, conversing with this sweet soldier of Henry's rather than seek out the king. She sought her breath, for she feared she had lost her voice, just as her knight had. My God, at their approach to Henry, even this kind man had lost his composure. And his stunning dimpled smile.

Was Henry so imperious, so impersonal? She had heard otherwise. But that was before he picked up Richard's crown from the dust of Bosworth. That was before, when he had needed friends and their donations. When he had needed her friendship, her money, her support. She prayed she was not too late and that Henry's power was not yet so great that he would refuse to negotiate. Please God, she recited as she marched on. On. Past her fear to the singular courage she knew came to one obsessed with the rectitude of a cause such as hers.

But when Henry's knight finally showed her into a vast room and seated her at the end of the rectangular oak table, Lacy wished for an armed phalanx to fight her foe who sat assembled before her.

Do not weaken now, not when you are so close.

Count your arrows. Thread the first. Aim it for its mark.

She clenched her hands, closed her eyes, and heard the whispered words of the man who had been so kind to her these last few minutes.

"My lady, these men will cause you no pain." He squeezed her shoulder lightly as he backed away and took up a position at the far end of the solar near the carved door.

She took heart at his comfort. If she could but deal solely with him, she might have greater hope of success. These men, nine of them, looked to be a motley crowd. Some wore partial armor; some wore threadbare clothes; only two sported rich brocades and thereby signified their superiority from the rest.

The door opened and her knight, gazing upon the short silver-haired man who would enter, bade him to the hall. He closed the door upon their conversation while for tense moments the others examined her and Anna, now seated behind her. At long last, her friend and the silver-haired man entered. Though the smaller man took a seat, her knight remained at the door, his thick-hewn legs astride the portal like a bold colossus.

Lacy tore her eyes from their appreciation of him to view the new arrival. Surprisingly, despite the shock of frosty hair, he was a young man of thirty plus a few years. But he seemed much older with worry. He was also their leader, for he sat at the head of the oblong table, opposite her. He took the chair that she expected Henry Tudor might have taken and began the interview at once.

"My lady Fletcher"—he folded his bloodless hands upon the table and peered at her with little tolerance

—"we will dispense with the formalities of courtly introductions. We are men laden with concerns of the country and we hasten about our multitudinous duties. We do understand from our good king that you wish his advice. We have come together at his order so that you might lay your cares before us for our consideration."

Anger at Henry's absence ate up whatever fear had flowered in her chest. Knowing the time was not ripe for its full blossoming, she spoke through tight lips, yet with honeyed tones coaxed the bee to her nectar. "I seek only King Henry."

The senior adviser's umber eyes flickered with courtesy and a man's contempt for a female's demands. "He entertains our good queen, his future mother-in-law. They discuss his marriage."

"I will wait."

"That may take inordinate time, Lady Fletcher."

"Marchioness," she corrected with winter chill.

He inclined his head. "I beg your pardon, Marchioness. I did forget your singular station."

She let her silence speak of her disapproval. She needed him to think her powerful, adept at men's games.

The man pursed his pouty lips, clearly hating to be led, especially by a woman. "Surely you understand the demands on our new king. He moves quickly south to London. We move the court as rapidly as logistics allow us. An army so fresh from battle requires time to bury its dead, collect and care for its wounded—"

"Your army," Lacy honed in on her target, "requires what I possess." She watched the ten shift in their chairs. Only her knight by the door crossed his massive arms and let the hint of a lopsided smile brighten those marvelous lavender eyes. "I wait for King Henry."

The chief adviser checked the expressions of his fellows. To a man, they nodded or shook their heads —all in sign of acquiescence to her demand.

"Very well, Marchioness. We will make you a promise. Please"—he flourished a hand in abandon, making sport of whatever words she would speak— "tell us what compels you to this stance, and we promise you we will set it before King Henry as quickly as circumstances permit."

"I need this done immediately."

"Very well, milady, as soon as his chambers are free."

Having no reason to trust this man, instinct sent Lacy's gaze to her knight's. There, across a room of ten unknown men, she saw upon that one handsome, compassionate face a confirmation that he believed the statement of the king's senior councillor. It was enough for Lacy.

She licked her dry lips, balanced the wicked hat upon her head, and prayed that no fleas might come to infest her coming speech. 'Twas bad enough she felt liquid beneath the layers and the furs and the burden of her quest. God, to have done with this and be gone from here and all her troubles!

"I am well pleased at our new sovereign's progress," she began and noted how the men frowned or marveled at her digression. Politesse, they dumbly assumed, was the province of men alone. She smiled, satisfied with her opening barrage, then loaded her quiver for another assault. "With Bosworth's victory not two days gone, Henry Tudor has inspired many in the countryside to believe we English may hope for lasting peace."

The chief councillor leaned back in his chair, wary of her ploy. "We mean to give it them. England has too long suffered from misrule—or worse, no rule."

"Aye, 'tis so in many villages. Although by King Henry's kind protection, my estate and my villagers have enjoyed peace—and prosperity."

The councillor sighed, clearly eager to be done with her circumlocution. He waved another imperious hand.

Lacy bristled but gave him more of the same. "My farms produce much wheat and my herds of sheep do fatten mightily. My villeins shear the thickest wool, and now from Flemish émigrés, they learn the art of weaving in this new form of embroidery we call lace. My gratitude to Henry Tudor for his protection of me and mine flows, boundlessly."

By the arch of the chief councillor's thin brow, Lacy knew he understood that her last word did not define her true meaning. She waited a cool moment and sighed.

"Were it not for Henry Tudor's uncle's decision fifteen years ago, my estate would not be intact. It would have long ago been meat to the Yorkist wolves surrounding it."

"Aye, Marchioness. Your estates sat in strategic territory. Had your vast legacy fallen into King Edward's or King Richard's Yorkist hands, we would have encountered too many problems to take the Midlands. Your alliance to our Lancastrian cause has benefited us all."

"The alliance," she enunciated, "secured by my marriage."

"Your marriage to us fifteen years ago took your estates from Yorkist affections to our own. You have received from us, by continued demands of your husband"—he glanced about at his ten cohorts and up to her knight—"the means to live a peaceful and profitable life."

"And now I wish to show my gratitude."

"How kind of you."

"And I wish you to display the extent of your own." Her heart stopped.

He sat forward in his chair, his brown eyes weary and wary of her game. Behind him, her knight dropped his arms and stared at her. The other nine squirmed with a few fleas of their own.

"My lady, I think we owe you no display of gratitude."

"You think wrongly, sir." Her heart pounded so, she praised the layers that hid her wild fear from view.

He slapped the table. "I will not parry with a woman."

If he thought to quell her with that masculine show of strength, he chose the wrong weapon and the wrong sport.

Resolve filled her body. "Allow me then, sir, to take my mark. Fifteen years ago, Jasper Tudor—our good king's uncle—joined with my cousin the Earl of Oxford and planned a marriage. I was four years old. One night a man dressed all in black up to his hooded eyes did enter my nursery with drawn sword. He, with his armed companions, tore me from my nurse's arms, the only loved one I had known since my parents' untimely death two years before. He abducted me from my home and placed me on his horse before him. As I sobbed my terror, he took me to a church. There, he held me before the door and proclaimed my union with a man whom I had never seen."

Looks ran around the table up to the sorrowing face

of her knight and back around once more. One would have spoken, but Lacy obliterated his weak attempt with her own words.

"They took me, where through my tears I did gaze upon a dark-haired lad of fifteen years. A priest did recite the vows that I have lived by for most my life. Yet never in all that time have I had the honor, the privilege—nay, the courtesy—of coming face to face with the man who gave me his name and very little else."

"My lady Fletcher, you have had much. I do protest!"

"As I protest the way I have been treated, sir."

"What would you of us, Marchioness? You want your husband rendered up?" He was feigning a chuckle, seeking to inspire humor in the others and her knight by nodding at them each in turn.

"On the contrary, sir. I want him cloven from me."

Men's mouths snapped down like the drop of so many iron portcullises. Her knight froze in icy shock.

The chief councillor cleared his throat. "This is most distressing, milady. You say the Baron Fletcher gave you nothing save his name, yet you admit to his protection. That has been everything, the very reason you sit before us, showing signs of your great . . . wealth." The skinny man did define her assets with distaste. "Ever in our military plans did we seek to surround your lands with our men that you might know how highly we treasure you and yours."

"Yet now, you need not ring my lands with such men at arms. Your prize is won. The crown secured."

"Aye, 'tis so."

"So you will leave me to my private life, having no need of my position—or my money—anymore."

He nodded very slowly.

"We both know Henry Tudor needs my latest rents to pay his soldiers, particularly his foreign troops. For the first time since my marriage, I did not remit my homage to our liege lord promptly. I delayed the transference of my funds because I had in mind this journey. To ensure that money does change hands and his men remain loyal, I ask King Henry for the honorable payment of his debt of affection to me. And a large debt of affection it is, I think. Though I be a woman, good sirs, like Henry's soldiers, my entire life has paid for Henry's coronet. Since my husband has also paid with like ties, I wish to free us both to live normal, peaceful lives. I ask kind King Henry to grant Baron Matthew Fletcher and me our freedom. I wish an annulment to a marriage that never was."

"My lady"—the man tried to smile and found it strained his taut mouth—"marriage is a matter of the church."

"Come, good sir, we know that is high jest. This marriage of mine is merely economic politics."

"King Henry gained his crown bare two days ago! You would have him anger the clergy?"

"I would have him use the clergy just as his uncle Jasper did."

"It cannot be done!"

"Annulments are achieved with proof that the marriage was never consummated. I assure you, sir, at the age of four the bed I slept in the night of my marriage was garlanded with no flowers, particularly none of my own."

Crimson faces diverted themselves from hers.

"My lady, I beseech you." Clearly now this opinionated councillor sought to use the deference and diplomacy he should have employed from the start of their interview. "Consider the consequences of such a decree."

"Oh, I have, I have. You will gain your money. I will gain my freedom, my integrity to chose whom I may for a husband. I will chose a bold man, an honest man, an honorable man who takes his vows seriously. For I have need of such a man, sir. I have need of one good man to comfort me, advise me, support me in my quest to administer my estates with equanimity. I have need of one good man to assist me in seeing to it my people gain their daily bread."

She felt the tears of years of loneliness rise and blinked them away. "I have need of a man to love me, give me companionship and children. I have need of a man to give me a normal life such as every other woman enjoys. You see, though I am rich in my own right, though I possess the largest estate in the Midlands, I am no different than the thousands of women who walk the earth. I wish for a true husband."

She shuddered, saw her feminine plea had captured some and alienated others. With steely purpose, she returned to her logic. "Yet, good sirs, in all the fifteen years of my marriage, never have I enjoyed such ordinary benefits from my husband. Never has he come near me, sent a letter, or offered any other personal sign that he intended to uphold his marriage promises. Were I less wealthy, I know I could not deliver this ultimatum to my king. But were I less wealthy, I would not stand amidst these circumstances. I want my freedom, sirs. I want my freedom from a man who never wanted me. And I want it now, today, from the man who would be king and who used me for my lands and money—and naught else."

Not one of them could find words.

So her quest had come to this final stand.

Lacy rose. She threaded the last arrow in her bow. "I will wait for King Henry's decision for one hour. Then, I will be gone, returned to my own estate."

The chief councillor rose, gauging her huge form and her giant determination. "Come, milady, let us not be rash."

"Rashness, sir, forms no part of my nature, for the necessity of living alone demanded I be deliberative. Therefore, I will speak bluntly. I will have my annulment assured me by King Henry in one hour or my money retires with me to my lands. Then, dare I you to come across my borders to retrieve it."

"You threaten the king of England, milady?"

"We all know the threats to his kingdom are greater without my financial support. Tell him of my need. I believe he is a rational man. Tell him. And then"—she inched from her finger the inscribed band she had worn since she had been old enough for it to fit her finger—"give him this. His uncle bought it. His knight, the elder Baron Fletcher, approved it. His friend and bodyguard, Matthew, used it. I have worn it in all honor and respect since I turned twelve. Yet its very inscription mocks me. 'You and No Other' it reads. Like some jester's double entendre, the words have ever implied how alone I have been and probably shall be if I continue in this farce of a marriage."

She examined each man, wishing she could meet every one eye to naked eye. "This ring, like this marriage, has done me some good but brought me no happiness. I deserve that. I wish that for myself and for that man who has never darkened my door. I pray good King Henry sees my plight and will, like a true knight, deliver me from my travail."

She placed the golden ring upon the dark table. To

her veiled eyes, it still sparkled ironically with the thousand hopes and dreams she had for years attributed to it. She bit her lip, reminding herself that those dreams were as vacuous as the vows the ring represented.

With tears clogging her throat, she swept up her skirts and sailed toward the door.

CHAPTER 3

He never came.

Lacy could barely believe that Henry Tudor never came for her! Never appeared to say aye or nay. Never sent any man, not even his knight who had been so kind. He let her rot in that room for far more than an hour. But before another hour passed, Lacy had donned her cloak and departed Henry's castle. She swore she would now find a way to escape his aegis as well.

Where had she misjudged his need of her?

She frowned at her folly and threw her head back to consider the smirking impertinence of the man in the moon.

How had she failed? By what poorly calibrated yardstick had she mismeasured her own ability to stretch Henry Tudor to her dire purpose?

Her unanswered questions loomed as darkly as the summer night. They ate at her as surely as the eternal question of why her husband had never come for her, either. Devouring her good nature, anger loomed that Matthew Fletcher had never appeared. It destroyed her composure as certainly as did the infernal fleas hidden in the riddled quilted doublet.

"I can bear it no longer." Lacy urged her horse toward the edge of the thick copse, flinging the offending cone hat to the ditch and tearing at the ties of her sapphire cloak.

"Milady! What are you doing?"

Raking her tumbling hair with greedy fingers, Lacy grunted in aggravation as she headed for the cover of brush and trees. "I will rid myself at least of the vermin in my raiment, if not my maiden's bower."

"But—milady!" Anna drove her own mount to close the distance behind Lacy. "This is a public road. Someone may chance upon us. You cannot disrobe *here!*"

"Who says I cannot, Annie? My king? Ha! My *husband?*" She slid from the saddle and suppressed the urge to pummel the uncomfortable seat to dust. "I will do as I wish." She shrugged from her cloak, which Anna deftly captured before it hit the dirt. "I will do as I must." She divested herself of her cote-hardie, which Anna also saved from ruin. "I will do what I can." She grabbed hold of the endless first gown and yanked it over her head, then captured the second and did it likewise service. Only the two items she had borrowed from men remained—the quilted arming doublet and a pair of smooth, soft hose.

Anna resembled a rooster on alert. "Milady, the night is dark. You cannot do this."

"Aye, the night is dark. I *will* do this now. Before we reach the White Swan Inn once more. I cannot"—

she swiftly undid the hooks down the front of the doublet—"bear another moment of this torment." She ripped the ogre from her body and flung it over her shoulder. "Ahh, God, what heaven." She ran her palms over her midriff, up the circumference of her breasts to her collarbones, across to caress—and scratch—her shoulders. In the next moment, she untied the hose at her waist and slid the item down to her ankles, kicked off her pointed little shoes, and stood, a naked nymph for the smirking sight of the celestial man—ha! the only man!—who had ever smiled down on her.

The sweet summer breeze soothed her ravaged senses. She closed her eyes in ecstasy. "Lord above, if I could only take a bath, I would ask for little more in life. . . ." Her eyes snapped open. "Except of course, my freedom." She stomped her foot. "Men!"

"Milady, I plead with you to clothe yourself. I did not like the idea of venturing from Renwick alone without a wayfaring guide. Now I fear the worst if robbers should beset us—and find one of us utterly at their mercy." Anna shot her head to and fro along the ancient road, her eyes round and bright with fear.

"Pah! I have already been robbed, Annie. Years ago, at the tender age of four. I have given money, loyalty, homage to a man I have never known. What else can I lose in the service of my king and my husband?" She sighed and then found two spots beneath her breasts where fleas had feasted upon her flesh. Abandoning herself to the gluttonous satisfaction of relieving their itch, she sank to a boulder while the air rushed about her refreshed skin. She arched her back, stretched out her legs to their full length, then extended her arms and flexed every muscle, every tendon to an elegant degree. As if the movement suddenly sapped her strength, she sank into herself. Her plight plumbed the depths of a sorrow she'd rarely indulged.

What had she done to so anger her God that he would deny her this one wish?

A tinkling response invaded her reverie. She lifted her head, narrowed her eyes, stood. "Annie! Listen! I do believe . . ." Lacy took a few steps into the thicker briers, swept back more branches, and paused, a delightful vision causing her mouth to drop like a drawbridge. "Why yes, it is so. Prayers are answered. A bath, Anna. A huge one!"

"My lady!" Lacy could hear Anna scramble through the forest, obviously crazed as ever to keep pace with her mistress. "I do object. This is not seemly."

"No matter." Lacy stood at the edge of relief, her toes testing the lapping water of a small but useful lake. "I fear for you, my good cousin." She began her descent into the shining silver waters, which salved her body's and her soul's gnawing distress. "I fear you will not be able to tame me to your prudent advice for quite some time. . . . Ah, this is divine respite. I never knew cool water could melt so much lumpy pudding, did you, Annie?"

"Milady, please. This is no time for jests."

Submerged to the tops of her breasts, Lacy gazed upon her maid, who stood wringing her hands in the moonlight. "Do not fear, dear. I will swim only a moment."

"This is not our secret lake at De Vere Castle, milady. We know not where we are or who might be about. We should never have left without hiring a companion. Such journeys are not taken without proper protection."

"Hush, Anna. All will be well. God has answered

my request for a bath and I cannot refuse such gifts as He gives me. Tether the horses. Better, bring them down that they might know some deliverance from their drudgery. Surely, activity will occupy your fear with useful deeds." And with that, Lacy turned from her faithful kinswoman and began to stroke the blessed waters.

Lacy had swum to the farthest shore of the odd leaf-shaped lake when she heard Anna coax the horses through the brush down to its edge. As Lacy turned, she smiled as the two noble beasts dipped their heads to drink. She swirled to her back and floated, buoyed upon sheer thankfulness. She had survived her ordeal. It was but one test along the rugged path toward her freedom to wed another man. She would do more, again.

She had been born with a hardy spirit and thus had always found a way to assault the barriers cast up by others to deter her. When she'd passed her eighth birthday, she had prettily persuaded her husband's kind nurse Lady Margery to let her ride her first horse astride. When she passed fourteen, she told her husband's emissary Robert Morris that she would henceforth reckon her own tenants' incomes and taxes due her. Though Master Robert questioned Lady Margery about Lacy's abilities to cipher, the woman assured him of Lacy's extraordinary talents. Lacy then proved her expertise by delivering to him his yearly due in protection monies two months before the scheduled date of the New Year. Thereafter, her requests met with a quick smile and a wave of his accepting hand. Robert Morris had grown older—and fatter—helping her monitor her estates and relaying to her errant husband news of her feminine achievements and her unfeminine abilities as manager of her vast wealth.

On his deathbed this past March, Robert called for her to come to him. There, he took her hand and pledged her his fealty and his respect for her steadfastness to his lord and master, Matthew Fletcher. When Robert died the next morn, she mourned him greatly. Over the years, his burly, increasingly friendly yet formidable presence oft deterred her greedy neighbors, the Arnolds, from seizing that which they coveted. As a man who had come to her blustering about his unwelcome duty to care for her, Robert died murmuring his praise of her and proclaiming his hope that his master might yet find it in his power and in his heart to do his sacred duty by her and claim her as his bride.

But hope was far from fact.

So that, of course, totaled two men who harbored not enough care for her to honor her by their presence.

She rolled to her belly and would have plowed the water to the shore when a cry curdled her blood. She treaded water and peered toward the only person who could have uttered such a sound.

Anna had been caught about the waist and lifted off the ground by one lanky crow who pressed her back against him and chuckled. She kicked at him to no avail.

His voice rolled across the surface of the water as he offered a few blatantly crude words to someone—who emerged from the shadowy cover of the copse.

"Come out, my lady!" the second raven taunted Lacy as he strode to the shore. "Come here. I'd like to see the whole of you, I would."

The other man grappled with a straining, struggling Anna and offered a loutish remark in parody of his companion's statement. The implication made Lacy blush and bristle all at the same moment.

What could she do to save Annie and herself?

Her taunter urged her in with a gesturing arm, which even in the moonlight she saw was clothed in rags. "Come forward, do. We wish ye no harm. Only a little sport. We have yer purse, o' course. No need to fret over that. Now, I wish to see the greater prize." He snorted.

His friend was retreating to the cover of thicker brush, dragging, by her waist and hair, her precious Annie.

"No, don't hurt her!" Lacy beseeched him.

"Aye, lovey. Not a red hair on her head," called the one who yanked her servant beyond her sight.

Lacy felt bile engorge her throat. If she could not stop him, the man would steal the virginity Annie had so diligently preserved and ruin her for the proper match her cousin had always pledged herself to make. But Lacy had no weapons, nothing as always, save her wits. Always her wits.

"Come out, my beauty. I would see what treasures ye hold without the hat and gowns I saw strewn near the road."

Lacy considered her options and chose the only one likely to gain her some hope. She trained her voice to the level she knew men preferred. "Why not come to get me?" she invited with implications that rippled toward the shore.

"'Tis cold."

"'Tis bracing."

"Me blood needs no bracing, lady." She could see him sneer in lusty expectation as he crouched and beckoned her with waggling fingers. "Come to me."

Lacy listened for sounds of Anna. When none met her ears, she caught back a spasm of fright. Still, to him she would give no quarter. "Have you never experienced the joy of union in the water, sir? 'Tis most rewarding. It fires the senses." What was she speaking of? "It enflames the soul."

He stuck one foot in the lake, then snatched it back. "It's not me soul that flames, lady."

"Then, come let me tend your fire."

Since he couldn't persuade her out, she saw him acquiesce to come in. Good. She treaded water more leisurely while she tortured her brains for her next tactic. What on God's good earth was she going to do now? Drown him?

She needn't worry. He had other problems.

He feared the water. And this not even the turbulent sea but a languid lake. She felt a frisson of triumph overtake her fear as he picked his way along the lake's rolling bottom.

"Come," she urged, a cat offering cream. "It is not deep." A lie God would forgive her for speedily, she thought. "You can walk to me." She fanned the water more serenely, hoping that in the midst of night he could not see how she supported herself.

He tried a step and then another. He grinned, displaying black teeth and a lust that plucked at her threadbare hope. Up to his broad chest now, he seemed suddenly confident. She let him take two more steps.

And then she arched back, her arms cutting the water behind her in a frantic dart to freedom. He followed with a bullying snarl—and a swift stroke of his own!

She panicked, swallowed a mouthful of lake, and came up, sputtering and flailing. He held her by the foot. And hand over insulting hand, he drew her to him, standing firmly in the turbulence they created.

"Thought ye'd fool me. Ye little bitch!" He hauled

her to him by the waist. "Christ in his grave, ye feel good." One cold harsh hand closed over a breast. "Ripe as late melons." He turned her and pressed her naked length against his giant body. "Ahh, lovey, am I going to enjoy meself on your morsels," he promised as he dragged her toward the shore.

A woman's cry pierced the summer night's serenity.

Norwich spun to Matthew. "Baron! What say you?"

"I heard it."

"Think you, sir—"

"I know not, Thomas." Matthew didn't take the time to complete his horrible thought to Norwich. He spurred his horse along the road he knew his wife and her maid would have taken to return to her castle. *Fool, fool,* he repeated and knew not whom he meant —her or himself.

The cries rose like a dirge as Matt reached Thomas and surpassed him.

"God's eyes! Look you at that!" Norwich's gray destrier pranced about a veiled hennin that even in the moonlight Matt recognized as his wife's absurdly tall hat.

The white horse with his wife's livery strode through two trees and affirmed his worst fears. "It *is* Lacy!" Matt's keen soldier's senses had him pricking his ears to the origin of his quest. "Through the brambles, there."

He kneed his horse toward the terrible sound. Then heard another woman's cry, more like a groan. "They've divided them."

Norwich nodded boldly. "I'll take this one."

"Good man." Matt drew his razor-sharp sword and instructed his horse with hellish impatience.

Despite his speed, Matt spied the secrets that might

aid him. His eyes picked out the richly brilliant sapphire satin cloak that had surrounded his wife's copious form. It framed one mellow blue kirtle, also cast carelessly to the ground.

Had the plunderers done their wicked deed before he could scarce perceive his wife's peril? He prayed, muttering vows of murder as his horse chose his agile way among the twining bushes. Urging the animal onward, Matt slid from his horse at the water's edge and dropped his saber. He blinked at the sight before him.

In the midst of the lake struggled one man with one writhing woman—one *naked* woman held aloft so that her skin shimmered silver in the moonlight.

Matt stripped himself of cloak, belts, and doublet. Tearing cloth, damning all restraint, he plucked at the points of his hose, then freed himself of thigh-high boots. He unsheathed his rondel dagger with the whistle of sleek steel. Clamping the Venetian triad razor carefully between his teeth, he plunged into the cold lake and cut the water like a silent creature of the deep. The other man who fought the thrashing Fury never knew he was hunted before Matt snaked one arm about his shoulders, snapped up his jaw, and neatly severed him from his mortal coil.

The swooning woman was sinking past her hairline when Matt caught her about her waist and lifted her lithe, listless body to his own. Still some instinct made her moan and push at him.

"Sweeting," Matt breathed as he turned her supple laxness into his embrace, "be not afraid. I am the king's man. And this poor excuse for a man cannot hurt you anymore. He is gone . . . forever."

Matt shoved the brigand's body adrift with one disgusted hand. Then he turned his full attention to the woman in his arms. Though the night sky spread a sprinkling of stars and lay bright enough with moonlight, Matt did not believe his eyes. Some part of him—nay, most every part of him this woman's body touched—had instantly and uprightly declared that this woman must be Anna, his wife's comely maid. Yet the woman he held was no auburn-haired Anna. No bulging barge of a woman, either.

This woman who coughed and sputtered, shook and cuddled naked to his chest . . . This woman who whimpered her relief and curled her delicate hands about his shoulders up into his hair at his nape . . . This woman who arched her slim back, pressed two ample breasts to his yearning skin, and shook back her thick blanket of pale, sopping hair was no servant nor a ship. She was incomparable.

An unrivaled beauty.

He cupped her neck and examined her as she lay back gratefully, compliantly in his arms. The man in the moon conspired to shine his light upon the stellar creature Matt held within his grasp. Her skin shone flawlessly in the crystal glow from the heavens. Her face, heart-shaped and open-mouthed, stirred his knightly ideals from their treasure box where pain and circumstance had contrived to lock them from his daily life. Her face was the content of troubadours' tales. Carved, wide cheekbones; haughty, upturned nose, stubborn chin. Two plush peaks on the bow of her upper lip. One succulent fruit beckoning below. This afternoon's excessive wife had transformed into this night's paramount beauty. And to think, she was his—and he had never wanted her. Until now. When she didn't want him.

He gently settled her against him, while sorrow drained his senses of the joy of finally holding her in his embrace. "Darling woman, you are safe. Rest in my arms, while I take you from your cares."

She offered some faint sound of surrender, and his heart swelled with bitter regret for all the years he had persuaded himself he could protect her from afar. He caught her under her knees, cradling her to his care. She settled there, as if she had done so for decades. He pressed his lips into the slick warmth of her hair at her temple, then crooned of safety and surcease.

"Hold fast to me. That's right. Now cough out the lake water. You would not wish to digest it, then find yourself ill abed tomorrow. In a moment when we reach the shore, I will find your cloak so you might not shiver so violently. The night is warm, but fright can chill the soul to its very quick. I know, for I have seen it so with many a man upon a battlefield. I would not see you suffer, my lady. In any way. I will personally make you safe and see you to a soft, warm bed where you might dream of better men than you have met this night."

She caught at a sob and pressed herself into his body.

"Easy, my lady. Your trials are finished."

"My maid," she murmured, and would have pulled away.

He caught her noble head with one splayed hand, running his fingers into her glossy mane, and tucked her against what security his body might provide. "My man has saved her from her foe. Fear not."

Indeed, Matt saw Thomas sitting on the ground beneath a shrub, rocking back and forth with a crying woman in his arms. Matt prayed his friend had arrived in as good time as he himself. He would not have his wife weep more for things she could not change.

Matt gladly trudged the last few steps to dry land and immediately sank to his knees in the verdant grass. Tenderly, he laid his burden down and arranged her elegant arms in repose across her splendid, heaving breasts. But when he would have left her to clothe her modesty in some propriety, her cry of *"No!"* tore him from his purpose. He dropped to one knee.

"Do not trouble yourself unduly." He stroked her brow and her tangled tresses. "You are safe. Your maid is, too. Look you upon her."

She did as he bid. She opened her eyes.

And the world skidded to a halt, then reversed its journey. Matt grew dizzy, gazing on spellbinding beauty. He clutched her closer, seeking to end his delirium.

But her eyes twinkled in a thousand deceptive shades of silver. Were they yet the bright turquoise of her childhood? It mattered not. Color could not enhance the endearing oval orbs. Nor tempt him more than manly endurance to keep himself from placing his lips upon them. For in truth, her helpless, pleading look seized his heart as surely as if she had hunted him down and used his rondel to carve that bleating organ from him. "My sweet lady, you are safe now here with me."

Recognition finally lit her eyes. *"You?"*

"Aye, my lady." He raised one of her limp hands to offer a lingering kiss to her dainty fingertips.

She shuddered, her eyes closing again in fearful aftershock.

"I would get you your cloak." He replaced her hand to her chest and made to rise.

Her eyes flew open. She gripped him by the wrist. Inexorably, her mighty will made him bend to her, cover her, his skin growing to infernal temperatures from the nearness of her tantalizing body. He glanced down to see how his golden chain, which now bore two wedding rings, danced above her delectable breasts. His nostrils flared as he watched her round, dusky nipples, beaded from the bracing water, pierce his chest hair—and his honorable resolve.

She noted nothing, sought nothing but pertinent answers.

"How came you here to me, sir?"

At the moment, the only response that filled his mind was the one his body longed to make to hers. A long, languid stroke from head to toe, with hands, mouth, tongue and turgid need. He'd show her his homage in a mate's primal rite of possession. Passion never-ending, all-consuming . . . Passion so enchanting . . .

No. He could never do that. Never! He had avoided disastrous passion all his married life. He had stayed far away from her and any temptation to live a normal wedded life. He would not break that most sacred vow to himself. Not now that he gazed upon his wife's lustrous beauty of body and soul. 'Twould invite those two devilish dragons to dwell with him eternally. And such evil he could never entertain. No matter his wife's endearing nature. For now, having seen all her glorious assets in spirit and in truth, he admitted he cared not so much for his own salvation, but his wife's he would secure by guarding her from his own curse, whatever the cost.

He caressed her hand with his own and smiled into those eyes he could swear resembled the finest turquoise of the Orient. "I came at the request of King Henry. And as luck would do, my man and I arrived when we did. You are safe now. I would have you recover all your senses, my Lady Fletcher. King Henry deeply regrets the delay, but he will see you. He bids you return to his castle."

Her expression drifted from wonder into incredulity. Then she arched up as galing laughter shook her frame.

Matt frowned, certain now that she suffered delusions from her plight. He rose, ran to the place where memory served truth, and found the unforgettable satin sapphire cloak and not one but two blue gowns. As he slid on his hose and doublet, he assumed both gowns must be hers because her maid was still quite clothed. Confusion reigned. But as he stepped from the cover of a tree, he noticed a soldier's quilted doublet upon the ground. Suspicion dawned, then died as understanding of his wife's game made him chuckle, then roar with laughter. When he returned to her, he draped her cloak over her shoulders, then circled her to hold up the gowns in one hand, the doublet in the other.

"I have found your clothes." He went on bended knee, remorseful that she concealed the spherical breasts and tapered hips, the shapely thighs and thatch of glistening down, all of which made his mouth water with need. "You have quite a wealth of them, my lady. Will you not don them all again so that I might feast my eyes on a lady pretending to be twice her size?"

She tossed her hair over her curvaceous shoulder and busied herself with arranging the cloak's folds. "I will not wear that doublet or those gowns ever again. The disguise profited me only a few advantages. Even the fleas from Bosworth Field found new homes in my good garments while I gained naught of what I need."

He stared at her, his eyes complimenting the way the cloak clung, his mouth twitching up in a smile he could not suppress. "I know the fleas of Bosworth are a ravenous lot. No wonder you took to jumping and scratching like a lunatic."

"I do not *scratch,* sir, and well you know it." She fought a smile and failed to suppress a captivating laugh.

He thrilled to see her so resilient to disaster that she could parry with him so soon after the dispatch of her attacker. "Aye, what I do not know is why such a gorgeous woman would conceal that which God granted with such bounty."

She blushed at his compliment, then grinned, flourishing a hand in frustration. "I wore them to warn men from me, but the minute I took them off . . . disaster!" She rolled her eyes, then quieted to a serious tone.

He raised her delicate chin with one finger. "Why did you dress like that?"

She shook her head, kneaded her hands, and tried to avoid his gaze. He would not let her go. He knew her reluctance to appear vain grappled with her need to be honest with him. "Why?"

"When first I meet a man, most likely he stands dumbstruck."

"Aye, my lady." He breathed deeply as he adored her pleading turquoise eyes and pink lips. "I would break the rack of truth to deny such a fact as this."

She searched his own eyes to confirm his even-minded acceptance of her words. "I wanted more from Henry Tudor than his gaping surprise at my person. I knew what I would ask would startle him enough."

"It did. He heard your logic with shock. And anger."

"Well, then, why are you here?"

"He bade me bring you back to him. He sends abject apologies for his tardiness."

She curled her shoulders protectively. "Did he send you to retrieve me so that he might now refuse me in person?"

"Do not misjudge my lord Henry. He is far more contemplative of his decisions than King Richard. Henry Tudor, from an early age, has survived and prospered because he considers every aspect of an issue with minute care."

"I ask the same for this one woman who has been his loyal supporter. Were I a man—were I Matthew Fletcher—seeking an annulment, I daresay Henry would not hesitate."

"Your logic did impress the council but did not compel them to risk Henry's wrath by interrupting him with his future mother-in-law."

"Perhaps I should have told them the whole of it."

"What more is there?"

She shrugged, then met his gaze with bravado. "I want a new husband—a man who will stand beside me and care for me." He stared at her, heartbroken for what neither of them had enjoyed. She evidently mistook his sad shock for challenge. She dropped her gaze to her lap and swallowed hard.

"You bear the demeanor of a woman who is afraid. Why? What is it? Tell me. I am ever your champion."

Her sad eyes flew to his. "I wish it were so," she whispered.

"It is, dearest lady." His fingertip skimmed her lower lip, and he wondered if she tasted as dewy as she felt. "Tell me."

"I want a man who will also fight for me because I need a man to ward off the attentions of a few of my neighbors."

"Who brings you their attentions?"

"The Arnold family."

"You are a married woman," he gruffed, both his dragons halting behind her to salivate in glee. "Neither these Arnolds nor anyone else should come to court you as if you were a maiden. Are these Arnolds not the Leicester cloth merchants who have prospered enough to purchase an estate from impoverished knights?"

"Aye, they are the same. They come across my northern boundaries regularly to use my streams, steal my cattle and my sheep. They began to cross in March after the death of my husband's agent. They knew, of course, that my husband could do nothing to assist me because he was imprisoned by Yorkist sympathizers. But, fortunately for me and mine, my villagers have lately become adept at guarding our streams and secretive enough to steal our animals back at night. My villeins more often than not win the day. But I want no more blood shed. I have few good men with me because many went to join Henry's army as free lances. I want them to return home to peace. I need a man to help secure it."

"I would say you need more than one man."

"Aye, but a husband would deter them. A husband who is ever present and who has a right to help me. That would keep the Arnolds from my door. Don't you see?"

"Aye, I do." He saw a woman beset by packs of men bent on robbing her of her birthright. Her peace. His anguish for her flowed to every corner of his soul. He'd help her gain her freedom. He'd move heaven and earth. But then he knew that to do it he would have to cut her from him completely.

She gazed up at him, her sadness as palpable as the

small hand she placed to his chest. "The council's flaunting of my request today shows you how much weight a woman carries."

He inhaled and shook off his doldrums. He rounded his eyes merrily. "Oh, *aye.* I did learn that quite well today." He would take her, as he had promised, from her cares. As many as he could. Beginning now.

He leaned forward and brushed drying tendrils of her hair behind one ear. "Do you feel recovered enough to sit a horse? I would have you away from here with me quickly."

"Aye." She beamed, eagerly grasping the sapphire cloak closed. "I think it possible. And Anna?"

He could not stop himself; he hugged her fiercely, the action bringing her warm cheek against his own. "She seems better. She has quieted and Norwich nods at me. I think all is well. Wait for me a moment and I will see to my man and your two mounts." Once more, he gently lowered her to the ground, clucking over her like a willful nurse.

When finally he rose, he felt her flowing gaze upon his every move. Honored that this one woman should find him appealing enough to favor him with her appreciation, he knew he had done so very little to merit it. Until a few minutes ago, he would have said he merited only her scorn. The thought made him weak with remorse, then wild with anger.

The red dragon, who stood just out of reach, roared in delight.

Matt cursed the fiend and pivoted away for his duties.

Conferring briefly with Norwich, Matt sheathed his dagger and sword, then dropped his cloak about his shoulders. With a confident gait, he returned to his wife. Helping her to her feet, he swiftly swept her up.

Once more enfolded to his care, Lacy snuggled against him, her face to his throat. His eyes squeezed shut at the joy her trust engendered. Beneath his doublet, his pulse did pound with his fond desire for this unique woman.

"Milady, I trust not your ability to sit the saddle alone."

She smiled so that he felt her soft lips curving against his skin. "I hate the sidesaddle. It wearies me."

"How did I know this?" He lowered his head to send her an answering smile as they came beside his destrier. "You will ride with me."

His gargantuan black horse nickered as he set her upon the animal's capable back. Deprived of her body, his own tried to cool. In the interminable minutes wherein he and Norwich acquired Lacy's effects and secured the women's mounts to trailing tethers, Matthew understood what it was to require another's touch. His every breath beat the message of her lack to every corner of his being. After eons of deprivation, he ended his duties and gave the final orders to Thomas. Surely, she could not yet be watching him.

He turned and her eyes met his.

He approached and she stilled.

He mounted and she shivered.

But when his chest pressed her sculpted back and his legs slid along her own, he groaned at the jubilance he felt. This was surely heaven.

Sin, Matt decided in a sensual daze, acquired new meaning. For it was surely sin to hold his wife so close. Yet this triumph he felt, this wild pride of possession filled his breast with raging longings to secure her from all harm—and to hold more of her . . . now.

His conscience reprimanded him. He ignored it and shifted, taking up the reins with one hand while the other filled with the glory of this woman who belonged to him. He was rewarded with her sigh and sent his conscience into exile. He circled her thin waist, while his hand—wayfaring fellow that he became—spanned her ribs to mold her flush to his need. Her satin cloak heated with the presence of his hand and with the rising temperature of her answering skin.

His horse, long trained to do his master's will at his slightest touch, took to the road with easeful purpose. Matt nodded at Norwich in the direction of Renwick Castle and watched his friend seat Anna before him on his war horse. In fond communion, Norwich and Anna now conversed as they took the road in front of Matt and his wife.

The four began their return journey amid the somnolence of a summer's sultry night. Matt commended the moon's glow for assisting them and thanked his God for leading him to his wife in good time. His heart swelled with gratitude. His lips found a surreptitious but seemingly natural repose within the lavender-scented hair, which in the moonlight took on a variegated sheen of blonds and reds and browns. All the colors in the world did display in this one woman, the only woman in the universe who had ever felt so damned right within his arms.

"Are you comfortable, my lady?"

She nodded. "You are as able a rider as a savior, my lord knight."

He smiled and planted a tender kiss within the drying, waist-length tresses that curled about his torso, arms, and hands. "Why did you leave Renwick alone?" he asked, his voice filled with the sadness he'd felt when first he had reentered the oriel and found her gone.

"I would not wait a moment longer. I was insulted that Henry Tudor cared so little for me that he would ignore my hour's requirement. More, I was outraged that he would flaunt his power over me, for I know he will try to collect his monies whether he frees me from my marriage or no."

Matt felt her torment like a knife to his throat. "You have suffered much at the hands of men."

Her head sagged forward. She seemed morose for one interminable moment. "Save for my husband's man, Robert Morris, of whom I told you, few men have ever shown me more than passing regard."

"So I realized this noontime. You deserve better."

She turned her face up to him. Braced against his shoulder, she admired his eyes and then his lips. She stared at him and suddenly placed a gentle kiss upon his cheek.

Matt stifled his groan of pleasure, lest Norwich and the maid hear his telltale cry. 'Twas God's truth, no woman could feel like this one. No woman could respond so well. Lean against him with such trust and make him want to slay those dragons who kept him from her.

He closed his eyes, purposely letting his sense of smell fill with the remains of lavender scent clinging to her despite the lake. His sin of holding her became his living hell.

His horse sidestepped some huge hole and set her jostling more against his aroused senses. To secure her, he enfolded her with both arms. One bore the weight of one full breast; the other bound her hips. His face nestled into her fragrant tresses. She made a little sound of anguish. His arms bound her more securely to his care.

"My lord," she whispered and he could not discern if she beseeched him or their heavenly master.

He could care not. He only knew he had to taste her.

His lips met hers and he groaned.

She trembled. Her mouth pressed to his, and just as he began to feel the soft contours of her plush lips, she retreated. "I have never kissed a man," she breathed.

All these years alone in her bower, no one would have touched the lady of the manor. No one had. He had seen to her safety so that now he could do what? Plunder what he had preserved? He pulled away and in a sensual agony of denial placed his lips against her temple. "Aye, and I am wrong to initiate you when you are not mine to teach."

She lolled her head upon his shoulder and gazed at him. Her unmatchable turquoise eyes glowed with a desire he knew she barely fathomed, much less understood.

"You are so sweet, my lady." He cupped her cheek and adored her exquisite features. "I knew you would be. From the first moment I saw you in the lake, I longed to prove it to myself."

She gasped and twisted into him, her lips a ripe temptation for the gods, let alone this very mortal man. "Once," he vowed to himself and her as his mouth descended and met hers, breath for breath. He rubbed his lips across hers to feel their incredible soft texture, their innocent longing. He gave her his tender homage and as his lips left hers, he mourned.

Suddenly, once was a pittance for the wealth of passion he bore her. Driven, he bent to her and, God help him, took her mouth in tender little nips. In luxuriant declarations of his ardor. He sampled her, cherished her, and knew at the touch of her warm lips to his, he had never kissed, never tasted, never cared for any woman as he did now. He kissed her frantically, leisurely, shamelessly. With open mouth and mingled breath, with years of loneliness and sorrow he meant to compensate her for, he delighted in her. He took her as if he'd never stop, never part. And she met him, tenderness for tenderness, as if she somehow knew how she had always walked in his dreams. She gave a cry of surrender and delight, then sank her fingers into the hair at his nape.

This time when he kissed her, his lips opened hers wider, and his tongue found hers. She shuddered in shock but pressed herself closer, nearer, dearer to his heart. Some unbidden logic screamed at him not to press his virginal wife to such passion, and he groaned in protest. Yet he struggled to pull away and relinquished her lips with a lingering elegance he never knew he possessed. She sank against him, her hand covering his erratic heart. His hand blanketed hers, then brought it to his lips.

He rested his mouth against her fingertips and gazed into her startled, passion-clouded eyes. "There will be no more, my lady. That was too much."

She trembled and whispered raggedly, "Too wonderful."

"Aye." He combed her hair with his shaking fingers and cradled her near. "Aye, but now I will remember who I am and what we are about. I apologize for so bold a transgression, my lady. You will rest here, safe and untouched from now on. Sleep. Allow me to be at your service. Allow me to return you to our king, who will grant you your fondest wish."

Weariness of the day's and night's events overtook her. She fell serenely against his chest. She slept, while he tortured himself that he had kissed her and thus robbed her of one more thing he could not replace nor justify.

The night grew softer. Cooler. The silence deeper.

He sighed, satisfied to have these few hours to embrace his wife with no one to nay-say him. No one to point out he had no right because she might not be his eternally.

This road they traveled returned them to Renwick Castle, where he would relinquish her to her own desires. Yet as the hours tolled on and he savored her nearness all the more, he rebelled at the prospect of parting from her. And suddenly his journey took him to another castle, darker in his memory, more dreadful to his sanity. For within that moldering castle's walls, Matt saw his three ghosts walk. One rocked, one wailed, one railed. Matt writhed to see them all again when he had banished them from his mind all these years.

At his discomfiture, Lacy murmured in her sleep and clutched his cloak. He stroked her back and cuddled her closer, as much to keep her safe from the world's sorrows as to block out his own. She sighed and slept on.

Yet he found no rest. He saw three specters rise in all their faded power before his horrified eyes. His mother, huddled on the stone floor, rocking silently in her agony. His sister, curled into a corner, crying loudly in her pain. His father, striding the dungeon's parameter to rant of indulgences and indecencies done against the purity of his good family's name.

Ah, Christ above, why did these three resurrect so

easily? At the merest thought that he might want a normal life with his wife, they stalked him. Where was the mercy he granted often to many on battlefields and craved now here for himself? Where was the surcease from painful memories he wished for, prayed for? Where could he find whole measures of it for this sweet woman whose wit and joy and devotion consumed his heart and mind?

No answers fell into his path. He cursed the lack. And soon, too soon, he saw the parapets of Renwick.

"My lady," he murmured into her lush hair. "My lady, do awaken. We enter Renwick's gate."

A guard approached, bid him declare his intentions, and then welcomed him inside the courtyard. Another man emerged from the inner gatehouse and told him a room awaited the Lady Fletcher and her maid. Drugged by her sleep, Lacy opened her eyes and blinked up at him. She flinched from the intrusive lights as he hugged her in comfort. He brought his horse to a stand, and another knight lifted her down from the black destrier. She tried to stand, then swayed. Matt, barely on his feet from his dismounting, caught her up in his arms. Bidding the guard to bring her goods and then stable all their horses, he strode inside the castle, lit now by small torches in their sconces.

Lacy wound her arms about his shoulders. Matt bit his lips, predicting that soon, far too soon, he must release her to the life she desired, naught of which included him. As he took the curving stone stairs, she pressed her lips against his throat. "I would I did not have to let you go."

All too aware that Norwich and Anna walked behind them, mere paces away, Matt kissed her ear and murmured for her alone. "My sweet, I would wish the same. But alas, what we have had must be all we shall ever share."

As he kicked open her door and slid her to her feet, she flowed against him. He grasped her hands and gave each a tender squeeze. "Good night, my lady, sleep well. Henry sees you after you break your fast."

"Do you see me then as well, dear sir?"

He ran the backs of his fingers along her cheek. "Nay."

She made a sound of objection and clutched his hand. "Are you married, sir knight?"

Her question shocked him like a splash of icy water.

At his silence, she elaborated. "I asked if you were married. Do you have a wife at home, sir?"

"Aye." He swallowed hard.

"She must be greatly sorrowed to live without you."

"Aye." He bit on his lower lip.

"She must greatly love you, too."

Feeling as if she had slapped him, he jerked away.

Lacy put a gentle hand to his jaw and turned his face to hers. Still, he would not look at her. "If you are as sweet to her as you are to me, sir, I would wager she mourns your absence with copious tears each night."

"I did not think she ever wept for want of me."

"She must be a fool."

"Or I am."

His bitterness struck her momentarily senseless. He watched as she raked his features, puzzled. "You are no fool, but a glorious man who came to my rescue in a perilous hour of need. I thank you for your service to me, sir. I would tell King Henry and have him grant you a boon. Were I to die, King Henry would encounter more problems than he could care for now."

"'Twas unsurpassed honor to serve you, my lady. There will never be an equal to the calling. Now let us part. It is so very late. Too late for problems such as these to find solution. I bid you good evening and good rest."

Matt spun on his heel, frothing with rabid ferocity to kiss her, caress her, seizing the joy they brought each other. But his conscience—that prickly, errant man who had so readily gone into exile upon the road—had returned to berate him after he'd kissed her. And as his conscience warned, Matt must never touch her again.

He left, let Norwich and Anna pass him, then shut the heavy door against his need to rush in and reveal all so that once more his wife would utter words of praise for him.

Come the morrow, he knew that would not be so. Come the morrow, she would stand before their king and hear the lie that her husband did not want her. She would then hear the bald truth that her husband would not claim her.

Curling into the wall, he pounded the unforgiving stones with his bare fist until his flesh did throb.

Pain brought sanity. He straightened, choked away all human weakness, and let his glance define his wife's door.

Aye, dear heart, come tomorrow, you will be more than pleased to see me leave you. Forevermore.

CHAPTER 4

Henry Tudor may have seized a throne, but he did not yet possess regally consistent grace. He grew red-faced—nay, more nearly apoplectic—at Lacy's intransigence. And that in less time than it took to sharpen her best words on the flint of his economic distress. The mere mention that he needed her money and she required her freedom in exchange for it made him jump from his chair to pace his solar.

"Sire, I beseech you to understand my position." Lacy threaded her hands together in her lap, trying to quell the trembling of her heart as she sought to soothe her sovereign. "I understand why your uncle wed me to your friend. Your uncle Jasper wanted to secure my estates and assure that my wealth went firmly to the Lancastrian cause. My lands' strategic position has helped you outmaneuver the Yorkists. My yearly rents to you have helped you feed and outfit an army. But you are now in power. The Yorkists have succumbed and will never rise again because they have no funds, no friends such as me to aid them."

Henry nodded, clearly not happy she stated his financial need of her so blatantly. Yet Lacy had to make her case as strongly as she could. This was probably her only opportunity to appeal to Henry, and time grew short before the Arnolds once again attacked her lands—or even her person.

"I have never asked any favor of you in all these fifteen years, Sire. Should you do this for me, I shall never ask another. I truly have valued your protection. My villeins prosper, my crops and stock flourish. My request is only the same for myself as that I grant my lowliest serf. I would ask a marriage partner who will stand beside me." She kneaded her hands and put upon her face all the passion she felt for this, her heart's fondest wish. She gazed into his gray eyes and pleaded. "I am young yet and capable of becoming a good wife to some fine man. Capable, too, I hope, of becoming a mother. I have often wondered why my husband has never wanted a wife, never desired heirs. For many years, I pestered my nurse and guardian Lady Margery to tell me. She told me she had pledged my husband her silence on this matter. I even tried to persuade my husband's agent Robert Morris to reveal the secret. He refused. The question troubled my nights and riddled my days. But never have I had an answer. And now . . . now I have come to the point where I want not so much an answer as those things I see every other woman possess. I want a husband I can live with for all my days and nights, all my years. I want a man who wants me."

Henry sat with a thud, his eyes sadly set in hers. "Your husband, my lady Fletcher, has always intended to stand beside you."

Lacy understood Henry's attempt at diplomacy, but it rankled. "His noble intentions never impelled him to actions."

Henry's eyes grew stormy. "They do for me."

Lacy faced the winds of fate Henry stirred. "You are far more fortunate than I. I have merited nothing from the man in fifteen years, not even birthday greetings."

"My lord Fletcher is a soldier. He does not flatter himself that he knows courtly ways. He has worked in my service and brought me the best results."

"Aye. As captain of your yeoman guard and sometimes personal emissary for you, Matthew Fletcher—as I have learned of him from others—is the worthiest of knights. Loyal, honest, bold. But only for his liege lord. For his wife, I must affirm, the man lacks any attributes that I might affix to his legend."

"You are angry. This I can understand. Matthew has served me most fastidiously all these years, never straying from the necessity of the day. While I sat in exile in the duke of Brittany's realm for these past fourteen years, Matthew Fletcher was first my squire, then my friend and confidant. He became my most trustworthy supporter and thus I sent him often on diplomatic missions. He brought home to me much I valued and needed. Money, affections, promises of men at arms and immunity. Now he is constantly at my side as captain of my guard and my personal assurance of protection from harm."

"He is valued by you. This I know. But was he ever at your side? No. You cannot lie about that. You and I know he was often in England. Under guises to further his missions in secret, he could still have come to introduce himself, to visit for a short space of time, to see—if only for an hour—how his wife fared."

"'Twould have been dangerous."

"My estates were well fortified by arms and by their natural defenses. Even De Vere Castle boasts the best of moats and two ringed walls."

Henry had no retort.

Lacy suppressed ripe anger. "Matthew Fletcher could have come to me yet never did."

"He was unable. Detained by circumstances. Why, just this past January, he was seized in Yorkshire. Imprisoned for five months, he could not come to you as he wished when his agent Master Morris lay dying. Matthew himself did sicken while in that Yorkist dungeon. I am amazed the heathens did not kill him. But he did at last escape."

Lacy knew the tale of how that had happened. Who did not? 'Twas the juiciest bone for any and all to chew over these past few months. The Tudor's Sure Arrow, discovered in his disguise and thus detained, had hit a Yorkist maiden's heart and she, in her besotted state, had defied her father and his friends to loose the Arrow from his prison and any bonds to her affections. Matthew Fletcher was once more free to roam the earth—but never did he seek out his wife.

Lacy considered England's shrewd new monarch. "Five months does not a lifetime make, Sire. And many say he won his freedom by seducing the woman to his cause."

"*That* is rumor only."

"Is it?"

"Your man is honorable. I swear it."

"You justify Lord Fletcher's absence from me so adamantly, I do wonder if all your advisers are celibate monks."

Henry snorted, caught between laughter and outrage. "I assure you, milady, I mean to rule an England where men may marry and then, into their dotage, may enjoy their families. I will begin such enjoyment myself, as soon as possible."

Lacy knew full well that this Lancastrian Tudor meant to marry the Yorkist maiden Elizabeth to sanctify his military claim to the throne. Though popular tales would have it that Henry loved the lady, Lacy knew the two had never met. Lacy's cousin and close friend of Henry, the earl of Oxford, had told her so. Henry married for legitimacy, quick and bald. If thereafter he could find some affection in his heart for his bride, all the better. He had fought to rule this isle; let him live with whatever consequences that brought him—including Lacy's need for joy of her own.

"Sire, let me take the other view. Had you not won your laurels at Bosworth and were I now a pawn of the ignoble Richard, my meaningless marriage would certainly be forfeit to the demands of his crown. Then would my lord Fletcher require more than your good concern for him to retain me in this contract."

Henry lifted his face like a lion smelling the air for loyalty. "You have a prospective bridegroom awaiting you, do you, milady?"

Amazed at his sagacity, Lacy picked at the folds of the turquoise gown—one of two packed to her saddle—which had escaped the ravages of fleas. "Perhaps. If he finds favor with you, of course." Lie that that concession was, Lacy had to let it stand. On visits to Lady Margery's family, Lacy had met her intended husband. The lady's nephew, Gerard Wentworth, bore a viscountcy, his sickly nature as a child keeping him from the courts—and wars—of York and Lancaster. Few in power knew him, yet many had heard of the scholar from Chester.

Henry frowned and steepled his long hands before

his stomach. "Who is this man and when might I meet him whom you would favor above my most favorite?"

She smiled, a look that brought a like expression to his own face. "The Viscount Gerard Wentworth did arrive at Renwick early this morning, Your Majesty. He came at my request, knowing I was here to ask this of you."

"A wise man, your Viscount Wentworth. Though, like Baron Fletcher, still not equal to your station, milady."

She arched a brow at the handsome Henry. "Few men stand above me in rank—or landed wealth, Sire. As a marchioness in my own right, only a handful of men merit my second glance. Are you saying you would free me from my baron, and then hand me upward? I have been a loyal subject, Sire, but not deserving of half so fine a coronet as duchess."

Henry could laugh! "Madam, with a tongue like that, I should hand you over to the first bold man who says he can manage your presumption."

Lacy inclined her head deeply in mock deference and glee. Bareheaded this morn, save for turquoise bands woven through her simple coil of braids, she felt her hair begin to slip from its restraints. Why was order ever her problem? "Thank you, Sire. I wager there are few such men."

"You win the bet, milady. The only man I know who can spar as well as you is the man you mean to leave to me."

Her heart thumped to a stop. "Have we an agreement, Sire?"

Henry turned toward the bay window and opened one hinged casement. August breezes twined about the room. "I must first meet Wentworth, milady. I cannot loose you onto an unsuspecting male populace, can I?" He turned slightly, giving her a civil smile from his rueful lips. Then he gazed once more upon the moors for endless minutes. Finally, he said, "I have a care for all my subjects, Lady Fletcher. Including the husband you claim has been none. He is my friend, my other self since I was nine and as lonely and despairing as he. You know him not—and though I fear that fault lies at my door—I wonder if I can compensate you for that loss. For whatever else I may become, madam, I will always attempt to be fair."

Lacy could have thrown her arms around him and kissed him. But knowing he would abhor the disrespectful display, she contained herself. "Sire, I would ask nothing more."

"A bargain then." He faced her, his eyes darting to a young page standing by the door. "Summon Viscount Wentworth, Stephen. I would we decide this today."

Lacy dared to allow hope into her heart. As they waited, Henry took to his cushioned chair and questioned her about the weather, her crops, the roads.

"I encountered no troubles from De Vere Castle to Renwick. Of course, I had hired a carrier to accompany my maid and me."

"You took many chances, Lady Fletcher. Although I daresay the combination of carrier and disguise did the trick for you." Henry lifted both blond brows in reprimand.

"Yes, Sire." She fought a smile. "Should ever I need to escape a rogue's touch, I will surely don as many garments as I did yesterday."

"My councillors tell me you made quite a sight, even down to furred sleeves in August! I would find you a worthy—and heavy—opponent in any tilt, as huge as they tell me you were. Though I confess I could not believe my ears when I learned about your narrow escape last night from brigands on the road, I suppose your appearance helped the matter along."

Two knocks came at the outer door, and the eager page Stephen thrust it open at Henry's command. There stood Gerard.

Lacy welcomed him with a broad smile. She had not seen him in two weeks, since last he visited De Vere Castle to converse on this issue which separated them. He looked none the worse for his journey of four days from his estate to Renwick. He beamed at her, then nailed his eyes to the man he had long wished to meet. He strode forward, full of all the golden glory and bright cheer she had come to appreciate.

Yet Lacy noted as he walked toward them that Gerard's grace and build did not compare to those of her dark knight. For that singular colossus had filled her mind with elusive fantasies since he had left her arms last evening. And though she sought to banish those visions, they would not go. In that knight's stead appeared this constant, caring scholar who wanted her and wished to spend his life with her. Though she could not say Gerard made her heart pound with excitement, nor did his words or actions thrill her to her toes, such attributes were not what mates were made of. Lady Margery told her so. So, too, did Robert Morris. Surely Gerard, who was such a gentle man, would make a worthy mate. He was jovial, considerate, constant, and predictable. All those characteristics a good woman wanted in her husband. Certainly, Gerard should be the one to fill her mind and heart. Not some married man with other duties.

Henry Tudor draped lax hands over the finials of his chair and eyed Gerard Wentworth with indifference. "Come hither, Lord Wentworth. Let us meet you at long last."

Gerard went to bended knee. "Your Majesty," he murmured, bowing his head. "I am honored to be called into your presence." His yellow curls fell about his brow, obscuring his best features of blue eyes and Roman nose.

"Come, sit here with us." Henry's sharp eyes indicated a huge armed German chair to match theirs. "We seek to know you personally since we have only read your treatise on Charlemagne's use of church to solidify his power. I seek to know the scholar whose work has given the world such insight and such pleasure."

"The pleasure will be mine, Sire. I have too long sequestered myself in Charlemagne's realm, far from the realities of our own kingdom. Yet abroad it is said you will do well by England and better than our previous lords."

Though Lacy knew Gerard was not given to flattery for idolatry or personal purpose, she shot a glance at Henry, fearful he might misinterpret.

He did not. He opened a palm. "We shall attempt to give the people that which they believe is so."

Gerard nodded. "Because they need it."

"Because we all do."

"You seem far different than I expected, if you will excuse my boldness, Sire. I foresaw a brutal man. A military man. Yet you are more circumspect. I would wish to know that which compels such a man as you to politics."

"Would you?"

Lacy felt the prick of Henry's displeasure, yet one glance at Gerard told her he took no such point. She flowed back into her cushions, her eyes honing in on Gerard's, her mind screaming alarms. No matter. Gerard did not see, could not hear aught but his new monarch's simple query. He took this as an academic debate between—good God—equals.

"Aye, Sire. I have studied Catholic canon for more than two decades and find it simpler to understand than the merits and demerits of the temporal necessities of princes. Why, this very controversy which has so torn our land asunder these past decades is a case in point. One scarcely knew who controlled the throne when or for how long or why. How then to decide who was right and who was wrong?"

"Right and wrong carry greater weight in ecclesiastical affairs than political ones, Lord Wentworth."

"Perhaps. But that is not to say right and wrong cannot be applied to the human condition. Sire, politics form the earthly basis of the human condition."

"I hate to shake the foundations of your knowledge of the temporal, good sir. But I would say the matters of God are best left to God. For me, I will rule as I must."

Gerard hooted. "Obviously. Because you employed mercenary armies to win your prize. But now that you are secure upon your throne, you may dismiss them. Pay them. Send them home."

"I grant you, Wentworth, I wish peace. I fought to win it. I hasten to London to secure it from all foes who would challenge it. But I cannot send every man home for I have need of an army. And I will have one, though composed of men paid through my own treasury. A national army, loyal to me and the throne."

"Some would say that bespeaks of tyranny."

"You call it tyranny. I call it prudence. I gained Richard's crown as it rolled from his brow into the dust of Bosworth Field scarce three days ago, sir.

Other Yorkist claimants rise up from that dirt like weeds, ready to grapple me to earth. Think upon it: If I let all my soldiers disperse to their homes, once more the plague of war will beset my land. My yeoman guards are few in number and strong in loyalty, yet they are not able to save England from the multitude of challengers to its peace."

"Expand the yeoman guards then, quietly, quickly. No one need know since you will pay them from your pocket."

"And if my pocket is, shall we say, not precisely brimming at this moment, where would you suggest I acquire the gold to fill it up and then pay these men?"

"Ah, Sire, we know that the wars over the Crown have impoverished many, most important among them the Crown itself. Many good families have fallen to penury and had to sell their lands to those who could pay. Why, even Lacy's neighbors, Earl Fitzhugh and his family, were reduced to poverty by their support of the Yorkists. They sold their estates to some worsted merchants, the Arnolds of Leicester, and a rumbling lot they are, too."

Lacy had gone to stone at the drift of Gerard's conversation. She knew where it should lead yet feared Gerard might tell too much. She wanted to settle this matter of the Arnolds' transgressions herself, with her own husband and her own villeins as guards. She had had enough of meddling by men who sought to order her life. She certainly did not want Henry Tudor taking it upon himself to march into her borders, order her world for her, and then ask more of her in tribute, or worse, ask for her payment in land itself. Her ancestors had owned her lands ever since Saxon kings sat upon England's throne. When one of William the Conqueror's knights had won the heart of the Saxon heiress, she took her husband's name, and ever since the lands have been known as the De Vere estates. Whatever they were called, they had been and always would be unique in the Midlands for their prosperity. That was in no small part due to the care the De Veres had taken to administer the lands with justice for one and all. Lacy would not see that change. If she could only marry Gerard, he had promised to add immediately his men at arms to her defenses and aid her against the ravening Arnolds. Yet, until she was surely married, she could not ask the Wentworth men into her borders, lest her own peasants rise in revolt. She would not see such disaster strike her beloved De Vere. She had to contain Gerard's ramblings or pay consequences she feared. She had to ensure Gerard not only endeared himself to Henry but also left her problems for her to solve.

"Gerard, do explain your thinking about the royal finances. I am certain your plan would interest our king."

Gerard cleared his throat and suppressed a grin. "Well, yes. There is one thing you can do quickly and with vast results to net a huge sum of money to your purposes."

Henry arched a blond brow. "To any suggestion about money I will always lend an ear."

"Since the dynastic quarrels began over forty years ago, not only have many knights become poor with the fighting but many of their lands have changed hands. Some of those lands have been purchased legally, some taken by right of conquest."

Henry shifted. "Aye, we agreed to this fact."

"So too has the Crown lost lands. None of them has been purchased legally, all of them have been taken by right of conquest. Yet even in my homeland near Chester, the number of royal lands taken astounds me. And so, I always asked myself, what if the Crown were strong enough to take them back?"

Henry snorted. "I have only recently won my right to wear the coronet. I cannot now ride off in quest of all those lands my predecessors frittered away."

"I would not suggest that. But what if you decreed they are to be returned to the Crown? At least in payment of yearly tribute?"

"Kings may decree whatever they will. 'Tis the enforcement that trips them up."

"Ah, but Sire, the back of the Yorkists is broken. Else how could you have won within a few hours at Bosworth? Why have so many Yorkists come to your cause these past few years? Because they are poor in spirit and in truth. One decree from you that royal lands must return to royal protection and the English will comply. They want no more fighting. They are impressed with your swift victory and will do much to see you sit for years without dispute. They do not know that your need for money makes you prudent." Gerard glanced from Henry to Lacy, implying the king's need for Lacy's money. "The English welcome you and will do what you wish, as long as it means no more war."

Henry's gray eyes shimmered with excitement, and Lacy marveled at the cause. "You, good sir, have just devised a way to let a military brute become a tyrant before the populace know their plight."

"History shows that much must occur between the conquest and the glory of absolute rule. You have won hearts. Use that advantage and claim those lands which are yours with all due haste. Let the current so-called owners administer them if they seem loyal to you. Or better, put loyal agents in their places. The money these lands bring will pay all your debts, build your army, and secure the crown for your descendants."

"Viscount Wentworth, you have just as good a head for politics as for religion. Is it the same for marriage?" Henry grinned as if the sun had entered the solar. "Let us hear why you do seek to marry this fine lady."

Lacy breathed in ripe relief.

Gerard cast her an assuring glance, then explained simply, "I love her."

"Commendable, and certainly an asset to this lady who has served us so well in so many extraordinary ways." Henry acknowledged Lacy's contributions with a nod, then turned a placid face to Gerard. "But surely somewhere in your reading, good sir, you discovered that the *chansons* lauded love for a damsel as proper only from afar. Love has no place in marriage, even according to the bards."

Lacy fidgeted to hear confirmation of this. Though she knew it, accepted it herself enough to contemplate marriage to the kindly Gerard, Henry's words gutted her. It was so difficult to accept the fact that a daring, darling man existed whom she might favor as a mate—and know that even if he were free and hers, he might not thrill to her as she did him. He might discount such feelings as unworthy of a marriage.

Gerard smacked his lips. "Our love is of a nature that the bards would find acceptable. But even if it were more . . . romantic, now in the new state to come, love between a man and woman should be acceptable. I should think, Sire, such passion should be highly desired, contributing as it must to every day's peace."

Henry chuckled so hard, tears formed at his eyes.

He pinched the bridge of his nose, then finally faced Gerard. "My dear sir, I have seen passions that burned cottages, killed children, scourged whole families. True love and passion are not always intertwined, nor should they be. Nay, my good sir, love—romantic love—is not the best emotion for the marriage bed. Respect often bodes better."

"Sire, Lacy and I respect each other's minds. And our love is based on that. We will be very happy."

"A prediction all bridegrooms should make."

"But I have proof, Sire."

Henry moved not a muscle.

Ooooo, if Lacy could have disappeared, she would have bartered with a witch. Where were Gerard's fabled wits?

Henry pursed his lips. "What proof is that, Lord Wentworth?"

"Lacy and I have spent much time together, Your Majesty. We are well suited."

Lacy dared not look at Henry. She dared not even swallow, breathe, or . . .

"Tell me more."

"I have taught Lacy a smattering of Greek. She reads Latin quite well as it is, so I did not have to tutor her in that. She has been helpful in my newest research."

"Research?"

"Into the temporal affairs of the papacy before the Second Council of Nicaea in 787 when the—"

"I know what the Council of Nicaea did. You mean to tell me," Henry said quite slowly, "that the two of you have passed hours together poring over books?"

"And papers that I have been most blessed to find and which recount in detail—"

Henry stood. "Lady Fletcher, you verify this?"

She could only blink her answer.

"Good Christ rolling in his grave!" Henry backhanded his brow.

Lacy sat aghast, never predicting such vehemence from the cool, collected Henry. He made her blood drain.

Meanwhile, Gerard only took umbrage. "Sire, it is not seemly that—"

"Lord Wentworth, it is not right that you spend hours alone with a married woman, let alone that you admit to them."

"My aunt, Lady Margery—who was Lacy's guardian—allowed it. She introduced us when we were young. Lacy had no children as friends, save me. Lacy has often helped me with my studies. Lady Margery condoned it. Lacy now helps me translate the documents."

"I don't care if she helps you fabricate them! You have been alone with a woman in her bower!"

Gerard huffed. "It was not her bower but her hall. And it was the lady herself who invited me in, Sire."

Henry narrowed his eyes at Lacy.

She knew Henry's question and somehow voiced an explanation. "Save for Lady Margery's instructions, I have always been left to myself, Sire. Only she and Robert Morris have ever come to say me nay. Furthermore, I have chosen well. Never has scandal haunted my doorstep. Affirm that now yourself."

"Aye, 'tis true. No scandal ever reached my ears. But this is unseemly, Lady Fletcher. If your husband knew of this, he would be sore distressed."

Lacy's mouth fell open. "Why would that be? My esteemed husband cares only if another man cares for me? That is absurd. My husband never showed distress over me for any other reason. I find it amazing that he would change his habits now."

Gerard nodded. "My Lady Fletcher is correct. Never has her husband been a factor in our thinking. Of course, we knew he was your man, but once you won the crown, Lacy and I felt assured that you would see this rationally and not delay the annulment based on private prejudices." When Henry arched two brows at that, Gerard hastened to answer. "We knew that Matthew Fletcher's father had always pledged his allegiance to your father and your uncle. We knew most of your advisers come from an elite corps of extremely loyal men. Though you need Lacy's money, we thought—"

"Enough!" Henry thrust up a rigid palm.

"Sire . . ." Lacy pleaded, mad to ameliorate Gerard's mistake of carelessly mentioning her money.

Henry looked to his page. "Stephen, summon Lord Fletcher."

Lacy sprang to her feet. "Your Majesty, no! I have no desire to meet my husband now. I wish only to be parted from him. Please, I—"

"Sit down, Lacy. Hurry, Stephen, do as I say and bring my Lord Fletcher to us immediately. I should have done so in the beginning, despite whatever Matthew requested of me. This marriage might have been created to my benefit, but it shall be debated to everyone's benefit. I refuse to make decisions that leave me vulnerable from all parties." Henry cast a warning eye on Gerard, who took the hint and refrained from reverting to a discussion of tyranny versus heavenly sanction.

Lacy drifted to her chair, drowning in a new nightmare. Long ago, she had prayed for the day when she would come face to face with her husband. On her knees or totally prostrate, she had spent hours on the cold, hard stones of despair before the altar in her private chapel. She offered prayers, promised obedience, even made delicate bribes with a God who never obliged, much less listened to her pleas. She wanted a husband. She had one. Why could she not befriend him? Enjoy him? Serve him? Comfort him?

Yet God gave her no answer. Soon she stopped seeking one. For a time, bitterness ate at her good nature. Her days grew weary and joyless. She wrestled with herself to be relieved of her resentment, and when she won her struggle, she rejoiced. Thereafter, she returned to her devotions and prayed merely for that which seemed appropriate—her husband's safety. When such news came, usually via Robert Morris, Lacy would thank her God but ask naught else. She knew that to ask was such a waste of knees and breath and hope. Still a child of her God, she feared that the lack of her attention might now cause Him to strike her down for neglect by sending her the very man she no longer wanted.

What was far worse was that He now visited her with a king who was less than pleased with her. And at this moment, Lacy feared far more the temporal than the heavenly hand of power.

When the little page returned and stood before his master, Lacy could not take her eyes from his cherubic face. When the boy departed, she stared straight ahead. To look upon the dark figure who stood at her peripheral vision would be to contemplate all those faded dreams of childhood when she had required a protector and all the failed fantasies of girlhood when she had yearned for a lover. Now a woman, she had put those silly illusions aside and sought those tangible assets within reach. A man who valued her mind. A man whose mind many acclaimed. A man whose very presence deterred those others who would use and abuse her.

She could not bring herself to look upon the one man who had denied her her dreams by his very absence. The very idea brought tears to her eyes and tremors to her lips. She fought both in a losing battle. She had girded herself so completely for this siege, yet she had not steeled her heart. Oh, how she had vowed not to show weakness before Henry. And here she sat, unable to show other than terror while her tears seeped down her cheeks.

"Sire," this husband who was none whispered in homage to his king.

Tears clouded her vision but not so completely that she couldn't detect how very large he was, how unsure how to proceed, how distressed by her sadness. She could hear him swallow hard. "Sire, what would you of me?"

Her gaze flew to Henry, who examined her husband intricately, then narrowed his eyes at him. "Lord Fletcher, know you that your lady wishes to wed another man?"

No introductions, no pleasantries. Only cold indifference to the agony of the years and frigid service to the matter of the moment.

Her husband shifted toward Gerard. "No. No certain man."

"This man seeks her hand. He is Viscount Gerard Wentworth, a scholar of some repute. A worthy man, though I must add he has spent time with your good wife alone."

"I see." She could feel her husband's eyes fall over her. "I would ask some time with my wife alone, Sire."

"Justly so, Lord Fletcher. We grant you a few minutes. Come, Wentworth."

As Henry swept from his solar with a startled Wentworth in his wake, Lacy trembled.

"Milady . . ." The man reached out a hand and as if he were a viper, she ran to the diamond cut window. She braced herself against the sill while sobs destroyed whatever serenity she had preserved for herself.

He came to stand behind her. Here, so close, she could detect his power, his heat, his huge body surrounding her, claiming her . . .

She felt his hands upon her shoulders, gently trying to turn her. "Lacy," he rasped, "look at me."

Her breath halted, her head shook.

"Lacy." He sounded as if he fought tears of his own.

His voice reached into the cavern of her despair to lull her. That it stilled her amazed her, and she froze.

"Lacy, please don't cry. My sweet wife, I would see you laugh." This time, his hands cupped her shuddering shoulders with strong purpose and pressed her back against his chest. He was so strong, so insistent, her sorrow had her sinking to him. In this man's arms in the exact attitude of hours before with that other man of her dreams, finer facets of that event returned to her. The warmth, the breadth, the muscular might of that singular man who also stopped her breath and her heart tormented her. She closed her eyes and bit back a sob for what she really wanted and could never have.

"Lacy, Lacy. I did not want it this way. I did not wish to prolong the agony. I told Henry to give you what you desire. I told him I would not stand in your way. Believe me, please." He bound her closer and placed a tender kiss within her curls. "I did not want us to meet. I told Henry it would bring no good. Only this. More tears for you, my darling. And I want you happy, laughing, loved, always."

His words made so little sense, but his voice . . . Ah, his divine velvet voice summoned visions of a man, the only man, who had ever stirred her body and soul.

Her head shifted against his broad shoulder. Her mouth dropped open as her eyes—her startled eyes—took in his.

"I must be mad," she murmured, her body frozen with the chaos in her mind.

"No, I am." He stroked away her tears with a thumb. His eyes traversed her features with tender agony. "Your skin, here where last night I kissed you, bears the abrasions of my beard. God, I have hurt you in so many ways, though for years and years I never knew it. I have much for which to ask your forgiveness—and God's as well, I fear."

She heard his confession with incredulity that had her turning in his arms and reaching up a quivering hand to trace his sculpted brow, his lush lashes, his high cheekbones, and trembling lips. He closed his eyes. He kissed her palm. She flowed nearer. How could this one ideal man possibly be her husband?

Shock came with the stroke of his lips to her sensitized skin. "How could you not tell me who you were last night?"

"Last night is the most heinous of my crimes against you," he mourned, while his eyes devoured hers and his fingers spanned into her hair. "I did not reveal who I was. I could not. For I am no fit man for the likes of you, my sweet. I wished you never to gaze upon me with any knowledge of my identity. 'Twould have made our final parting simpler. Yet our king did see fit to bring us together despite my plea of this morning. I would that you not sorrow. I would give you that which you desire."

Anger uncoiled in her mind. He had given her kisses and caresses, leaving her with false impressions and heartbreaking turmoil. Yet from experience she knew anger always brought her less satisfaction than facts. "Why be concerned with that after all these years?"

Avoiding her eyes, he combed her hair with languid fingers. "Because now at last Henry wears the crown, and the need of each of us for the other diminishes. You said that yourself yesterday."

Logic banished her anger, leaving utter wonder to trail an equanimity that astonished her. She knew she should have stepped from his embrace, accused, screamed, berated him for years of loss as well as last night's actions, and yet . . . and yet, she could only marvel at the sight of her dream come true. "Last night . . ." was all she could manage in her joy.

"I will take the memory to my grave."

Echoing his thought, she burrowed into his massive chest and warm concern. She hiccupped, calmed, and reveled in the feel of his large hands stroking down her back, the way she had so enjoyed last night. The way she had so longed to be coddled by a man. By her husband.

"Aye." He perched his jaw on her head and fit his body's broad valleys and hollows to the complement of hers. "Whatever you want, you shall have it."

"A true husband. In name and deed."

Matt stopped his hands. "This Wentworth, then?"

Lacy gulped, unable to answer truthfully. For though she had wanted Gerard for her husband, she wanted this man more. And for reasons none, ironically, would find acceptable.

Matt resumed his stroking. "Do you care for him?"

Lacy's head fell back and her eyes met his in leisured scrutiny. He was so very handsome with all that blue-black hair and swarthy skin, those absurdly luscious lavender eyes, and a bone structure across cheeks and chin and shoulders that mocked classic statues for their so-called perfection. She wished she could trace his jaw, caress his hair, kiss his mellow eyes. She wished she didn't have to speak of Gerard. "Yes, in the ways one cares for an old friend."

Matt paused, seeming not to breathe. "Many marriages are made of less."

Soundlessly, she said, "I know."

He let his head fall back and cursed the air blue. Then he crushed her closer, his one hand thrust into her hair at her nape, his lips buried against her crown. "God, this is wrong of me to hold you, I know it." With a cry of agreement, she wound her arms around him and pressed her mouth to the strong column of his throat. "If marriage to Wentworth is what you want, then you must have him. I will see to it. Fear not, my lovely Lacy. We will overcome Henry's wrath. I will help you. Come . . ." He dragged her from his embrace and smoothed her hair behind her ear. Then he smiled so sadly she thought she'd give way to sobbing again. "Tell me, have you spent time with Wentworth alone as Henry says?"

"Aye, but I did nothing with Gerard except read and translate papers."

Matt clenched his jaw. "I believe you. Still, Henry is appalled. We must find a way to calm him."

"Why is it his concern?"

"Because, married to me, you are as much his ward

as my own. He is a very honorable man and sees to his responsibilities with diligence."

He took her hand. "Come. I will call Henry and see he knows your desires."

She pulled him back as he turned. "I have one request of you before you go."

"What is that, my sweet?"

She wished for one favor from this man before she could never ask another thing of him again. "Kiss me as you did last night."

"No, I don't think . . ."

She tilted her head at him. "Please, once before we no longer have the right. I would not walk the rest of my days on this good earth wondering if what I felt last night were merely hellish delusion or truth."

"Lacy," he groaned, "we can't. Honor prohibits . . ."

She cast her eyes to the floor, began to turn . . .

His powerful arms caught her, bound her like chain mail. "No! I won't leave you thinking last night meant nothing to me! Last night *was* real. I scarce believe it myself." His eyes lowered to her mouth. "Shall I tell you how I felt when I held you? Tasted you?" She could only swallow painfully and meet his eyes with terrible hope. "Ah, Lacy, you unravel my every thought and string out all my noble intentions."

He bent to her, cradled her head in his hand, while his other hand forged her to him from breasts to belly to thighs. He placed his mouth on hers and gave her his breath. She took it, returning to him her own joy in his surrender. He moaned and kissed her liberally, tracing the contours of her lips. "Lacy, last night, I felt like this. I felt like a man gone to heaven. Lacy," he implored between explorations that made her head spin, "last night, I thought I would die if I did not kiss you, have you once. And now"—he took her lips endlessly in ravenous little nips and luxuriant, stroking, wet kisses—"now I know once will never be enough. For you are scrumptious. I love your mouth." He made her melt with the delicate play of his tongue with hers. "You give your mouth so freely and you taste—ah, you taste even better than last night. You are a banquet for a man who starves only for you."

She swooned, dizzy with his ardor, delighted with his words, his passion. She clutched at him, clung to him, moaned, and kissed him back.

His fingers found the firm fullness of her breast. His thumb circled her nipple, and through her fine gown, she felt a showerburst of stars.

"Matthew, Matthew!" She plunged her hands into his hair, anchored herself, and then arched to his conquering moves.

His mouth traveled to replace his thumb and suckle through the filmy linen gown her begging breast. At the first warmth of his lips, Lacy felt flames lick along her senses to every corner of her being. She writhed, afire with his desire and her own need to have more of some elusive, unnameable surcease.

"My Lord Fletcher!"

Matt stilled at the sound of Henry's outrage. Lacy sank to Matt's chest, aflame still and searching for a way to douse the conflagration her husband so easily ignited.

Henry stomped across the room. "What is the meaning of this, my lord?"

Matt turned to face his sovereign and Gerard, while he kept Lacy securely behind him. "We were saying farewell."

Henry glanced at the two of them. "Fare well, *indeed.*" He frowned at Matt. "That was no parting embrace, sir, but a welcoming one." He turned his back on them all and went to his desk to ponder.

When Henry raised his face, Lacy detected some change in the atmosphere. Lightning streaked. The air calmed. A storm was about to break and she knew not why or how. She glanced at her husband and knew from his expression he felt the coming tumult. She wished she were as serene as he, for Matt would know the nature of such disasters, having served his liege for all these years. Lacy was not so fortunate. She came to stand beside her husband and mentally braced herself.

Henry eyed her indifferently. "My good lady, I have listened to your plea. And those of these two men. I hear your logic. Now hear mine. I wonder if the three of you really do know what you want. Your happiness is precious to me, for as your sovereign I wish all in this new kingdom to be happy."

Lacy heard Matt grind his teeth in vexation. She understood. She did not think Henry a pompous ass. Why was the man prattling?

"Therefore, for the next month I shall take this matter into advisement. So should you all. To make this more expedient, we shall decree a few . . . changes. My lady Fletcher, you shall attend me here at court. We move on toward London tomorrow and you shall come with me. Here, under my guardianship, we shall see you daily and discuss this affair."

"But, Sire, I did not prepare to remain long with you. I have few clothes and I must return to my estates. I have pressing matters."

"None so pressing as matrimonial matters, eh?"

She was checked. "Yes, your majesty."

"As for you, Lord Wentworth, we do find your

insights useful to our new directions of statecraft. We bid you stay with us, if you can."

"I would be delighted, Sire. Though I do wish a speedy end to this issue of my lady Fletcher's first marriage."

"We shall resolve it with all due speed, sir. And as for you, my lord Fletcher"—Henry threw a wan smile at his friend—"you have served me well and long for so many years without reprieve, that I do think relief from your duties for a spell might improve your disposition."

Matt's brows shot to his hairline. "I need no rest, no finer disposition, Sire. If anything has ever *in*disposed me, it has been this matter of my marriage—"

"Aye, Matt, *that* is very clear to me. Therefore, I relieve you of your duties for the next month. Save for the posting of the guard night and day."

Matt mashed his mouth together. Lacy knew he strangled words he might regret.

Lacy smelled the air. The lightning gone, the air grew rich with new elements. All at the command of one man. And so, what had they here?

Henry gave with one hand and took with another. A ploy to protect the king against the interests of others. Henry appeared cornered, checked by her own needs and Matthew's compliance. Yet, at the same time, Henry maneuvered to gain the help of Gerard. Was this a tactic in a game she only now knew she played?

Matthew huffed.

Lacy's gaze flew to her husband. His face grew red, his hands clenched and unclenched, his gorgeous eyes snapped lavender flames. He understood, as she did, that they were compelled to play Henry's game, whatever it was. And she was sure Matt understood that game's rules better than she.

He inclined his head to his sovereign. "Sire, if you will excuse me, I have much to accomplish before we begin our journey on the morrow."

At Henry's upturned palm, Matt left the three as silently as he had entered.

While Lacy watched him go, she pondered how well she had learned the game of chess.

CHAPTER 5

"LORD NORWICH SAYS WE MOVE DIRECTLY TO LONDON tomorrow, though the journey would normally take two days or more, especially with women in the train."

Lacy noted Anna's quotation of Lord Norwich for another countless time today. It nettled Lacy that the man buzzed about this flower who was her responsibility. Save for the fact that Anna's father, Lacy's uncle, died of the sweating sickness before he could marry Anna's mother, Anna would have been Lacy's fully recognized cousin. Anna had always served Lacy with a light and happy heart, and Lacy meant to do her cousin the return favor of not allowing anything—or anyone—to hurt her beautiful red-haired relative.

Lacy threw her maid a comforting smile. "I shall be pleased to move quickly and be settled. Then we will send home for more goods that we might live more comfortably."

"Lord Norwich says he knows not how suitable the accommodations will be in London. They are not certain if they must fight outside the city to overtake King Richard's palaces."

Lacy felt Anna's gentle but stern pull on her hair. "Do not fret, Anna. I feel Henry Tudor has won the day in many ways. He will assume few risks and probably has sent a force ahead to make a show and quell the need for more battle." Lacy sat stoically while Anna attempted to coil her hair up into a gold mesh crespin, a task difficult to do because Lacy's strands did ever escape confinement. "If Henry allows women in this train, I doubt he predicts more armed strife. I do wonder how many women there are."

"Norwich says there are five, including us. I wonder if the queen dowager, King Edward's widow, remains."

"I would like to see her. It is said she is the loveliest of women. So blond, so bewitching she was that he married her against the wishes of his brothers and his councillors. Marrying her, poor as she was, was one of his worst political mistakes."

"Nevertheless, their oldest daughter, Elizabeth, is said to be even more comely. No wonder Henry Tudor wants her."

Lacy frowned. "From what I heard from Henry Tudor this morning, he does not believe so much in romance as in politics. He is a realist, although he strives for the ideal when he can."

Lacy entertained no doubts about Henry. He was cunning. He was observant. He was wise to combine the two, which he did in her presence this morning with her husband and her suitor. The king saw all. Saw first all the ramifications of an issue. Saw certainly more than Gerard did, perhaps even more than Matthew, although she would not lay good money on that.

Certainly, King Henry had taken her measure. She was sure of it. He saw her distress and analyzed it. Further, she had no doubt now, Henry combined that with what he knew of her husband's. Matt had probably told his king much—but she prayed not all—of what had happened on the return to Renwick. Henry had seen more than she herself could fathom, because Henry knew more of his loyal servant Matthew than Lacy could. He probably even knew why Matt did not want her. Henry held so many advantages. Too many.

For better or worse, the king liked Gerard. By tying all three of them to himself for the next few weeks, Henry had accomplished the impossible in one stroke; he had satisfied every person's objective by neatly sidestepping every objection. Clearly, Henry wished to see how the course of true love flowed. But as he watched, Lacy knew the king would also ponder his own best interests. She had so little time to resolve her predicament.

She fingered the folds of her apricot gown and wondered what power, if any, she held within her own grasp. Tonight's dinner would offer her the opportunity to measure its strength. For Henry could do naught but seat her near her husband and her suitor. Meanwhile, she would go to supper and during its courses learn more about her position.

"There, milady. I do believe the crespin will hold the curls in place. 'Tis a pity that for your first public appearance with King Henry you have no headdresses or veils, none of your handsome jewelry, either."

Lacy nodded into the hand mirror and approved the upswept arrangement of her hair. Pulled severely away from her face, her thick chunks of curls appeared to have disappeared. If the evening were short, the devilish strands would hold and she, for once, might appear in the best of fashion. Though Lacy disdained shaving to become strongly browed, she tried tonight for the classical look so favored by the French and Roman women whose sleekness formed the stuff of bards' ballads.

Lacy rose and let the apricot tissue wool swoosh about her legs. It, like one other turquoise wool, had been packed to her saddle and thus was the second garment remaining in tact after the disaster of last night. She thanked her saints this was one of her most complimentary. The gown hugged her breasts in the current style. Cut round in front, the golden-trimmed neckline hovered at the crest of her nipples. The dictate was to dare the depths, of course, and though Lacy knew this, she could not bring herself to bare all her private assets. Shyness would have made her shiver and then her breasts would shrivel, just as they had this morning when Matthew put his hands and mouth upon them.

She shuddered violently with the potent memory and picked up her pace to the hall. Fashion take the devil. 'Twas enough of a burden to have such large breasts when women with smaller attributes breathed more easily in their tight bodices. That is, whenever they did not bare them entirely free, like the French king's mistress who had set the style for complete display. Lacy's bow to fashion was the dip of her gown down her back. Bared in a vee to the waist, the gown gave a lattice-work glimpse of her shoulderblades and spine through a lacing of golden threaded tethers tied at the small of her back. She might not make the bare-breasted picture of virginal fashion, but she would create a suitable impression as a woman of some importance.

Taking to the graceful winding staircase, she preceded Anna to the great hall on the first floor. Unlike her own De Vere Castle, built by her Norman ancestor for defense against Saxon raids, Renwick Castle had been built by the Yorkist King Edward less than ten years ago as a showpiece of his royal power in the Midlands. Its structure and decor stood to display its master's need for prestige and comfort. With many apartments for the housing of retainers, Renwick resembled a garden maze of corridors, solars, oriels, and a hundred cozy nooks for reading or contemplation of the countryside beyond the glassed bay windows. These last Lacy found to be Renwick's most appealing feature, and when she went home, she would find the means to create one such bay for herself. Cuddled into such a sunlit corner, she could read or embroider with her dogs at her feet. Alone.

No, no. No longer alone.

She wrung her hands, pausing at the open doors to the great hall, surveying the more than one hundred people, most of them soldiers, milling about in conversation and laughter. She'd never seen so many people assembled in one place. One such small space. Though she liked people and craved more company than she usually had, somehow she felt more alone now amidst these men of war than she had ever been. The urge to run—run all the way home to her beloved De Vere—shook her frame.

But not her resolve.

Never that. She had lived too long alone. Too long without companionship, affection. Too long without hope of love.

She had come for a man. She must leave with one.

If she had her wish, she knew now which one she would prefer. But being honest with herself, she acknowledged her preference was only important if she played out her own advantages upon this chessboard. As when she arrived, her wealth led her list of assets in this game. Her need for a speedy resolution closely followed. But after that short list, she panicked with the void before her. If only she could discover why such a wonderful sweet man as her husband could hold her and kiss her, caress her and praise her, but still not wish to claim her as his wife in deed. If only she knew this phantom reason, she might call out this foe that kept her from her heart's desire. But to open a frontal attack by asking Matt to name the beast might find her easily subdued. How could she discover and defeat such a fiend with only money and a few weeks as her shield and sword?

Her eyes scanned the huge room for Matthew or Gerard. But in the crowd of equally tall, brawny soldiers, to find two specific men became an endless hunt. Yet as she strode across the room toward the dais, heads turned, eyes clung, hands were no longer washed in preparation for the meal. Norwich appeared and took Anna to a table with him. Lacy sent her cousin a warning look while Norwich sent Lacy an answering assurance that he would never hurt the maid. Lacy acquiesced. Murmurs rose. A path appeared. Some men swept themselves low in a sign of homage; others whispered to their companions. Tones of praise for her grace mingled with words of delight for her beauty. To be so openly and brazenly desired left her suddenly feeling naked, frightened . . .

"My lady."

Lacy wanted to hug her husband for appearing now. Relief washed through her, and she knew he saw it.

He offered his arm. "I will escort you to table."

"Thank you," she breathed through trembling lips. "I did not know what to expect."

"I know. I saw trepidation on your face." He looked straight ahead, avoiding her perusal. "They are gentle men, but so long in the saddle that their manners are less than they should be. Come sit here. Henry is delayed with matters of state. Perhaps some wine would calm your fears." He sat beside her and lifted his chin at a servant with a large earthen jug.

Lacy sank into the sumptuous chair Matt offered. While the servant poured her a goblet of red wine, she let her eyes revel in the matching glow of her husband's black velvet doublet to the ebony satin of his hair. His swarthy skin shimmered in the candles' sheen. He had barbered himself closely for supper. The sight of his smooth, angular jaw made her long to kiss it as she had this morning. Prudently, she chose the wine and downed a satisfying draft. "I do like good company, though the size of this did seem daunting." She raised her face to give him a smile she only now began to feel.

His answering gaze told her much. His lavender eyes caressed her face like the whisk of spring blossoms against her eyes and lips. He examined her cheeks and finally her mouth. "Your apartment is sufficient, I hope."

"Completely." She held her breath as his gaze descended to her throat and shoulders, and then to the swell of her breasts where beneath the tissued wool her nipples rose to beg release and praise.

He saw and would not take his eyes away. "You do not wear the virgin's current mode."

"I am a wife." Her breasts tingled with the swath of his eyes. She writhed as her skin puckered, and she blushed, wishing she could hide her overt physical reaction to him.

His gaze rounded on her florid declarations of desire and then rose to caress her blinking eyes. "Though I have no right to be," he rasped, "I am pleased—nay, thrilled—at your modesty. In truth, thrilled at everything you are."

She parted her lips and breathed heavily. "And I, you. Though Robert Morris told me tales of a brave warrior and loyal friend, I see a kind and gentle man before me."

He clenched his jaw. The dimple of his left cheek was now displayed in deep, rueful crevices. "Robert was authorized to tell you only pertinent things. Nothing personal was to be discussed."

"Why is that, my lord? You are no ogre that I see."

"Still, Robert was given explicit instructions not to reveal anything about me. Not habits. Not exploits. Nothing."

"You cannot blame a man for what he tells while wine still sits in his cup."

"You plied him beyond his capacity?"

"Only to have news of my husband. And what he told me was very satisfying. It seems the Tudor's Sure Arrow is not only Henry's most accurate archer, he has also targeted many a new friend for his liege lord and brought him alliances and wealth with dukes and princes throughout Europe. He has endured beatings and imprisonment for his lord's sake, even saved him once in a blinding snowstorm by offering up his own cloaks to shield the winds of fate. Such tales warmed my heart to think this man could belong to me. Young girls dream of knights, you see. That this man was mine in man's law and in the eyes of God made him so much finer than those heroes who merely move upon the pages of a romance."

"Lacy, you dreamt of a man who didn't exist. Those pages of your books contained more true knights than I shall ever be."

"I have read those romances, my lord, and no man is your equal."

"Lacy," he breathed while he shook his head in torment. "You must desist. You lay me open with your tender sword and tempt me to emotions I must not claim."

"My lord," she whispered, her eyes upon his in mellow frankness, "you tempt me to emotions I barely understand."

His eyes flared wide. "You must not. We will not."

"Tell me *why* not."

His gaze flew back to hers and once more they became the lavender pools of desire she longed to bathe in to the end of her days. "Lacy, Lacy. You tantalize the saints."

"You know whom I seek."

"You mean *what* you seek."

"My husband."

"*A* husband."

She arranged her skirts. "You have shown me you display those qualities I seek."

He growled. "*Any* man can show you lust."

Her chin snapped up. Her eyes defied him. "None has shown me such compassion. Save you. None laughter. Save you. None has kissed me as you have and shown me heaven with only the touch of your skin to mine."

He pounded the table with his fist.

She saw him wrestle with a fiendish anger.

Men stopped to watch the head table's pewter plate clatter with the saltcellars.

Matt cursed between clenched teeth. "Robert Morris told me you were unique."

"He told me you were just."

"I am. That is why I can let you go so easily."

That cut to the quick of her pride. Her eyes drifted from his to scope the hall, the men who took their seats and chuckled, the same men whose attention turned en masse to the three women who entered and stood posed in the archway.

Like triplets, the women appeared to be imitations of each other. Each was pale blond, lightly boned, of middling height with the taut, toned bodies of the young. Each woman wore the fine hauteur of station, grace, and money. One, the oldest by but a few years, appraised the scene before her with indifferent calculation. By her numerous rings, her high-necked green brocade and her shaved eyebrows and forehead, she declared she was a married woman of great means. Not so her sisters.

They came displaying other attributes—and to Lacy's wide eyes—other intentions. No man in the hall missed them, either. Including Matthew Fletcher.

"Silliness," he seethed, while his eyes focused on two sets of pale pink nipples.

Lacy could have screeched. Mother Mary's nightgown. Who were these two women that they came so blithely to this hall chock to the rafters with men horned by battle?

The three made their way to the head table as Matt swung his eyes to Lacy. "Thank God you do not wear the fashion."

Lacy gulped, unable to take her gaze from the sight

of those four small circles that advanced on her and him. "I would die of cold within a fortnight."

He chuckled, a warm rush of soothing waters to her chilled distress. "My dearest, look not so avidly. Those breasts are not worth such scrutiny. I would venture yours are more to a man's liking."

Her eyes slid to his, her reaction—to reprimand him for such worldly knowledge—transforming at his half-lidded appraisal of her mouth and eyes. "You say you want me not, my lord, and then you brand me with hot words of praise. What would you of me, sir? Total madness? I am no playmate for your amusement. No pawn to your knightly maneuvers."

"Aye, sweet wife. I do you wrong. Forgive me. I meant only to console you that you need not compare your attributes to such thimbles and spools as these. Though I have not seen the plush pillows we speak of, I have tested with my lips what turgid comfort must exist beneath. Were you to bare your breasts, my darling, I would be cut down by each man in the kingdom as they scrambled over my corpse to embrace your wealth."

"Fortunately for you, I need only one man."

He shot both brows to his shock of wavy black locks. "Fortunately for you, I give you leave to gain one."

Tilting at this quintain wearied her. She turned and sought a more sedate game. By now the three women stood near the head table, servants fluttering about to seat them. "You must introduce us, my lord."

"Aye, come. They speak some English."

There was no time to reveal more for he had risen and taken Lacy's arm and did his duty nicely. The three were ladies of his long acquaintance. The married woman awaited her husband's arrival from Brittany, where they would become Duke Francis's representative to Henry's court. Her two sisters, the two virgins, flushed at the sight of Matthew, whom they eagerly declared they had long admired.

"We have so many years wished to meet the lady who was wife to Lord Fletcher," said Thérèse, a frail maiden whose almond-shaped, azure eyes were her shapeliest feature. "He is a man of hearts, *Marquise* Fletcher. When my sisters and I were very young and we were the only children in the duke of Brittany's court, your husband took pity on us and our boredom. He taught me how to ride."

"Oui," cooed her milk-complexioned sister, whose name was Isobelle. "He taught me how to use a bow."

Lacy lifted one slippered foot and ground it atop her husband's.

He woofed in pain and gripped her elbow in warning.

"My husband is a good shot, I do understand," offered Lacy with social aplomb and feigned serenity.

"Absolument!" gushed the pale Isobelle, while her white breasts blued and her nipples pebbled in the drafty room. "I hit my mark each time." She gave Matt a puppy's loving look. "Matthew says the trick is in the sighting."

"Is that so?" Lacy shot her husband a glance of tolerant challenge. "I have for years been off the mark. Only lately have I been able to spot it. Must be my eyes have become clearer. Perhaps now, my husband can teach me the value of sighting."

His fingers digging in her elbow told her he would teach her the value of strangulation.

The married sister, who watched and waited, assessed Lacy coolly from her chair. Unlike the other two, who, as unmarried women, had no titles yet, she was a *marquise* equal to Lacy and therefore entitled to sit if she chose. She also chose to dissect Lacy as if she were an animal carcass readied for the cook's sharp spit.

"I should think that now you two are reunited, the Tudor's Sure Arrow would find quick applications for the continual wealth in his quiver."

The ice of her innuendo froze Lacy instantly. Of the five, only Matt found words to cover everyone's distress. Those he managed came out clipped and hot.

"Sybilline, please do not use that old rumor against me. I have only met my wife recently and I would not have her prejudiced against me by things I cannot disprove."

The woman's glassy cerulean eyes met his in defiance. *"Mon cher,* many things I can prove. So many I remember."

"Sybilline, I thought we settled this in Brittany. Come, Lacy. I see our Henry at the door. We will to supper." Matt's fingers now demanded that Lacy accompany him quickly.

Once more standing before their chairs, Lacy swallowed bitterly, her eyes straight ahead. As Henry swept the room, stopping here and there to grasp hands or converse, she wanted to sob. It was one thing to hear from Robert Morris that her errant husband drew women to his charm with no effort; it was galling to face such a woman and hear her jealous tirade recount his exploits.

"Please do not cry." Matt kept his eyes trained on Henry's progress. "She torments you with words that imply falsehoods. I never touched her. I never wanted to. It angers her, and she seeks to spear us both on the blade of her resentment. If you cry, she will be so proud her words drew blood that she will try again. You would not wish that. Nor would I."

His words gave some salve for her wound. When Henry finally approached, Lacy was sitting with more circumspection. And when she noted that Gerard came in Henry's wake, Lacy knew objectivity would accompany him to her other side.

Henry took his place at the center of the damask-covered table. Above the throng of lusty men of war, the new English king sat while the priest offered the blessing. Then Henry graciously nodded and smiled as the pages and squires brought forth the numerous courses. Though the usual was to serve a heavy meal at noon, Henry's needs demanded that his army officers perform their various duties until sun no longer guided their actions. This supper therefore resembled a copious noontide dinner. Through a delicate soup of braised onions, baked trout, and a blancmange of chicken and almond rice, Lacy fought despair.

By rank, she had been seated, as she suspected, with her husband on her one hand and her suitor on the other. Yet, by custom, she had been paired to Matt, who served her from the platters and tureens. Gerard, whose academic chatter she had craved to cure her sorrow, by order of the seating had been paired to Isobelle. And clearly, Isobelle's thimbles capped other assets Gerard wished to explore.

Henry's wine tasted remarkably good. Better than the food. More soothing than the tense silence.

"Drink any more of that and I shall have to carry you from the hall."

Lacy's eyes flew to her husband's. Finished with his meal, he reclined in the huge chair, one arm carelessly flung over the back. Lacy took another sip of the very tasty burgundy.

He watched her swallow. "Have you always gotten what you wanted, Lacy?"

"Much of what was important. Except a true husband," she said as she reached for one ripe peach from the bowl before them. "Have you?" When he didn't answer, she stopped her peeling and asked, "Well?"

He considered the far wall a moment. "I suppose so. I wished to leave my father's house when I was sent into a knight's household at age six. I wished to become a good marksman when I was introduced to the bow. I wished to serve Henry from the moment I was introduced to him at age eleven."

Lacy was not surprised that Matt did not list their marriage. Given such a question, she would not have listed it either. "Perhaps a more telling answer is to list what you have wished for and never received."

He straightened, his eyes upon the door where minstrels gathered. "Perhaps it is."

He shut her out. Whatever his past, whatever his present desires, he would not let her see them. Why? Robert Morris had revealed no hellish aspect to her husband's character, no irredeemable qualities that might deter a woman from cherishing her husband. The only element that she knew Robert carefully hid from her was the reason her husband had never appeared, though he did let slip that Matthew had had a few good opportunities.

"Did Robert tell you tales about me that discouraged you from seeking me out?"

Her change of subject had him blinking at her. "What? Nay. Nay, he did not. If anything, his stories made me long to see you in the flesh."

Since the next logical question would gain her nothing, she jabbed at her peach, sliced it to the pit, and offered him a sliver. The juice dribbled down her fingers. "Eat if you want it," she invited impatiently, her challenge the words of Eve. "I cannot wait forever."

Lavender eyes understood her message. He snapped open his mouth. She shoved the fruit in a bit too far, anger and desire warring for control as she plunked the fruit between his lips and startled as he clamped them shut to suck her fingers clean. The act made them both swallow hard.

"Lacy," he said raggedly, "you always were the perfect mate."

She speared the peach viciously. "Odd for you to say, since we have never mated."

"You play word games with me. I meant, from what I heard from Robert, you seemed wonderful."

"Never wonderful enough to prompt you to my side."

"Wonderful enough to keep you all these years."

That gave her pause. She stared sadly at her hands. "But why keep me?" She turned her face to him and saw how her sorrow eroded his resolve. "Please do not recite the military importance of my lands. Nor speak again about Henry Tudor's need for my yearly tribute to pay his army. Instead, fill my tired ears with some reason that sounds new. Tell me why this man, this legendary knight I knew as Matthew Fletcher, would remain married to a girl he had not the slightest curiosity to seek out, not even for an afternoon's discussion of the weather."

"Ah, Lacy, don't you know that like you, in my youth, I had no choice? My father divined the match to gain your dower portion to benefit his own crumbling castle and estate. My lord Henry and his uncle sanctioned the union because, frankly, you were an orphan, weak and alone save for hired servants paid from your estate coffers by your guardian and cousin, the earl of Oxford. The earl himself had recently come to our cause and at my father's suggestion to Oxford of the marriage, the Tudors thought it a worthy strategic alliance. It would ensure the loyalty of Oxford, your cousin, whose forces and influences we needed as badly as we needed your money."

"And so you abducted me—"

"Nay, not I. I took no part in that dastardly deed. I had objected loudly, you see. So vociferously, in fact, that when I refused to marry, I was, shall we say, persuaded by my father to the rightness of his decision. Nay, my little wife, 'twas not I who took you from your bed. I was chained to my own to prevent my threatened escape from our nuptials."

Her mouth dropped open.

"Look not at me that way. Such cruelties happen. You must know it. You are a lady of a vast estate. You must have seen or heard of persuasions by violent force."

She swallowed repeatedly. "Yes, I have heard. Seen. Only last month, my bailiff brought a man to my leet court for trial. He was one of my serfs. He had beaten his wife for failure to attend the fields with him. She was eight months gone with child when he thrashed her. She came to her time early I'm sure as a result of his torture. She lost the child. I sentenced him to my dungeon."

"He deserved to be hanged," Matt seethed.

"He pleaded with me that he repented and could change with time."

"He lies. He will not change." She watched him

descend into the dungeons of his own mind to view some private torment she could not imagine. He snapped his eyes to hers and covered her hand briefly. "I suppose you remember little of that night you were taken."

"Aye, the night was dark and I was only four." She valiantly tried to return to the subject of their wedding. "I remember only a man dressed all in black."

"The earl of Oxford."

"My cousin?"

"He planned it all. He knew the lay of your castle. He is the one who did disguise himself and his men to charge De Vere's walls and pick off your guards. He had to don a guise because he knew if your men recognized him, they would never adhere to his orders again. An abduction by an unknown force was preferable to raising an alarm among men fiercely loyal to your dead father, who wished you to marry one of King Edward's barons."

She fell back, stunned. "I was to be given even by my father for political ambitions."

"And economic advantage. Aye. An heiress is too often married for her future husband's and her father's benefit. Even my mother was an earl's only daughter, and she was sent to marry a man she thought she loved, yet who also gained financially from their union." He offered her a comforting squeeze on the hand. "I do not condone arranged marriages. Not when I was fifteen. And not now. Marriage should begin in mutual respect and love, not the terror of an abduction such as yours."

She shook and clenched her hands, white to the knuckles. "I remember only a hooded man who took me from my nurse's arms to carry me out and seat me upon his saddle. He rode away with me, quelling my fright by crooning to me. . . ."

"You were so mistreated, my sweet wife."

"All so that when the deed was done, my cousin the earl could proclaim me wedded to the Lancastrian cause, and my father's retainers could do naught but accept it." She turned her eyes to her husband's mournful ones. "And you had no hand in the abduction."

"None. I was as much a pawn as you. Forced to do my father's will, I was released from my chains one night and told to mount my horse. I rode out of our fortifications with Jasper Tudor and my father to a church I had never seen. With the dawn as we three waited at the church steps, your cousin the earl rode over the horizon bearing a sleeping angel in his lap. I recoiled at the injustice of what was being done to you."

Lacy noted how he spoke only of the injustice done to her. "And what of you, my lord? What was your mind that morning of our marriage?"

He shifted, rage making him inhale raggedly. "Had I been given a choice fifteen years ago, I would not have married. Not certainly a baby, four years of age. You cannot remember me at the church door. But I was tall as I am now and, though not as solidly hewn, I was fully a man in many ways. I had bested an older man in a joust, boasted at least two Yorkist deaths to my archery skills, and knew quite well a tanner's willing daughter. I did not want a wife. If I had, I assure you at that point in my life I would have demanded one I could take to my bed, not my nursery."

Curiosity about her wedding day drove her nearer to him in search of comfort.

He traced a forefinger down the bones of her hand to the tip of her finger. "I will never forget you. Until the day I die, I carry with me the vision of a silvery-haired angel awakening from her sleep to face four huge men. An angel crying from incredibly large turquoise eyes. Eyes I likened to a Turkish sultan's turquoise stones, which my Fletcher forebear brought home from his travels on crusade. I shall never forget you, my darling. That sight of you crying as your cousin spoke for you your marriage vows—that vision of you helpless and afraid made me promise myself to protect you from anyone who would ever make you cry again. I pledged I would never be the one to hurt you. And so I have not come near you to ruin your days."

The sweet pain of his revelation ripped the shreds of any serenity. And to ask why he would ruin her days might present again too frontal an attack upon his defenses to gain her any knowledge of why he did not want her as his mate. "You came near me last night and then again this morning, knowing full well who I was, and yet you did not ruin me."

"Ahh, but you know if we had continued, I could have ruined you completely."

"As is your right."

"All the worse."

"Why?"

"Because, I say, I am no good for you." He leaned nearer, his features aflow with sorrow, his strong mouth so close she felt his wine-warm breath. "You deserve a man who deserves you. A man who without reservation wants you."

"Speak a lie and say you want me not."

His eyes defined her every feature, hair, brows, cheeks, mouth, breasts, hands. "Aye, I want you. So sorely my every muscle aches to hold you, my very blood sings for the elixir your joy and beauty bring me. You are a delight for any man. Were I any other man, I would harangue Henry to let me near you, barter my soul to gain you, challenge hell to keep you. But I am what I am, and there is no changing that."

She covered his hand. "My lord, what are you that I do not see? A profligate? A mercenary? A beast by night?"

Something about her words flailed him. Raw despair suffused his sanguine handsomeness. "A little of each."

She sank to the back of her chair. "Now you lie."

He stared at her.

She swept out a hand in protest, a laugh of outrage piercing the room where minstrels strolled and led the throng in song. "I believe you not at all."

"You do not know much of men."

"I know enough of one man to say your words are false."

"You must let this die!"

"You give me nothing save generalities for proof!"

"Henry knows what proofs there are."

"Good for him! He is not married to you."

"He will dissolve this marriage no matter what you now say."

"Why then did he not do it this morning?"

"You know as well as I that he seeks to play the diplomat."

Lacy examined her husband and then her sovereign. "Aye. But I have too long been a pawn. I will play as queen upon this chessboard." She trembled and rose, an abrupt move that sent her chair crashing to the dais. She stepped over it toward a surprised Henry. "Forgive me, Sire," she said as she inclined her head in a homage she did not feel. "I am ill and wish to retire."

"Of course, milady, do by all means rest before our journey tomorrow."

Lacy pivoted and sailed from the hall as gracefully as her torment could allow. But instead of her apartment, she turned for the inner courtyard beyond the great hall. She sought the garden maze she had glimpsed from her window.

Here, hidden by the squared boxwoods amid the heavy scents of late summer's flowers and the moon's hot glow, she wandered amid the moist summer night into a maze and gave in to the frustrated tears she'd stopped up during the meal. In her misery, she paced the narrow corridor and swiped at tears that would not stop.

Damn the man! He was hers, by all that was holy. And she wanted him, by all that was sacred—and secular. She wanted his good humor and wit. His charm. She wanted his lavender eyes for their children. His power to protect and impress their daughters. His strength and moral certitude as a model for their sons. She wanted *him*. Preferred him, God help her, to kind Gerard.

"Lacy?"

And so it was Gerard who sought her. Why would she hope for the other? Gerard was all those qualities she craved in a mate. Hadn't she said it was so only yesterday? Hadn't she donned scores of garments and a silly hat, borne fleas and the attack of two larger roadside vermin to free herself so that she might take Gerard to husband? Why, then, would she be disappointed that this fine-looking scholar, her friend of years, would now pale before the might of the man who had ever left her alone? Because yesterday she had not known Matthew Fletcher. And today, having met him, enjoyed him, kissed him, she knew him. She knew him to be the best mate for her hungering soul.

"Lacy! I saw you come in here." Gerard's footsteps passed her and looped back.

She should tell him where she stood. She should.

She took two steps to the corner of her corridor. "I'm here, Gerard." She sniffed, shook off her doldrums, and smoothed her skirts. "Here. Can you hear me? Follow my voice."

"Talk more to me. What an intricate puzzle this is!"

She spoke little words of encouragement so that soon he stood before her, his hands cupping her face. It was the first time he had ever touched more than her hand.

"You've been crying. I thought it would be so. I overheard some of your discourse with that husband of yours. I tried to intervene, but the two of you went so hotly at each other. I was distressed when you left." He reached into his belt and extracted a handkerchief. "Here. Blow your nose. . . . There. That's better." He smoothed two fat tears from the rise of her cheeks.

Lacy noted the delicacy of these fingers and how lightly they conveyed their message. Not like the bold, strong stroke of long, lean hands tempered by war.

"He hurt you," Gerard said simply. "I don't want him to hurt you anymore."

She gave a little smile of gratitude, then prayed for courage for what she was about to do. "Gerard, I must talk with you. I need to tell you how I feel about what happened this morning. It was then to Henry when you discussed how you feel about—"

"Aye, I know we have not spoken much of my views of secular power. I have always thought a good government would need the counsel of avid scholars. And I have strong opinions about the role of the tyrant versus—"

"No, I mean your revelation about our time together and how you love—"

"Oh, you must not worry about that. I have spoken with Henry at length this afternoon about our time spent together and he understands."

"He does?"

"Of course. He knows that men and women may be in each other's company and not rain down the wrath of God for breaching the bounds of moral conduct. He knows how fond I am of you and how I would not mar your reputation. I told him how we enjoy the quiet hours we spend together, silently combing our records for the truths of the past."

"And what did he say?"

"He thought we might make a good marriage. We respect each other and have many of the same desires to spend our days and to raise our children in a peaceful, prosperous kingdom."

"I see." She walked away from him around a corner to come face to face with a startled Matthew, just skidding to a halt. "And what did Henry think of such a marriage?" She turned her back on Matt and once more rounded the corner so that Gerard might answer and think naught amiss.

"He said marriages made of friendship like ours were certainly the practice." Gerard's eyes danced as he met her steady gaze. Behind her, no footfalls denoted Matthew's departure. "He said we would be wise not to wish for more than we could create together. He thought our passions were engaged elsewhere. I know my passion is my study. But yours? I told him you have ever only shown passion for want of a husband."

"Aye, one true husband."

"But then, the call to supper came and as we left his solar, Henry made me a promise."

"Really?" Her heart stopped, fearing to hear her king's plan. "What was that?"

"He promised he would see us all granted that which we require for a happy life." Gerard moved forward, his hands drawing her near, his eyes speaking of affection. "I know I would be happy with you." He bent over her, his mouth descending, and her blood raced in panic. She turned her cheek, stepped back, and collided with the granite wall of a man's chest and the feel of two powerful hands steadying her on her feet.

"Lord Wentworth, I think it is time you retired for the evening."

Gerard's eyes snapped blue fire as he looked above her to Matthew. "I think it is time you retired completely, sir. From all battlefields. The day is mine. You do not wish her."

For the first time, Lacy saw anger light her suitor's features. The sight astounded her—but did not strike fear into her soul as much as the feel of her husband's wrath as his body went rigid and his voice rose to a roar.

"Good night, Wentworth!"

Gerard's gaze dipped to Lacy's in question.

"'Tis all right for you to go, Gerard." When he hesitated, she put a palm to his heaving chest. "Please!"

Gerard fixed upon the sight of her husband's hands on her shoulders. "You forget yourself, man."

"You forget I am captain of the king's guard." Against her back, Lacy felt Matthew's chest expand like bellows. "Shall I call them?"

Gerard's nostrils flared. "Lacy, if he tries anything, scream like a fishmonger."

Lacy nodded. Unable to say a word, she bit her lip as she watched Gerard spin on his heel and leave.

Matthew turned her to his arms and she gasped. She thought she had seen rage before. She certainly had seen jealousy, but never over her and, in God's truth, never so rabidly. Never did she wish to see anger or jealousy on his handsome face, yet she'd seen them twice. Last night as they spoke of the Arnolds. And this morning when they spoke of his need to let her go.

Matthew held out his arm. "Come. I will escort you to your apartments."

"No. I will find my way alone." She pivoted.

He caught her by the arm. "Lacy, you try my soul."

"And you, sir, try my good nature. What mean you to treat Gerard so? He did naught to you."

Matt blinked. "He meant to kiss you."

"He can if I say he can."

"You are a married woman."

"Now who plays word games?"

He softened, more contrite. "Has he? Kissed you?"

"You think I lied then when I told you he hadn't touched me. Wonderful." She blew a tendril of hair from her eyes and advanced on Matt. "But if he has, why would you care?"

He searched her eyes a moment. "He hasn't. God, I'm glad." He sagged. "Forgive me, Lacy. I am sorry. I should have known you told the truth this morning, and he did just now when he said he felt only friendship for you."

That made her shiver in her own anger. "'Tis what many good marriages are made of. And so shall mine be."

He reached out one shaking hand to curl one wisp

of her hair around his forefinger. "I watched a hundred men tonight gaze at you with longing."

"I saw no such men." She knew she had eyes only for him. "Other ladies revealed more virtues, sir, than I."

He cupped her cheek and whispered, "None of them shines with the glory of you. Every man there went blind at your brilliance."

His eloquence brought tears to her eyes. "Why, oh, why are you so sweet to me, my husband?"

"I cannot help myself." He drew her flush to his chest while one hand crept to her nape. "I never knew you would be so lovely, in soul and body." She shuddered as he placed little kisses on her eyes and across her cheek to her ear. "My Lacy. My delicate, delicious Lacy. I want to leave you to your own desires and find I cannot leave behind my own. I care for you," he admitted on a ragged breath, and trailed hot lips down her throat.

Her world reeled. She grabbed at his shoulders and plunged one hand into his rich, silk hair. "My lord, you do me wrong to kiss me so and tell me such endearments. I cannot endure this maelstrom of emotions."

He paused, his face buried in her neck. "Aye, my love. I do you wrong. Again."

He straightened and grasped her hand, then led her out of the maze.

Never meeting her gaze, he took her along the garden path and the stairs to her rooms in silence. At the door, Matthew opened it, and when she would have bid him good night, he placed a finger across her lips. "I promise you I will not touch you again. I will instead do you the service of describing how very wrong I am for you. Tomorrow, ride beside me as we go to Bedford. Then shall I begin to tell you why our marriage must . . . could not ever be."

"But I—"

"Please, Lacy. I am a man of honor, though with you I have never seemed so. Ride beside me and I will describe to you the person I really am. And never more will you wonder why I did not come to you, claim you, live with you as my own. Meet me and this torment will be ended."

CHAPTER 6

BUT PLANNING AND DOING BECAME TOO DIFFERENT things. Matthew could never have predicted the innumerable obstacles to conversing with his wife along the road south to Bedford. If his duties to his men did not occupy him beyond measure, the extra demands of his sovereign did. Carrying messages to Henry's commanders in the field, deliberating march procedures and discussing the distribution of limited supplies meant his morning went to riding up and down the column as far back as the baggage wagons. By the time he had settled all of Henry's matters and rode forward past a company of archers, Matt saw Lacy speaking softly with Anna.

Once more, his wife's golden beauty sent lightning streaks to his every nerve. And he was mesmerized. Oh, he had first truly glimpsed her in moonlight, naked and nymphlike. In that sylvan setting, she shone with a silver glow. Inside Renwick Castle's hennaed halls, her complexion creamed with the complement of peach lips and coral cheeks. But here in the brilliance of an August sun, she glistened with a blooming radiance that robbed his breath.

Her hair, uncovered save by a turquoise satin crespin, sparkled amber with streaks of sunlit gold racing through its wealth. The strands reminded him of embroidery thread his mother had oft used to decorate satin pillows for Fletcher Castle's comforts. But her eyes, flashing now as she cast a tremulous welcoming smile at him, twinkled with those incomparable blue-green facets, so similar to her turquoise gown and reminiscent of the precious stones still locked away in his castle's dungeon hold. Her mouth opened to bid him welcome, and he considered her lush lips, blushed to ripe perfection in the sun. He had been right that first night when he'd thought she displayed all the colors in the world. She looked like a glorious rainbow, shining above the agony that was his life without her. Her perfection made him grip his pommel and clench his teeth. It made him regret everything he was, every flaw ever visited upon him, and every moment he had never savored her as he should have and did now.

Oh, God deliver him from what he had to do. She deserved better than he, and he would see her gain it. Or in this case, *him.* Though he admitted grudgingly that he rather liked Gerard, Matt thanked the heavens that the scholar did not float about Lacy this morning. In fact, Matt thought the man might have come to court Henry Tudor, so much time did he spend in the king's company. Evidently the feeling was quite mutual, for Henry remained so engrossed he looked reluctant to surrender Gerard for even a moment. Could the scholar say that much which Henry had not yet heard? Matt doubted it, but then, he had doubted much, including how much he could care for this woman who was his.

"Good afternoon," Matt bid his wife as he pulled his black steed alongside her white one. "I am sorry I have not had the opportunity to do as I promised before this."

"Please, do not apologize," she said with a small voice. She trained her eyes upon the road south while her maid Anna fell back from earshot. "The ride has been quite pleasant."

"The sun is not too hot for you?" he asked as he examined her delicate cheeks with concerned eyes.

She grinned. "Not today."

"Fewer garments make for a lighter load?"

She cast him a playful look. "And make it easier to sit this sidesaddle."

The banter died as he gazed at her, remembering what had happened when last she sat a saddle in his arms. Evidently, she too recalled and snapped her head around to contemplate the crowded thoroughfare, dusty with soldiers and their supplies.

"Lacy," he began and knew not how to continue. He had lain awake all night, tossing upon his thin pallet and thinking how he would broach this difficult subject. He, of course, thought he had found the words. But now they fled his mind as easily as the birds that flew overhead.

"Lacy, this is as difficult for me to tell as it is for you to hear."

Her spine straightened. Some odd emotion suffused her features, and she suddenly began to prattle like one possessed. "I have always been eager to hear anything you said. Anything. You never knew it, though. I waited for you, prayed for you, yearned for you to come to me for years and years. I would have listened to anything, for what did I know? I was only a foolish girl who dreamed of a husband who didn't dream of her."

"That's not true," he said, heartbroken. "I did dream of you. The real you."

Her eyes met his in turquoise defiance.

"'Tis so. I swear it. Robert Morris did tell me tales of this intelligent girl-bride who begged to ride at an early age and who for amusement tallied her yeoman farmers' rents. I heard of this and laughed. You brought joy to my days, though you never knew it."

Her expression mellowed, her chin trembled, and she faced the road again.

"Then Lady Margery would write me about how you were so very agreeable."

A smile curved Lacy's lips though she did not turn her head. "In most things."

"Aye. Most that were important to make the days a joy. Lady Margery said you were born to the nobility but that your every move showed you embodied its finest aspects. And then she said how very beautiful you grew."

Lacy shook her head and swallowed.

He knew he shouldn't but he did elaborate. "She confirmed my only memory of you when she wrote that you became a golden angel. With hair one thousand shades of blond. With a face one hundred blind men would beg to commit to memory with their fingertips. Her descriptions and Robert's surprised praise did compose a picture for me too intriguing to ignore. I fantasized and found you walking my dreams and then, too soon, my desperate days when I was alone or in need of some small solace. You—or the very thought of you—became my best refuge from the horrors of wars and countless other bitternesses I could not conquer."

When he turned, she stared at him, tears on her lashes. "You allowed me to be your comfort when I was no more than a phantom. Do I in the flesh not match the imaginary woman then?"

"No, no, that is not what I meant."

She winced. "Tell me no more of your visions. I would hear instead what you meant to impart. The foundations of your denial of me."

He flexed his shoulders and realized he did so as if he prepared to thread his bow or take up a lance. By Jesus' copious tears, he was not doing battle with her. Nay, but with his dragons once again. With those two churls who sought to find a way to prolong their torture of him. He could not let them win, for to do so meant his wife's unhappiness.

"Lacy, the reasons I never came to you reside in my past. When I was young, before I went to serve the Tudors, I lived with my family at Fletcher Castle, not far from here. My father held a barony, longstanding from before the Conquest, and held by the family outright since William the Conqueror's time with fealty only to the Crown." He licked his lips. "My mother was a sweet woman. She had been an earl's daughter, much tutored in music and her mother's native French language. She was an attentive mother who played with me in the nursery and taught me French from an early age. So too did my sister."

Lacy considered him now with some eager thought drifting across her features. "I did not know you have a sister."

He grit his teeth. "I don't. She's dead."

"Oh, Matt, I'm so sorry."

"She died years ago. One year before we wed. She

was married to a baron, who has too since found his grave, thank God." Matt cast a look at Lacy who frowned. "He was a heinous brute. I hated him the moment I first saw him. Burly and boisterous with his retainers and surly to our servants, he played the gentleman with my mother. But I was in his company with my father, and I saw every hideous characteristic he possessed. He was a drunkard, you see. A dicer. A gambler who would bet large sums, even over the gender of a new foal. I loathed him." Matt forced himself to meet Lacy eye to eye. "I prayed he would die. One day, he did. But not before he killed my sister."

"Are you certain? Such an accusation—"

"Aye, Lacy, I am well aware of the weight of my words. Yes, the man killed my sister. I had it directly from her in letters I kept for years."

"How did he hurt her?"

"He beat her. Regularly and often. Even when she carried his child." The very words seared his common sense, and he muttered old curses against the man he had so hated. "She died in childbirth. So did the child. I did hear that a few years afterward, with no one else to endure his whippings, the man did take to inflicting physical tortures on himself. From his own perversions did he sicken and die. He suffered long. He should suffer for eternity for what he did to Marian."

He felt the sudden grip of Lacy's hand. He covered it with his own as she called his name.

"Ah, Lacy. Marian is sixteen years dead and still I remember her. Her blue-black curls and violet eyes. She was a beauty. My father could have married her to any man—*any* man—she was that beautiful in spirit and appearance. But he gave her to that devil."

"But your father could not know how ruthless he

might be to her! Taking too much wine and gaming are not always indicators that a person might murder—"

"No!" Matt seethed so vehemently that a few guards who rode before them turned to stare at him. "My father knew. He approved."

"Oh, my sweet heavens, Matt! That could not be!"

"Oh, aye, my innocent wife. It could. I heard him say so many a time. 'A wife is to be tamed, a falcon fit to the temperament of her master. Fit by any means at hand.' My father married her to that excuse for a man and did it for the same reasons he married me to you—with no forethought of her happiness or heirs. All his thoughts centered on his own political and economic gains. They didn't merit him much, though, I am pleased to say. The lands he won were soon swallowed by the Yorkists. He never won them back in his lifetime. When my sister's husband died, the yearly payments to my father ceased. The Fletchers were as poor as before. Poorer still, for now they had no lovely Marian to call their own. My father died three years ago, his sole surviving relative hating the very ground on which he walked. I shall never forgive him, Lacy. He made all our lives a living hell."

"Matthew," she mourned, and squeezed his hand. "My sweet husband, you must not say this. Not to forgive is such a sin."

"Ah, my love, but what care I for sin? I have no life. Have never had. Not one to call my own. Without a life, what pain can death cause?"

"Such talk is blasphemy."

"I have seen what miseries God allows and cannot believe he intends good."

"You must not speak thus."

"I tell you I walk this earth without fear of God."

"If that is so, then it must be because you are so very noble, my dear husband." Her eyes melted into his in confirmation of her belief.

"Lacy, Lacy. I am not noble. Were I so, I would have freed you from your bonds to me long ago. You asked me last night why I did keep you, and I did not answer. I do now. I kept you out of selfishness. Simple selfishness. I wanted to keep my dreams of you, you see. I wanted to have a bright vision of someone pure and golden who was mine, all mine. I wanted—I enjoyed the very idea that someone waited for me. Aye, in my darkest hours, with the blood of my enemies upon my hands, I did transport my mind to visions of one angelic woman who waited for her knight to come home to her." He tried to dam the tears that flooded his eyes and found that in the bright light of day, his vision refracted—and beneath his tears this lovely woman shone through to sear his wounds with salving words.

"My darling man, if I served as a beacon unto your desperate hours, so too were you to my lonely ones."

"Lacy . . ." He lifted her hand to his mouth to place a tender kiss within her palm.

"My lord Fletcher."

Thomas Norwich brought his horse alongside Matt's. With a nod of deference to Lacy and a quick smile at Anna, Thomas set his gaze on his commander's.

Matt relinquished Lacy's hand with remorse. At his friend, he arched his brows and blinked to hide the evidence of his distress. "Aye, what is it, Tom?"

"Henry bids you come forward. We have had a few sightings of bands of Yorkists. Henry needs your advice."

Matt mashed his lips together. Of all the infernally

poor times to meet a band of rebels, this had to be the worst. Even more disturbing was the sight of Gerard Wentworth directing his mount toward them.

"Very well. I shall go." He whipped his head around to see Lacy raise her face, her apricot mouth parting, her compassionate turquoise eyes sparking a flash fire of regret in his heart. "I shall return, Lacy. There is more you must know."

Gerard came apace of the three and pivoted his horse.

"Good day, Lacy. Lord Fletcher." Gerard offered Matt a sliver of a satisfied smile. "Henry bids you go forward to him, sir."

Matt wished he could tell Gerard where to go. Instead, he rounded his eyes at Lacy and kneed his horse into a gallop. Damn the man! Damn every man who conspired to take Lacy from him just when he began to want . . .

Christ, what was he thinking?

He mustn't want her, couldn't keep her!

Not even for a moment's conversation. Why would he feel this possessive about a woman who could never mean anything to him?

He drove his horse faster.

No! That was not correct either. She *meant* many things to him. Like peace. Contentment. Children. Love.

He sneered at his folly as he reined his horse to a canter. He had no right to love her. Not ever. And so the sooner he told her all, the sooner she'd reject him. The more peacefully he'd live. With a clear conscience. Without his two dragons.

Why then did the very idea of loving her and never having her make breathing so damned painful?

* * *

Matt pressed his fist into his breastbone. The pain of wanting her returned with every move he watched Lacy make. Now she strolled along the lower wall walk of Southborne Castle. Attired still in her turquoise gown, she brought bright color to the dove gray stones that sparkled in the dying rays of the day.

Throughout the afternoon, his labored breathing became nothing to the torture of not being able to touch her or talk with her again. Nothing to the gutting jealousy of seeing her talking with Gerard or conversing with Anna and Thomas. Nothing to the knowledge that he could only glimpse her while all through the afternoon he went about his duties for his king.

And those duties never ended, either!

He'd sent a contingent of his yeoman guard to aid a unit of Henry's archers to disperse the score of Yorkist rebels. He'd discussed with Henry the disposition of the prisoners they'd taken from the band. He'd even assisted Henry in deciding whether or not they should rest here at Southborne Castle for the night to scout the countryside for any more roaming Yorkist bands.

"Matthew, what say you to this plan of dividing our forces to enter London?"

Matt took himself from his musings at the window and peered over his shoulder at his king, who bent over a set of maps. He rubbed his jaw, stirring a nagging toothache to life.

"I think our commanders have given you their best information and plan. We meet no resistance. But prudence demands we be prepared for any eventuality."

"And you agree we should wait here a day or two to let our spies scout the area before we go in to London?"

"Aye, 'tis best to know the full report lest we diminish our current advantage by too much haste." Matt turned back to see Lacy bend and smell red roses planted in a garth's turret. She would never wear red. White roses, perhaps. Gardenias, aye, they would complement her better. Just like the lavender scent that clung to her, gardenias were fragile and—

"Matt! What interests you more than my blather about men and armies, eh?" Rolling a map, Henry strode over to peer out the window himself. He turned, a smirk pursing his lips. "Ah, I should have known." He walked away while Matt's gaze did define the delicate beauty of his wife's profile. "Have you told her yet?"

Matt did not face his sovereign, only the bitter truth. "No, not yet. I will. I vowed I will. Before supper."

"Think you she will run from you?"

"If she values her life."

"What if she values being your wife more?"

Matt spun and fixed Henry with a look. "She won't. She can't. What woman would?"

"I have no idea. Do you?" When Matt faltered, Henry slapped a rolled parchment in his hands. "No. Because you have never told another soul, save me. Now you must tell Lacy. Gerard is a very determined man and, albeit a kind one, he will not wait long. He cares for her, though mayhaps not as you do."

Matt shook his head. "I . . ." He shut his eyes but pivoted once more to the window. "I cannot lie to you. I do care for her. Who could not? She is . . . incomparable. Sweet. Loving."

"Gorgeous."

"Aye, that too, inside and out."

Gerard stepped out onto the wall walk and called

and waved to Lacy. The two sat on a stone bench. Gerard took Lacy's hand.

Matt felt his stomach clench.

"Have done with this which takes your mind from your work."

Matt tore his eyes from Gerard laughing with Lacy to face Henry with a frown. "You have a problem, Sire, with my performance of my duties?"

"Since she appeared, your mind has drifted more to her than to your responsibilities. Oh, I find no fault in your attention to detail. As ever, you are fastidious. 'Tis less a matter of where the mind is and more a matter of where the heart is. Actually"—Henry relaxed in his chair and leisurely surveyed him—"I have often wondered when the day would come that you would falter in your service to me because you need to deal with the past. With this wife. With the means—and the people—who brought her to you and decided your fate. I have long wondered, my dearest compatriot, when you would begin to deal less with my foes than with your own."

"Henry, Lacy is not my foe. Neither are you. You have been my boon companion and given me much."

"Aye. But has it been what you wanted?"

"Not always," Matt admitted truthfully and matched his sovereign's rueful grin. "Whatever my lot, I made the best of it."

"For a certainty, you have. You have also been my trusted right arm." Henry fingered a map for a moment and then nailed his gray eyes to Matt's. "I hate to see my Sure Arrow off the mark. Tell her all of it, Matt. And do it quickly, will you please? The tension of not revealing all is killing you."

Matt dismissed himself with speed. But when he

thrust open the armor-plated door to the wall walk, Lacy was alone. His torture transformed into one of watching a glorious smile spread upon her face for him and knowing he had no right to kiss those lips that welcomed him.

She glided forward, her eyes aglow, her hands seeking his. "Good evening," she offered and then cast her eyes away, obviously remembering his promise to return and reveal more horrible facts. "Lady Southborne's maid told me of this garth. 'Tis a lovely allure, do you not agree? What with the view and the roses?" She extricated herself from him, going to the parapet's edge. There the red roses spilled across the stones with a wild abandon, ruffling in the breeze to send a musky perfume to the air about them.

Cognizant that they could be seen from the room he had recently left, Matt followed her to contemplate the bronze cast of the sun across the green fields. Here, so close again, he could detect the lavender signature upon her skin. Here, so close, he could remember the feel of her skin beneath his questing fingertips. She embodied so many glories most men would thrill to claim as their own . . . though he, of all men, could never take her and make her his.

"Lacy . . ." He struggled with his own fear and knew hers made her keep her back to him. "Lacy, I am sorry I could not come to you sooner. The afternoon has been filled with so many duties."

"I have kept well occupied." She kneaded her hands. He could tell by the way her shoulders flexed and her posture remained rigid.

"Darling," he said, and cursed himself that he had no right to call her by any endearment. Despite who might see, he put his hands to her quivering shoulders.

She curled away from him. "Why touch me so tenderly when you seek to tell me things to make me leave you?"

He swallowed this new pain of rejection. With hellish agony, his knees began to buckle with the blow. "I knew it would be so with you. Once you understood what I came from, what a hell my family lived in, you would not want me."

She spun, fearful tears beading in her beautiful eyes. "You think what you told me today sends me from you? Oh, Matthew!" She put a hand to his chest where all his pain whirled like a cyclone. With her touch, calm euphoria took its place. "My wonderful man, you are an idiot. What you told me this noontide tells me nothing of you that I should fear. Only of some nameless baron who took a whip to your sister and of your father who condoned it! Those are not your sins!"

He grasped her arms. "Listen to me. They *are* my sins! I tried to stop both men and couldn't!"

"You were a boy! What would you expect?"

"I was as tall as I am now. As skilled in archery and a battle ax."

"Skilled at many things, but not at holding back the inevitable." She floated closer, and the need to thumb away her tears from her flushed cheeks overtook his fine resolve. "Oh, Matt, there was nothing you could have done to prevent those events."

Just as there is nothing I can do now to hold back the tide of love that floods my very soul with need of you. He brought her flush to him and raised her chin with gentle fingers. "Lacy, your absolution fills me with humility."

"I wish it gave you peace."

"Only you give me peace, my love."

Her eyes flowed over his features. "'Tis said a kiss is the greatest sign of peace."

"Ahh, Lacy." His trembling lips skimmed her warm ones. "You are so right. You are my peace, my joy. I fear you are my everything." He caressed her mouth tenderly, testing the measure of her plump lower lip and the delicate art of her upper. He kissed her lingeringly and then took her mouth once more in a consummation that had her moaning and him aloft in a storm of desire.

She came with him, wildly pressing herself to him, giving herself to the tumultuous waves of their mutual ecstasy. This time, his kisses came in a gush of heat. They went deeper, faster, surer, tasting her texture, tangling with her tongue. Of a sudden, he knew he needed to anchor them both while this torrent raged around them. He lifted her, catching her under her knees and taking her to spread across his lap as he sat on the stone bench.

Splaying his fingers into her hair, it fell about his hands and arms. The curls, amber waves with brilliant lighter streaks, wound around his wrists with a will of their own. His burning eyes beheld her languid ones and enjoyed the look of longing on her lovely face. His thumbs traced the perfection of her cheekbones and her chin. She was so ravishing, so achingly beautiful. Wanting to trace all her features, he drew her near and with parted mouth defined her smooth forehead, her fine brows, her dainty eyelids, and her nose. With every reverent stroke, he longed to prove how avidly he adored every inch of her, how dearly he wished he might keep her, cherish her not just now but all the days of their lives.

She sat still, her eyes closed, her mouth open to his, her head moving as his lips found and nuzzled the delicate skin behind her ear.

"My darling wife, how I wish you were truly mine."

She quivered as he blazed a trail down the elegant column of her throat, bending her back over his arm. This time, the feel of cloth between them made him impatient to see and feel that which he had once admired. With a swift, small pull, he lowered her gown to reveal the creamy expanse he longed to savor. He gazed at her full, high breast with its roseate nipple.

"I knew you would be perfect," he crooned as he took her mouth with his lips and her full breast with his questing hand. "Your body is so pretty." He outlined the circumference of her breast with the backs of his fingers, then stroked and shaped her aureole into a peak. "At my touch, your body reaches for me. How can I not cover you with my response?" His mouth wended down once more. "You are God's delight in so many ways."

She shook back her hair, groaned, and abandoned herself to his ministrations. "I need only to be your delight."

Her admission made him wild. This time when he dipped his head, he sucked her large, satiny nipple into his mouth and laved it endlessly. It rose and firmed as he molded it higher with his lips. His hand drifted to her leg, and his fingers gathered up her gown. Her skin along her thigh was taut but soft. She cuddled closer, clamped her legs in want of him while his hand palmed her moist hair. She called his name in embarrassed objection and delight. Gently, he threaded his fingers through her tangled down, tugging her legs open with tiny exhortations. On a little cry from her, his fingers parted her and slid inside where she was slippery with need. She gasped and curled her body up into his hand. He exulted—and railed against his selfishness and his stupidity that Henry could oversee this were he up and about the room he used as a study.

Matt withdrew gently, reluctantly. He pulled down her skirts, smoothed the gown, and all the while he kissed her, purposely lessening the intensity so that she might not suffer.

He drew her to him, put her head to his shoulder, and placed his lips against her cheek. He shut his eyes at his own willfulness, unable to find words to explain his remorse.

She stirred. "Is that how tender it is between a husband and wife?" she asked, her silken voice muffled as she spoke against his throat, her hand nestled into the hair at his nape.

"Aye. I would say it must be so since it is thus with the only wife this husband ever had."

She gave him a little hug. "'Tis wonderful."

"'Tis but the beginning." No sooner were the words out than he wanted to kick himself. Why speak of a beginning when there could be no ending?

"There *is* more, isn't there?"

"Aye, my sweet," he murmured. "Much more."

She moved away a bit to gaze at him from his shoulder. "Is it always so exciting?"

He brushed back her hair from her face and avoided meeting her passion-filled eyes. "No."

He knew it wasn't. And that knowledge roiled him, too. He'd had other women in his arms, in his bed. He'd taken them as a green boy or as an overeager youth. He'd taken some out of sorrow over his battles, others from the vapors of too much wine. All of them, he knew, he had taken in lust. For that reason, over the years, fewer and fewer had graced his bed. He had come to hate the impersonality, the hurried imitation of the act for an emotion that ever eluded him. This act—incomplete and unsatisfying though it had been and had to be—this act with this one woman had confirmed the searing difference between hot carnal pleasures and the blissful act of love.

Matt lifted her to her feet and helped her rearrange her bodice. Upon her cheeks, a flush of shyness spread. "I must say, my love, I like this gown. The color is the best for you. But I have something I intended for you from Flanders that just might do for the dress the very thing I think appropriate." When she lifted her face, he could tell she was curious and still a little embarrassed by their actions. He gave her his most congenial smile. "It is a bit of Flemish lace. Many women wear the yardage now as trimming for their gowns."

"Aye. I know of some patterns. My weavers in my village do attempt to imitate it. But"—her eyes twinkled in a thousand turquoise stars—"you got this lace for me?"

"Aye. I have it in my baggage with the train. It was to be my birthday present to you. I would you have it now."

"Why would you give it me? You never gave me any token of your affection before this."

He dropped his gaze to the points of his shoes. "I never felt correct using your own money to buy you presents. This lace was given me by a Flemish lord for a diplomatic service I performed between the man and Henry. But more than that, I would give you this present because I knew last winter we would try to take the crown from Richard's head. I thought, perhaps, if we won, I might approach you and . . ." He forced back all the tender fantasies he'd nurtured of her. The reality of her far surpassed any dream. "But then, I had to enter England to reconnoiter. On a bad move, I was captured and imprisoned by a Yorkist faction. Henry prepared the invasion without me, until I escaped. But he saved my gift for me to give you when we landed, and I . . ."

Lacy put her hand to his arm. "You *did* think of me."

"Aye. You'll never know how much, how often."

"I'd love to be told, though. Especially about how you wished to bring this gift to me."

"My courage failed me—or should I say my audacity. But if you would like it, I could bring it to supper." He didn't trust himself to seek her out in her apartment. Being alone with her always ended with them entwined like lovers. "Perhaps Anna is good with a needle?"

"Aye, very good." She reached up on tiptoe and placed a tender kiss upon his cheek. "I thank you now for I won't be able to at supper."

He smiled down at her and squeezed her hand. God, how he adored this charming, giving wife of his. "What say you to a game of chess?" Perhaps, if he could put something between them—a board, a wall, one million miles—he might be able to find the objectivity to tell her what he must.

Her turquoise eyes blinked up at him in gratitude. "I would like that. I am a very good gamesman."

He smiled. "I bet you are. Very well, I will retrieve one from the solar. I think I saw one there this noontide. Shall we play the match here?"

"Aye." She straightened and composed herself enough now to grin at him. "A quick game before the sun goes down."

"You think you'll win?"

"I always do. Robert Morris said I was superb."

"Ahh, my love, how right he was." Matt tapped her pert nose with a forefinger. "I'm off to find that chess set."

The ancient armored door creaked open and there stood—of course—Gerard. He held a book and an inquisitive look. "Lacy? What are you doing with him? I thought we were going to read poetry?"

Lacy's wide eyes flew in apology first to Gerard and then to him. Matt knew 'twas the best form to act the gentleman and relinquish his wife to the man who had the prior claim upon her time, but he hated the very idea. He clenched his jaw, making a needling toothache a dagger's pain.

As he turned, a movement from the corner of his eye drew his gaze upward. There sat his king, reclined upon the window ledge, his arms folded. How long had Henry perched there?

Matt flexed his hurting jaw and left his wife once more to the man who wanted her. As he slammed the massive castle door, he knew he now must seek out the man who held his wife's fate in his hands. And who held his own future as well.

CHAPTER 7

MATT WAITED AT THE ENTRANCE TO SOUTHBORNE'S GREAT hall with impatience. Henry's commanders had long since sought their seats inside the cavernous oak-lined room. Henry's allies soon followed. Those drifting toward the hall last were those who only recently had come to the conclusion that this Tudor was a man to court. This come-lately ragtag crowd included not only one Yorkist sympathizer from the next estate but also a few merchants from major towns. Matt listened to their chatter with distinct unease, folding and unfolding his arms, fingering the package he'd wrapped so carefully in the French parchment. Where *was* Thomas, and why was it taking him so long to complete a few simple preparations for a sojourn for two?

"I tell you, Lord Everett," mouthed one fleshy, piebald man to Henry's chief treasurer as they waited in the long hall to go in to supper, "I think His Majesty's estates should be returned unto him."

Matt clenched his jaw and winced in recognition that Gerard Wentworth had risen so quickly in Henry's favor. Gerard's idea had won approval not just with Henry but with his financial wizard as well. Magician with money that he was, Lord Everett had often wished for an easy way to fill his liege's coffers. Well, Gerard Wentworth's bold idea had provided the means to fill Henry's privy purse as well as the national treasury. But Matt wished to God the noble scholar would simply disappear. Gerard would, too, in a few hours now that Matt would have his way. For one short but precious day, Lacy would be his. Totally, undividedly his. And then he would not only be able to find some solitude to tell her why he could never keep her, he would be able to show her why.

"'Tis easier to say than do, Master Arnold."

Matt spun to view the fat man with the lascivious smile. Arnold. The same Arnold who was Lacy's neighbor?

"Easier than collecting new taxes from those of us who are trying to remain in business. As I told you before, our wool industry is thriving."

The two went on at each other, pointing and nodding, moving forward slowly with the throng bent on good supper seats. Matt, meanwhile, took in every detail of the squat man whose tinny voice made Matt's ears ring. From the man's discourse, he was none other than that Arnold, that merchant who had bought the Fitzhugh estate close to Lacy. Matt could imagine such a whale of a man raiding land that was not his. How could he sit a horse? He seemed so grasping with his rings bulging his fat fingers and so obsequious with his small eyes darting about the crowded corridor.

But looking at Arnold became no contest when Matt spied the splash of apricot wool weaving through the masses. He took two steps around and smiled down into his wife's sweet countenance. How he had missed her!

"Good evening, my lady." He had the insane urge to sweep her close and kiss her, hold her to him, and claim her, caress her. . . . He cleared his throat and tore his eyes from her joyful ones to consider his gift. "I brought my present as I promised."

She clapped her hands in glee. "May I open it now?"

He chuckled. "Do you desire all gifts this avidly?"

"Only gifts from my handsome husband." She let her head fall back as her eyes flowed into his.

He put the tiny package into her cupped palms. "Open it quickly before I drown in your eyes, my sweet. The crowd does move more rapidly to supper." He found he could not tear his gaze from her face as she licked her lower lip, ripped at the satin ribbon and the ivory parchment to reveal a length of lace that made her glorious features beam like the sun.

"'Tis the loveliest treasure," she whispered as her fingers brushed its pattern, and he wished she stroked his body in its stead. "Thank you, my dear husband. I shall wear it with great joy."

He arched a brow. "And with greater modesty than we have been treated to in that riot of a gown. I much prefer the turquoise of this afternoon."

She tsked, then set her hand upon his doublet's sapphire brocade sleeve. "I shall have Anna sew this to my bodice immediately when supper is ended." She asked him to tuck it into his belt and keep it for her until then.

He nodded agreeably, thinking to himself how impossible Anna's service would become once his plans took full motion.

"My good marchioness!" The fleshy Arnold stepped aside Lacy, and Matt's nostrils flared with the rancid smell of so much suet. "How fortunate to see you here at Henry's court."

Lacy moved not a muscle. Yet with her body this close, Matt felt her freeze like a petrified animal. With narrowing eyes, Matt focused on this man who dared to take what was his wife's—her land and her time.

"The marchioness goes in to supper, sir."

"Arnold. Master Alphonse Arnold." The man introduced himself, inclining his head while the king's treasurer looked above the throng of those before him in the line.

"Master Arnold"—Matt ruminated over the name a moment as if considering some fouled food—"excuse us. The marchioness is famished."

Arnold's long, thin brow crumpled like a rag. "And whom might I have the pleasure of addressing, my lord?"

Matt felt his anger boil, summoning his dragons to this fray. The red beast licked his chops while Matt suppressed the urge to take this meaty Arnold by his neckless body and throw him out into the courtyard. "I am the marchioness's husband, and do believe me when I tell you, Arnold, you take no pleasure in meeting me."

That made the man fall back, covering his initial reaction of surprise with his second one of fluster. His third reaction was a mighty blow. "Fletcher. The king's Sure Arrow." He looked Matt up, down, and across to nod finally at his opponent's power. Lacy melted against Matt's side, her body screaming at him to rescue her from this menace. "Interesting, isn't it, that you have finally appeared after all these years."

Everett intervened, his expression aghast that someone would criticize Matt, who was his friend. "Lord Fletcher has served King Henry extremely well."

"Ah, yes," said Arnold through pursed lips. "I'm certain he has. We have heard of your exploits in our towns and byways. The King's fabled Sure Arrow, it is said, makes many a man whimper at his power and many a woman arch like a bow—except his own wife, that is."

Lacy recoiled at his crudity, pressing her hand to Matt's chest. "Please," she begged.

"Aye, my love, we leave this man to his own base thoughts." Matt circled his arm around her waist and led her past the hideous man. As they walked forward, he crooned to her, "Don't think of him. Don't let him know he hit his target. Come, I will see you seated and a cool glass of wine in your hand." When he had provided her with both, he took the seat next to her and reached to loop one escaping golden ringlet around her dainty ear. He took her freezing hands in his. "There. You are safe with me."

"Why is he here?" Lacy gulped and turned to seek out the devil in the crowd.

Matt put a finger under her chin and brought her lovely face around to his. "Darling, he cannot hurt you."

"*Aye,* he can! He has!" Tears sprang into her eyes and began to dribble down her cheeks.

Matt fished out a handkerchief from his belt and wiped her flushed skin.

"Oooo, look! The son came with him, too!" Her

silken voice threaded to a wisp of despair as she turned from them. "Why are they here?"

Matt examined the son, who resembled the father not in the least. He was tall, well hewn in shoulders and legs, and sported a mass of carrot curls atop his not unhandsome head. "They've come, like so many others, to seek new favors from a new king."

Her eyes shot to Henry, who just now entered the hall. "They've come to plead for the rights to my land."

"Lacy—"

"They have, I tell you! I know these brigands. They threatened for years, but after Robert Morris died, they became bolder. Taking my villeins' animals, abducting and threatening and hurting my people and . . . others."

"Why do they want these portions of your land so badly that they would risk charges of trespassing and thievery to gain them?"

"The portion they desire sits beside a swift-flowing stream, which they might use to wash their wool before weaving. If they have this, it means they need not pay to come across my boundaries. Hence, they are richer faster."

"Do they claim any legal right to this parcel of your land?"

"The Fitzhughs, from whom the Arnolds purchased the land, received their land grant from William the Conqueror at the same time as did my ancestor, the first De Vere. Evidently, there was a boundary dispute even then, settled only by the king. William claimed he owned the disputed land by the stream and divided it between the Fitzhughs and De Veres to manage for him. But the Fitzhughs did poorly manage their portion and in my father's time, the old King Henry reclaimed it for the Crown. He let my father keep the De Vere portion. In our latest wars, the Fitzhughs supported the Yorkist cause and won their portion back from the Yorkist King Edward. That's how the Arnolds bought their land, which comes close to the stream but does not touch its banks."

"I see." He squeezed her hand and rose. "Wait here a minute or two. I shall return to you."

She caught his sleeve. "You will not tell Henry? He does not know. I did not tell him for fear he would confiscate all our lands. I wanted to settle this myself."

"Aye, love. I see that. I promise you I will not reveal your fuller motive to Henry. There is something else I would ask of him that could aid your cause." *And mine.*

He strode to Henry, who settled in his seat. Then he bent to his ear. "Sire, I would ask another favor of you. Small but important to my peace of mind."

Henry's gray gaze fell over him. "This totals two today. Since you have asked naught of me before this day, this second must be important as the first. Ask it, Matt. It shall be yours."

"There is among us tonight a man who has lately come to court your favor. His name is Arnold. I would beseech you not to give him audience until I return. Then Lacy will have Wentworth's support to counter any issues."

"This Arnold causes problems for your wife, eh?" He tapped a finger against his cheek. "Why do I suspect I should know the reason? No matter, for now. It shall be as you require."

"Thank you, Sire."

"Thank not your king but your friend, Matt."

Matt grinned at the man who had been his confidant since they were boys. "I appreciate it, Harry."

"I have appreciated all you have done for me, my Arrow." Henry slapped him on the back. "I wish you godspeed. When next we meet, I hope you are a happier man."

"I will be, thanks to you."

"I doubt that, but kings must take all credit, especially that which is not due them. Eat. Go. And take as long as you need, will you?"

"I shall return within a day, two at the most."

"If you need more, the time is yours. Ah"—Henry hoisted a hand—"no arguments. Your second in command has been well trained by you for these five years. You trust him. Therefore, so do I. Take the time you need for this. I have my plans for London ready, thanks to you, and I predict, as do you, our forces will meet small, if any, competition."

Matt returned to his chair, feeling as though Harry had implied more things than Henry would acknowledge. But fond memories of Harry and him fishing in Welsh rivers and climbing through French caves were fast supplanted by the terrible sight of his wife kneading her fingers white.

"I have spoken with Henry. He will not see these ruffians until I give the word."

Her terror ceased. Her head turned and her mouth parted as her grateful gaze delved into his. "How do I thank you?"

Visions of a thousand things she might do to thank him flooded his mind. She could kiss him or let him kiss her, caress her, lave her rosy breast, take her to some wide bed where both might drown in the oceanic passion they bore each other. He gulped back all those illusions and smiled pleasantly. "You might walk with me in the courtyard after dinner."

That brought joy to her face as nothing had so far

this night. "I will." She scanned the room with eagerness. "Where are the servants with the food?"

He roared with hilarity and kissed her fingertips. "Starving, are you?"

"Aye." She laughed. "I'd say I have a strong appetite."

Not half as strong as his, he'd wager. Thank heaven, he had asked Henry for only a day, two at the most. He could not risk being with his wife alone for longer than that. He already felt caught in the intricate delight of having her entirely to himself. Aye, he would take her with him to Fletcher Castle, but there he would untangle himself from her loving web, not enmesh himself further!

But his wild joust between his desire for her and his duty to tell her all ended as he watched her become stoic.

Now, dished up with supper's endless courses came a new terror for him. Lacy—his charming, witty wife—turned to stone. Repeatedly she would glance down from the advantage of the dais, seek out the fat pigeon named Arnold and his smirking son. And each time Matt sought to bring her attention back to him, she tried to shake her leaden thoughts. Too soon she would begin again to pick at her food or stare at her lifeless hands. Even Gerard, who sat at her other side, could not draw her from her brooding.

Gerard's frustrated blue eyes met Matt's. Matt arched his brows in vacuous response and wondered what, if anything, Gerard knew of this struggle Lacy had with the Arnolds. He also pondered what advantage a scholar might bring to a dispute over land. Husband or not, Gerard looked the type to win either with a war of words or with a few hired men-at-arms. Matt prayed Gerard had many strong yeoman to protect Lacy. He would hate to turn her over to a man unable to save her from this slavering duo who lived too close to her for comfort. Therefore, before he bowed himself out of Lacy's life forever, he would assure himself of Gerard's powers of persuasion, both in might and word. He'd set Thomas Norwich to the task while he was gone. Tom would welcome the work for it would keep his mind and his hands off Lacy's maid, Anna, whom this afternoon he declared he loved beyond all measure.

But when supper ended and actors assumed the stage at the other end of the hall, Matt knew his time had come. He glanced at his wife, lost in her own terrors, and acknowledged one of his own. What if she would not come with him? What would he do? He could never force her against her will. She had been sore abused by others in that way before. He wished her only joy, evermore. And if she would not come? What could he offer as the bait? He had nothing. Nothing . . . For it was God's truth, the finest treasure —the only treasure—he had ever possessed was one he had never so valued until now when he had to release her.

Tom Norwich bent to him. "My lord, I come to inform you that all is prepared."

"Thank you. I shall not forget you for this." He glanced at Lacy, who had risen from her chair to converse with the lady of the castle, Lady Southborne. "I want you to do me another service while I'm away."

"After I return Anna to De Vere or before?"

Matt lowered his voice so that the fretting Gerard might not overhear. "During, I would say. I need to know how well armed certain households are." His eyes pierced Tom's brown ones and led them to an unaware Gerard.

"Aye. 'Twill be done. You will send me word if you need me?" The young man seemed anxious.

Matt put his hand to Tom's shoulder. "If that were necessary, you would be the first I would summon. But this battle"—he inhaled and let his eyes trace the woman from whose charms he would free himself—"I fight alone."

"Are you certain, my lord?" Tom blurted and then, shaking off his embarrassment, walked into the maelstrom he stirred. "I do watch you and see you bear more the demeanor of a man who loves than one who seeks to live alone."

"You know not the reason, Tom, but I swear to you, I cannot live and love with this woman. Nor with any."

"Is there a fault? If it were so, why have I not found it these past two years I have served you, my liege? And assuming it does exist, is the fault so massive? Even I do find a means to breach the wall between my station as a knight and the woman whose status some would say should bar me from her."

Matt winced. "Ah, Tom. You can surmount your barricade. Mine is too high, too wide, too ancient."

"For a soldier with such skill and fame as you, I find it difficult to believe a barricade so formidable exists to deter you."

"It is one not of my making, yet one I often tried to cross to get to my wife. It seems I cannot find the means."

"Be you certain, my lord, I pray you. For by the looks of you when you do gaze at your wife—and too by the way she responds in kind—I would say if you reject her this time, she will never come to you again."

"Aye, and justly so. Too much time has she lived without a man to love and care for her properly. But I swear to you, I release her from her marriage vows because I care too deeply for her to hurt her by my continued presence in her life."

Tom's somber eyes blinked with tears. "I bid you well, my lord. I will see you in a few days."

Matt watched his retainer leave the dais for the floor where he did take Anna's arm. The maid stared at Matt for an interminable moment, bit her trembling lips, and took one last look at her mistress. *Take care of her,* Matt swore she mouthed. At his nod, she turned to Tom and let him lead her from the hall. Matt saw them go and wished he could take his wife's arm as easily into a paradise similar to that he recognized around Tom and Anna. Alas, he could not.

He strode forward, bowed to Lady Southborne, and took his wife's arm so that he could begin to lead her into hell.

He snapped his jaw together, winced in pain at his aching tooth, then half-smiled, discoursed, played the courtier, and wished to God he could extricate his wife from the eternal pleasantries to begin his journey.

"What ails you, my husband?" Lacy peered into his eyes as Lady Southbourne politely passed on to another guest.

"I have a toothache, but that is naught compared to my other ailments."

"Which others?" Alarmed, she put a hand to his brow. "You have no fever."

"Aye. I have a raging fever."

She tilted her head. "Do your eyes burn? Your muscles ache?" The backs of her fingers skimmed his cheek. Her palm pressed his chest.

"Aye, my love. My eyes burn at the sight of your beauty. My arms ache to hold your perfection."

"Matt!" It was a long, slow moan of joy and wild embarrassment as her eyes circled those near.

"Come with me now." He tugged her hands. "I need you."

"Henry?"

"I told him we're going. He expects no courtesies."

The stars of the heavens twinkled in her blue-green eyes. "Well, in that case, let's go."

They wove through the guests—and past two staring Arnolds—with quick ease. Past his archers, who smiled with envious eyes at their commander's comely spouse. Past four sleepy guards and then out into the inner courtyard. The night formed a black blanket across the sky while the huge moon glared down upon them.

"Where shall we stroll?" Lacy hooked her hand around his upper arm and inadvertently pressed close.

He knew now, as he had not that first day they met and she had done it, that this was one more expression of her affectionate nature. That it should be for him when he could never deserve such kind regard roiled him. He covered her hand with his own. "To the outer courtyard." But having once said it, he halted.

Lacy became confused. "What's the matter? Don't you want to go now?"

"No. Yes."

She blinked. "So . . . we won't go and we will, eh? My dearest, would you please make up your mind?"

"I can't."

"I will do it for you." She pulled him by the arm. "'Tis a warm and pleasant night for a walk—to the outer courtyard. Come along." She was teasing him now, drawing him with her devastating smile and dancing eyes.

But once through the inner wall, she stopped at the sight before her. The groomsman, who had held two sets of reins, looped them over a post, then trundled off with a doff of his hat. Lacy had not moved. "Your horse and mine are saddled." Because he dreaded to confront her straight on with the truth, instead he admired how moonglow lit her features from earthly beauty to divine. "Why are they here, Matt?" She lifted her serene eyes to his.

"I wondered if you would consider . . . I did want to know if . . . I . . ." He raked his hair and spun away from her. Jamming both hands on his hips, he threw his head back and shut his eyes to the problem he'd invented.

He heard her approach, felt her circle him. The next thing he knew she reached both hands up to cup his face and bring it down to hers. "Look at me. Aye . . . that's better. What did you wonder? If I would ride beneath the stars with you?" She smiled so radiantly that it seared his heart. "I think 'tis a fine idea. Come with me, isn't that what you said?" She gave a little chortle and tugged at his hands.

He dug his heels in. "No!"

At his vehemence, her expression fell.

"Not merely a ride! A journey! A necessary . . ."

She dropped his hands and with that considering tilt of her head, she examined him a second before turning to their horses. She patted her mount's nose, crooned sweet words to the animal, and stroked him before she went to do the same to Matt's own beast. The creature, which had known the charge of lances and the hack of axes on so many battlefields, also understood affection when he felt it. He snorted, pawed the dust, and nodded his elegant ebony head in acknowledgment of this woman's care. Lacy left the stallion to walk between both horses. At the rolled baggage strapped to each saddle, she ran her hands over their bulk and seemed to stop breathing. Without looking at Matt directly, she rasped, "Where would you have us go against King Henry's will?"

Matt swallowed repeatedly. "He gave his permission."

She took that in with a hard blink. "Where then, my husband?"

"Fletcher Castle," he whispered, weakness gnawing at his knees.

She heard him though, by the shake of her head, she appeared at first to disbelieve him. "I cannot go and leave the Arnolds to harangue Henry with their views."

"I told you he will not see them until I say the word."

Her gaze softened. "Henry loves you greatly that he would do such." When Matt did not reply, Lacy asked, "What of Gerard? He will take this as a slight."

"Henry promises to smooth the way with Gerard, telling him we will return soon and occupying him by proceeding to absorb all thoughts on politics and money."

Lacy grinned. "To the Crown's great benefit, I am certain. But then . . . why is Anna not here?"

"She will not come. That is, I did not think initially that she would . . . Ah, hell, Lacy, when I first devised this plan, I thought I would abduct you, lure you from the hall, and sweep you into my arms and over the saddle . . ."

Of a sudden, a smile played about the corners of her mouth. "What? Not throw me over your shoulder?"

"Lacy, this is no jest. I would never treat you like a sack of wheat. I wanted you to come with me to my home . . . or what passes for it. It's really just a set of buildings. A hulking thing. Not a home to me. It never was." He was punching his fist into his palm with the memories of what had occurred at Fletcher years and years ago, before he understood more than the meaning of terror.

She stepped forward, the touch of her hands atop his own ceasing his misery. "I would like to ride with you to Fletcher Castle."

Incredulous, he narrowed his eyes at her.

A smile broke upon her features like the sun after a storm. "I have one request, though." She fought mightily to stop up her laughter.

"Name it. It is yours."

She leaned to him conspiratorially. "I would like it very much if you would do all those things you did intend."

"You mean—?"

"A lady lives a quiet life, sir. She does ever crave one noble knight to, as you put it, lure her from a crowd and sweep her into his arms and over his saddle. A woman needs adventure just as men do." She sent him a ravishing smile. "I would be swept to your arms, my knight."

With a hoot of delight and fathomless relief, he scooped her up as if she were a sack of grain. He cradled her to him with reverence as he strode toward the horses. "You always make me laugh." *And want and need.* "You amaze me, my lady Fletcher."

"Do I?" she managed between chuckles and a tender caress of her hand along his jaw. "I return the compliment, my lord Fletcher." At his approach to her horse, she snapped her head around in surprise. "To do this correctly, weren't you going to *sweep* me over *your* saddle?"

"As my lady wishes." He pivoted with a rolling gait and gently deposited her atop his mount. Gathering up the reins to her horse, he lifted her sapphire cloak from across the animal's back. Then he hoisted himself behind her with one agile heave. As his arms closed around her to clothe her in her cloak, he knew once again the sublime delight of conquest and possession. To feel such happiness was so wrong, to adore her worse. But to delude her into thinking this journey would bring her joy was such a sin.

He kneed the horse and led them from the outer courtyard, beyond the gatehouse, and down the drawbridge to the road. Unlit by torches, the night seemed blacker. As dark as his mood. The sounds of the horses' hooves grew louder. As loud as the voice of his conscience. He sagged.

Her gaiety stilled. "How long is our journey?"

"An hour at the most. Are you tired? Hungry?"

She shifted back against him and he caught her tighter to him. "No," she said. "I sought only to know how long I might enjoy this feel of your arms about me."

"Ah, Lacy, I would that you stay here always." The allure of her lavender-scented hair drew his lips to her curls, as ever.

"Why then do I feel the fear that haunts you return, my husband? I wish that whatever troubles you, you would share with me." She slid her head across his shoulder so that she could consider him from her natural repose. "I am your wife, and I want to help ease all your sorrows."

"Aye, Lacy. That, I promise you, you shall know. For at Fletcher Castle, there is much to learn, my darling."

She smiled, some secret satisfaction spreading across her features. "This I do believe," she said.

"'Tis an old, ugly place. Filled with cobwebs and dust and lined with mold. Yet there are a few good rooms I bade my servants keep up to readiness standards. You will be comfortable, though not probably to your usual level."

"I have no fears," she offered simply. "You have not visited recently?"

'Twas an odd thing for her to ask. "No. Not since . . . I frankly can't remember when. Possibly, the year before last." The time he'd crossed the Channel as an emissary for Henry to the Scots king. The last time when he had ridden to Lacy's estate border to gaze across the hills toward De Vere Castle and all for which he hungered.

How long had he sat his horse atop that knoll, and how often had he sallied forth only to retreat? He wanted then to put this sham of a marriage to the test. He had come to so hate warfare. To so despise his endless soldier's duties. He had wanted so badly then to ride across the plain, introduce himself, and see if he and his wife might find some companionship together. But, he argued with himself, he had nothing to give his wife—just as he had for all the previous years of their marriage. Nothing. Not security nor hope of any. His liege lord Henry remained, as he had for many years, an exile in another land, and Matt, as Henry's retainer, must abide with him. Though that condition had certainly changed, the one Fletcher Castle personified in all its moldering ruin had not.

Lacy idly traced a pattern in his brocade doublet. "Mayhaps it has changed."

He snorted. "I doubt it, my sweet. Servants cannot work miracles."

"There is the possibility you do her wrong, you know. Mayhaps beneath her exterior is a lady of some dignity."

He caught her chin between his thumb and forefinger. "You mean like that one woman who so recently came to me? That charming little dumpling who weighed no more than a feather?" He clucked his tongue. "An odd event it was, too, to encounter such a woman. Beneath her flowing garments, I found her flesh measured more than my legs did tell me I supported. Then, when from beneath her swath of veils the voice flowed over me like the stroke of silk, I was curiously drawn. From trailing tippets, her fragile fingers emerged to chase an errant hat." He took one hand and brought it to his mouth where he branded her palm. "Aye, my dearest lady. I saw a woman the other day, and though she appeared extraordinary, I could not imagine what a rare jewel she was."

"How will I ever recover from all the compliments you shower on me?"

"They are not compliments but truths."

"You are so sweet to me." She captured his eyes.

"You are the sweetest woman I have ever known." How could he want to strike her from him when all he could think about was taking her to him? He bent over her and knew her lips were too ripe a temptation for any mortal to resist. "Were I a starving angel, my love, I would ask God to let me sup at your lips. For one touch of your mouth can nourish a dying man and make him believe that all things do come aright."

He placed his lips tenderly above hers and swirled his tongue around the soft edges of her mouth. She opened wider for him. He touched the tip of his tongue to her shy one, and she whimpered. In her move, she jostled the saddle, and he sought to steady her with one helping hand. He cupped one pliant thigh. Her strength, her feline sleekness filled his hand and then his mind.

His fingers splayed. His thumb found torrid heat. The others sought to follow. He pressed plump flesh and felt her arch up and back, rushing like hot lava against his body and moistening his startled, probing fingers. God above, she gushed so relentlessly, her humors doused the satin with her passion.

He growled in anguished delight. He'd never known a woman to respond so fiercely so instantly. Her compliment filled his mind with humility—and some wild dream that he might more fully see her satisfaction. If only they were in a bed, he might enjoy those attributes he had denied his hungering soul. Then would he, like a gentle man and grateful mate, teach her the full extent of her body's response to him. He would put his lips upon her breasts and belly, and here, at the source of her femininity, he would drink at her font.

His fingers—eager little men with appetites of their own—crinkled up the wool to its edge. Then, as his open mouth gave her sweet cheek a measure of his homage, his palm cupped the fire of her desire. His longest finger found her molten cleft and sank into swollen ecstasy. She strained backward and in her writhing, turned her face more toward him so that he now viewed her abandon.

He would die if he did not taste more.

With one smooth stroke, he took both sets of lips.

Her nether lips engulfed his caressing fingers, bathing them in her natural joy in him, swallowing him in her throbbing turbulence.

He moved time and again to take little kisses. "Sweeting, though only my fingers may attest, you are so gossamer soft and hot."

In answer, she hid her face in his throat and clutched his doublet with violent desire.

"Let me help you, darling," he urged as he parted her legs wider to give him access to his prize. Claiming that, he rubbed his fingers into her flowing core to let her feel the volcano's rumble. He found easily the hard little rock of her need. He shifted her, tilting her so that his forefinger and his thumb might tend the tiny pebble.

"Lacy," he murmured, "you need relief from pain."

She moaned, open-mouthed against his throat.

"I will take care of you. There is no other surcease like this. No salve its equal. I would show you joy to replace the sorrow of this night—and all the nights you have been alone and needed a true man."

"Show me anything," she urged, and he suddenly knew she was as delirious now as he to have him put her from her fiery misery. "But please don't take your hand away as you did this afternoon. I felt so . . . so *lost* without you."

"No, that was unfair. I would have you replete in my arms. Satisfied. Soaring. Christ above, you are a succulent woman. Feel . . . hear how your juices flow into my hand. My fingers drown in your ambrosia."

She writhed.

Breathless, he kissed her forehead, her elegant brow, her lovely eyelids while his fingers played in her magic. "I do wonder how you taste here. . . . Spiced and boiling. . . . As delicious as you feel. . . ."

Feel? He had never felt like this! This unearthly heavenly rage to let his mouth brand her, to have his hands claim her and make his mark upon her as his own. To put his hands upon her everywhere, inside, outside. All at once.

She lolled her head against his shoulder and ground her teeth.

He soothed her with fervent kisses and dexterous hands. His own body strained to rip its material confines. He felt harder than fine Augsburg armor and more eager than an untried youth to help her approach her eruption with wild pleasure. "You want to press me in, I know. I feel the power in your pretty thighs. Let me remain inside, love. There, this is where I belong. Here where the fire rages and only I can tend proper flames and give you peace. Ah, yes, that's right. There now, burrow tight to me. There is the first of the convulsions. Moan. No one can hear. Wondrous, I know. *Yes.* And I am strong enough to hold you through any turmoil. Yes, now there is more to come. I know you feel it. There . . . there."

She began to moan as his seeking, ravenous mouth captured her jubilance.

"Sweetheart. There is much more. I know what you need and I would have this for you. Give this to you."

Her body arched, bucked. She exploded in his arms. Convulsions of such power, such rage, such unheralded glory shook her delicate body that he marveled at her ability to withstand the quake. He squeezed his eyes shut to revel in her utter abandon. She shuddered for eternities, while he stroked the last of her tremors to their rest. She then settled into his care with shaking lips to his throat. He laid a hand to her face and kissed her brow. She murmured.

"I know. 'Twas wonderful. You are a giving, generous woman, my darling. So inviting. Any man should fall on his knees to hold such a treasure in his arms."

She shook her face against his chest.

"No, my heart, turn not away from me." He lifted her face. "Look at me. I beg you, look at me. *Aye,"* he breathed, and kissed her nose. "You are so lovely in your desire and your completion of it. Were I the man to make you soar to such heights each night, I would call myself blessed. Now should you rest from all your cares here with me. We will soon arrive at Fletcher." He settled her securely to him and her cloak about her, while he fought down the pounding demands of his own body. "Close your eyes. Sleep."

As she did his bidding, he berated himself. Then found the red and green fiends who were his constant companions slithering along the dark road. Each licked his lipless gums in joy that they returned to the heinous place where both had been spawned.

CHAPTER 8

NEITHER SLEEP NOR REST CAME TO LACY. STIRRED PAST THE boundaries of her innocence by his passion and thrilled from her hair to her toes by his endearing declarations of his affection for her, she approached Fletcher Castle with a thousand mixed feelings.

He cared for her. She could not escape the knowledge.

He desired her. She had recent and repeated evidence, both verbal and physical.

Still, he jousted with stubborn devils from his past who held forth banners declaring that Matt must not care, should not desire her. Each time her husband clashed with his foes, Lacy saw her cause gain some small ground only to retreat. How could she obtain some permanent advantage?

At this castle where Matt had grown to boyhood, she would meet his foe and hers. Here, she would descend from the spectators' seats and enter the fray from which Matt sought to keep her. And she could win. She could. She felt it to be true. She need only admit how she loved him. And oh, how she loved him!

She shifted in his arms and felt the massive, sturdy comfort of his form. Down to the marrow of her bones, she reveled in his care of her—and yearned that he might love her. If he could, if he did, then surely the power might make the day theirs—and their years might become their haven amid the outrageousness of earthly woes.

She twisted so that her face nestled into his chest. Absently, he kissed her forehead and rearranged his arms about her. Little could he know how her admission of her love could thrill her and frighten her. She loved him. When had she not? From the time she was old enough to ask Lady Margery for stories of her husband, she had cared for him. For his bravery and his loyalty. Aye, they were commendable traits any true knight should possess. But now that she had met her husband in the flesh, she adored him for all those other traits that were so uniquely his. His humor, through the agonies of their first meeting. His chivalrous regard of her with Henry and Gerard. His affectionate kisses and caresses. His remorse that he could not tame his body's want of her. Aye, she loved every one of his traits. Every inch of him.

So now he took her to his home, where at long last he would summon forth this demon to strut before her. Somehow she would help her husband conquer this brute who divided them. Somehow, with her love upon her every deed, if not aloud in every word, she would grapple with the fiend who wrested her husband from her and the love she bore him.

So, as she relaxed in Matt's arms, she feigned serenity. She also stopped up the joy that bubbled through her veins. Surely, she feared to see that which he promised to show her. She did not want to know this evidence he would present. But neither could she suppress the burgeoning hope that, once seen, this terror in his life would end. And certainly, she knew that whatever his secret, he would see other things at Fletcher Castle. Things that would surprise him—and, she hoped, delight him. For this would not be the first time she came to the Norman fortress. And though it might still possess those attributes that led Matt to call it a hulking thing, it had acquired a few other qualities since last he'd visited. She squirmed in his arms as she anticipated his reaction.

Burrowing into his broad chest, she folded her cloak more about her and peeped at the road. Ebony night offered few lights—the waning moon, the twinkling stars, and one hazy glow that sphered the horizon.

"What can that be?" she asked Matt, sitting forward.

"Torches blazing at Fletcher's gatehouse, I should think. Across this ridge sits the monstrosity I call my home. 'Tis my steward who raises a watch for us."

"You sent word we were coming?"

"Aye." His somnolent voice drugged her with joy while he nestled his lips into her hair as was now his unerring habit. "I had Thomas hire a messenger because I seek for you the best comfort Fletcher Castle possesses. It is not much. God knows, I have never spent a farthing here if there was no need."

She opened her mouth and snapped it shut. She'd almost said, "I know." Instead she gazed up at him. "You also spent little of what I sent you to maintain your person, returning to me much you could have used to improve your daily life."

"I felt like a thief taking your money to help me buy clothes and horses, even my suits of armor."

"'Twas what our marriage was made for—mutual help."

"Nay, my darling, 'twas made for baser things than that and well you know it. You said so yourself before the council." He threaded his fingers through her hair and adored her eyes. "Our marriage was made as many others are. 'Twas a suitable arrangement between a rich female who required protection and a male who had need of her money and her land. We fit the cast, my love. Still, I hated taking that which you gave so freely, so lavishly. I returned what I did not use for myself, and as for the other monies . . . aye, I spent them on necessities."

"A man's home *is* a necessity!" she objected, thrilled by his confirmation of the nobility that she had long suspected in this matter of his use of her money. "I sent you a yearly stipend via Robert Morris to care well for the castle. Why did you not use it on that for which it was intended?"

He shrugged. "Other needs were more pressing."

"What other needs?" She knew, of course, but had to ask lest he detect something amiss in her behavior—and that before he saw the evidence of her actions.

"The dovecote, two centuries or more old, did last fall burn with all the chickens inside. I had my steward build another one so that other animals might grow to feed his family, who tend the castle. Later, in the family chapel, new cloths were needed for the altar. The Franciscan friar from the village told me I owed it to God to replace them in honor of my ancestors. The only reason I did so was because my steward, David, and his wife, Bess, appealed to me to keep the old church in order for the few villeins who do still attend mass occasionally here."

"The household allowance provided so much more money than new altar cloths and a dovecote could ever cost, my husband." She was grinning at him. "I sent money for new tapestries, even thick Spanish ones to line the floors. I included money for panes of diamond-cut glass and new volumes for a library."

"I know. I ordered all that spent on new woolen cloaks for the people of the village and hearty Christmas dinners with good wine. Two years ago, after Richard of York killed the two princes in the Tower of London, I thought all villainy supreme in our land and feared for it. I took your money and pensioned off all the household staff save two of my father's retainers. My steward and his wife, who is the cook, remain and live within the lower apartments near the old great hall. I could not bear to turn them out because they were newly married when I did decide to take this castle down to its basest existence. I wish all your amenities were here for you now. But I did never think I'd ever meet you, much less bring you here."

He snatched at a ragged breath as his horse topped the ridge and halted. Though Lacy knew that his home stood before them in all its aged Norman splendor, she could not tear her eyes from her husband's visage. If ever hatred stood upon a sweet man's brow, it did now on his.

"Oh, weeping Jesus," he growled, "how I loathe this wretched place."

Lacy turned to view the octagonal Norman structure she had seen once in her life—a year ago August when she had come against Robert Morris's wishes. Silhouetted against the dying moon, the monolith of the square keep towered above its crumbling curtain walls. To many, Lacy was certain, the compound looked foreboding. To Matt, she knew it hid some terrible deterrent to their love. To her, it meant naught but a place to rest before enjoining the most significant battle of her life.

She put a hand to his heart, determined to probe his wound, cut the infection, and let her husband live free. "Are those all gone who made you hate it so?"

"Aye. All dead. Every one." His eyes delved into hers in remorse. "I do you wrong to frighten you unduly. No one is here to hurt you."

"Or you," she added meaningfully.

"Aye. You are right." He nodded, as if trying to convince himself, but failed. "Here live only the ghosts of my past. But they do walk with such menace I wished to tear the castle down stone by stone. That is why I emptied it of all innocent people years ago. The place is cursed. I would wish no evil to befall anyone who lived here."

At that, he directed his horse and hers down the path past the thatched cottages of the quiet village to the now-dried-up moat. They crossed the narrow drawbridge into the outer bailey. A scuffling down the stone steps from the battlements and a torch soon revealed a brawny young man about Matt's age.

"My lord Fletcher!" The pale-haired man fell to one knee. "We are pleased to have you with us again." He rose, his eyes sparkling in greeting to his master and then to Lacy, who warned him with round eyes not to reveal their secret. The man gave her a little wink but covered it with a quick grin at Matt.

"Good evening, David. How are you?" Matt dismounted, then turned to offer Lacy his help as she left the saddle.

"Well and getting fat, sir. But not as fat as Bess. She

awaits our second child next month." The moon-faced man took both horses' reins and turned to survey his master and his mistress. "We're very happy you've come home, sir." His eyes spoke in mute eloquence as they met Lacy's.

"David, this is my wife, Marchioness Fletcher."

"Aye, sir. I know. Lord Norwich's messenger said you would be bringing her with you. Bess and me, we were grateful. It's been too long you've been married and not brought her to her home, sir."

"Aye . . ." Matt jammed his hands on his hips and surveyed the shadowed courtyard and the giant keep with impatience. "Did you have enough time to prepare for us?"

"Absolutely, my lord. Right this way." David spread forth one meaty hand and walked beside Lacy, though he spoke to Matt. "We have been preparing for the winter. Now that our Henry has won the throne, Bess and me said we felt better about the coming cold months. We need not fear armies marching across our lands. What say you, my lord? Will there be more war?"

"None. Richard is dead, David. His army is in shambles. Only this morning we met upon the road a small force, which gave us little trouble. England's woes are at an end. We shall live in peace." Matt spoke with reassuring words while studying every cobblestone, every beehive, every haystack. "You have kept the old place in good form. I stand in awe that it could so improve." He halted and so brought them all to a stop as he stood, one foot upon the first step into the keep.

Lacy shuffled, eager to have him see the inside.

David's broad face split in a grin. "I think it is a comfortable home, my lord. Bess and me have tried to make it so. Come, let me show you more." He led the way, opening the hefty armor-studded door into an arched hall alit with sputtering torches.

Lacy walked slightly ahead of her husband but felt attuned to his every move, his every breath drawn in remembrance of this or that. As they strode up the spiral staircase, she heard him mutter about the lack of light here and how it had always been thus upon this stairway. But once in the great hall, more light flickered up from candles upon the banquet table, sending dim lines to dance upon the wall. The huge fireplace lay barren at this hour of the night. Then from one corner emerged a comely dark-haired woman, rounded with her unborn baby and grinning at her lord and master.

"My lord Fletcher." She gave a little curtsy—all she could manage with her girth—and a generous smile of glorious welcome. "My lady. Let me take your cloaks."

Lacy nodded as Bess came forward, tears glistening in her huge blue eyes."We never thought to see you again," she said to Matt with truth and then to Lacy with larger eyes and greater implication. "My husband and I are delighted you chose to come here now. We are grateful for the opportunity to show you how we can serve you."

Matt reached out a hand to help her up. "My dear woman, you need not do any great services for me, I assure you. You have already done so by staying in this horrid place all these years, though to what end I think we all know."

Bess's broad brow wrinkled. "Nay, my lord. Say not now that you still think of shutting up the keep or of razing it to the ground! 'Twould not be seemly, sir. Not when your wife has—"

"Please," Lacy intervened with smiling terror, "cite me not as motive for your hard work. You have kept the castle in good repair long before you ever knew I existed, isn't that correct, Bess?" Lacy peered into the friendly servant's eyes and willed her answer to be the right one.

Bess grinned, on to Lacy's divergence. "Aye, madam. 'Tis so."

Lacy beamed, reprieved for the moment. Turning, she found her husband surveying a tapestry over the fireplace wall. She swallowed hard. This was the first of her hurdles to surmount. "Bess, I wonder if we might prevail upon you to do Lord Fletcher a favor. Have you any potions for pain? He suffers from a toothache."

"Aye, my lady. I have some sage to boil."

"Thank you, he needs it."

Matt had not moved. "What richness is this?" He stretched up to glare at the expansive scenery embroidered there. "I recall no such cloth in our stores. Where did you get this, David?" The steward shifted from one foot to the other. "David, I would like an answer."

"Well, sir, that . . . ah, that came from Flanders."

Matt scowled at the tapestry, then at David, and on to Bess, who bit her lip. Lacy gulped.

"Flanders. Interesting." Matt spun to take a long taper from the table and returned holding it aloft. "A scintillating rendering of the marriage at Cana. One of the best portrayals I have ever seen. In fact, only one other like this have I ever viewed. The Baron Hohenstein owned it, and he claimed his was made by the best weavers in Arras."

"Was it really?" David asked, his voice creaking.

"Aye, David"—Matt drew near to narrow his eyes

at his steward—*"really.* How came you by this piece? This is no ancient family treasure of the Fletchers. We are too poor."

Lacy stepped between her husband and his man. "I bought it. Lady Margery and I traveled to Leicester to the open fair the spring before she died. We stayed with the earl of Canmore and his wife, who is Flemish herself. She recently had visited her family and brought back this and another. I offered her a good amount for it."

Her husband's jaw flexed, defining all the powerful ridges of his sculpted visage. "Why?"

"I thought it lovely," she said, avoiding his eyes.

"Aye, that it is. Lacy, why buy it and bring it here?"

"The Canmores had suffered much in the recent wars over the throne. The earl lost the use of one arm in hand-to-hand combat with a Yorkist at Barnet Field. Afterward, the family fell on hard times. The Arras tapestries were gifts to the Countess Canmore from her parents, who thought the works might bring some joy to their everyday lives—and some money to their empty coffers if she could but sell it. Lady Margery heard of how the countess came by it, and I begged for us to visit, taking many gold sovereigns to pay for it."

At his bark of surprise, she raised her gaze to find him raking his hair and smiling no smile. He strode to face her. His luscious lavender eyes, like his mind, battled whether to give in to anger or more amazement. Somehow, curiosity won. "And how came it here?"

Lacy cupped her fingers together and considered the stone floor. "I brought it myself. I brought it here and had David hang it there where obviously once, from the smoky outlines on the stones, a similar one graced the wall for all to enjoy while at their meals. I asked David what happened to it, but of course, he said that it must have disappeared before his time because he never remembered one there, and so I—"

"Lacy, darling"—Matt lifted her chin with the tips of his fingers—"it's beautiful." Her mouth opened at his mesmerizing expression of devotion. "Tell me, my wife, when were you here?"

"Last year, about this time."

David stepped forward. "My lord, I would that Bess and I depart so that—"

"Remain, David. You also have questions to answer."

The steward fell back to loop his arm securely around his wife.

Lacy licked her lips and strained at a smile for her husband. He could not cease his perusal of her features.

"Lacy, tell it all, will you, love? I weary of this hunt and peck for facts I should have known from you as well as my own staff." He threw David and Bess a weak frown.

Lacy lifted her shoulders. "I tired of never seeing you, never hearing from you." *Always wanting you.* "I came to see . . . aye, to pretend you were here." Her voice breaking, she spread her hands in supplication. "Don't you see, I mourned never knowing who you were and I thought if I came here, I might see where you live, how you live, and know more about you."

He captured her hands between his own palms and brought them to his lips for a tender kiss.

She gasped at his gentleness as she gazed down at his dark curls. "I came unannounced and was welcomed by David and Bess. I came soon after Lady Margery died in July. We had planned the journey together, you see. She had so wanted to accompany me. If she had lived, the visit would have been her first since your mother died. She said—"

Matt raised his head and his eyes grew wet with sadness and some lurking terror. "What did she tell you?"

"That she was a friend of your mother's. They had grown up together, and after your mother married and Margery did not, they grew apart, touching only by letters." Matt winced. Lacy swallowed. "Margery told me that when your mother married your father, she loved the man deeply and that over the years, her health flagged often. She died young. When you were ten, I do believe."

A curtain of steel clanged down between Lacy and her husband. He dropped her hands and strode to the fireplace, staring into the abyss with dead eyes. "My mother was an angel. A black-haired, violet-eyed angel with the sweetest disposition. Her laugh was like the rushing of a gentle brook and her smile, the kiss of a hummingbird. I have seen no woman her like, save my sister, until I did find you." He turned, his mouth open with his struggle to draw air. "Lacy, 'twas wonderfully giving of you to try to make beautiful this awful place."

David stepped forward, twisting his neck out of his doublet in his embarrassment to witness this intimate discourse of his master and mistress. "My lord, you have not seen the half of it!"

Matt's expression tore from pleasure to disbelief. "There is *more?*" His focus on Lacy made her lift her shoulders. "Well, let me see it then. All of it."

Bess clapped her hands as David grinned and both began a recitation of the improvements. Even though it must have been well past midnight, Bess took great pride in pointing out the thick silk ruby cushions upon the dining chairs and the new Fletcher family banners of red and gold furled over the archways. She took them to the kitchen, where she gleefully carted out the silver plate Lacy had commissioned, which had not yet been used except by David and her. She opened a cupboard and withdrew two of forty Venetian rose-glass goblets for Matt to examine. Finally, she displayed forks, knives, and spoons of such delicacy that he either stared or gasped at the workmanship.

"Everything the marchioness bought is such a treasure, my lord, that I do hate to mar their perfection with use."

"I wanted you to use it, Bess. I intended you to enjoy whatever was here, not keep for . . . some future day." Lacy lost her nerve to reveal that she had hoped one day to use it for Matthew's return to his home. But Matt looked so shaken, so undone that she feared his response.

"Aye, my lady, as you said before you left, I should make use of it and so I did for David and me."

David grinned. "Except for that which you placed in the lord's chamber, my lady, we have enjoyed it all immensely."

Matt flapped his hands to his sides. "Well, by all means, do let me see what awaits me in my chambers."

David took one step forward, only to be halted by his wife's grip of his wrist. "I will prepare your potion if, by your leave, sir, I could keep David to help me. My lord, your chambers are prepared, as your messenger requested." She inclined her head, a knowing smile tugging at her lips as Matt nodded in agreement.

While the couple turned away for a mortar, pestle, and herbs, Matt stood silently surveying Lacy. With courage, she caught a glimpse of him and exhaled at his tender gaze. He took one sputtering candle within its holder and lifted it. Without a word, he held forth his arm, and she gratefully glided forward to walk beside him from the kitchen to the great hall, up the curving wide stone steps to the master quarters meant for the lord of the house and his lady. At the door, they paused as Matt stepped forward and lifted the latch. He let the door fall open and stood there a moment, his back to her, as he took in the room laid before him in the glow of scores of candles. She froze at his small sound of utter surprise. Then he turned and, with outstretched hand, waved her toward him. "Come here, my wife. This room's decor needs great explanation."

She stepped inside, filling with joyful pride that the room was as awe-inspiring as she remembered. Huge as the great hall below, this master chamber boasted the best of Norman architecture. Bold symmetrical walls arched to the domed ceiling. Windows deserved less that name as they did the term arrow slits. Still, the stars did twinkle in the cracks where she had ordered glass be set to complement the beauty of the two-hundred-year-old structure. But as she walked upon the plush ivory silk Chinese carpet, she let her fingers trail the tall oak stands and sturdy chairs cushioned lavishly in reds. She smiled at the warmth of the blaze David had set in the twenty-foot hooded fireplace. She grinned at the massive beauty of the room's centerpiece—the broad bed she had had especially built by the local carpenter.

It stole her breath away. Flickering in the candle glow and set against the Fletcher family colors of red and gold brocade upon the back wall, the wide platformed bed sparkled with beauty that brought tears to her eyes. She walked its circumference, feeling the fire's heat at all points, as she had intended. She surveyed the bed's twelve-foot-square bounty and admired the delicacy of the Fletcher coat of arms, its two crossed arrows, stitched in gold to the vibrant red brocade coverlet. She became as pleased as last summer when she had first thought of the idea to replace the old poorly tufted pallet and its threadbare woolen cover she had found in this sparsely furnished room.

She strode forward and touched the handsome carved posters that supported the ornate mahogany canopy. All about its copious edge, the bed's variegated hangings soothed its strong lines in a cascade of sheerest creams and pale pinks, translucent reds and shining satin ruby brocade. Drawn back in invitation, the swaths of exquisite Italian hangings beckoned her to test the golden velvet cords. The swish and slide of so much fabric sent a shiver to her toes, just as she had intended. Just as she had ordered.

She had spared no expense to make the bed a haven for the master from the turmoils of his day. She had required the very best for her husband and she was not sorry then, nor was she now. So no matter what Matt said, she had wanted to do this then and she wanted him to have this now. He deserved comfort and beauty—whether he kept her here with him to enjoy it or not. He deserved it and she would see him have that which he required. Though he might not ever require her—not in the total way she wanted—she still loved him. She always would. And however he spent his days, wherever he went, he would remember this room and her generosity, if nothing else. Hoping that he might want to spend his days with her, she filled with the courage of her convictions and slowly turned to face him.

All the while she had reacquainted herself with the chamber's fittings, he had stood with his back to the closed door, his arms crossed, one hand to his mouth, his eyes never leaving her. He spread his arms—speechless—and dropped them to his side.

"Why?" His word whispered around the ancient room.

She spun in a lazy circle, remembering the inspiration that had flooded through her last summer. "I fell in love with the idea." She drifted to the gossamer veils spilling from the bed and pooling upon the carpeted floor. "I wanted to show you how I could care for you, how I could make a home for you, become a real wife to you. The tapestry was a lark of an idea. When I brought it here and saw how you had not spent my stipend on the castle's improvement and heard how you had spent it on your villeins, I improved the castle myself. I could give more, so I did.

"I ordered the plate and the cutlery from the village. I sent to London for the Luccan silks, the Venetian goblets, and this carpet. My first gift led to these others so easily. For what have I to spend all my wealth upon but the husband I did ever want? To what better use could I spend it, I asked myself, than to make your days more comfortable? If I did it without a finer knowledge of who you were or what you were, I argued to myself that did not matter. Perhaps this, if no other gesture, would persuade you to come to me. You and no other I did wish to meet. And in the wake of wishing arrived another dream.

"I wanted to witness the expression that must hit your face when you saw this. Though then I had no idea of what you could truly look like, I know surprise and pleasure when I see it. And I wanted to surprise you, please you. I wanted to impress you. I knew you would come home to England soon. You had to. I knew King Richard abused his power and lost his supporters. He was not long for his throne. There was no other claimant with as strong a force or personality as Henry Tudor, and I knew you would accompany him when he invaded. I wanted you to see this and know instantly what I wanted of you." She strode about the room, her adamance sparking more courage. "I wanted a true marriage last summer. After Lady Margery died in July, I had lost in her my best friend, save for her nephew Gerard. I knew Henry planned his entry to England, and I told Robert to send you word of how I needed a real husband home with me soon."

"Aye. He did."

She halted. "I stand amazed. He was your faithful servant, my husband, and never did he take lightly to any requests I gave him."

"He wrote me often that you were terribly stubborn—and inventive. I did not know how inventive, though."

"Well, at least I know now he did do two things I asked of him—he told you I wanted you with me soon to form a true marriage and he never told you about this refurbishment of Fletcher Castle. I suppose I should be grateful." She considered the pristine carpet. "I did this with all good intentions. Accept it as your due or not. I did it because I . . ."

She blushed furiously. It was so easy to sit in her bower and admit she wanted to share a bed with her husband, wanted to share affection and create children. But it was so much more delicate an issue to tell him to his face. For her exposure to the activities one found in bed began with conjecture and ended with what that hideous neighbor Charles Arnold had attempted last month. From her awful memories of his seizure of her in his mother's solar and his rough gropings, Lacy knew that whatever happened between a man and woman was not always sweet or kind. Certainly, friendship of the sort she shared with Gerard was to be prized and could contribute to congeniality in the physical matters of a marriage. But after taking flame in Matthew's arms, beneath his reverent hands, Lacy speculated that what could occur upon a marriage bed might contain more bliss than her heart had ever before imagined.

Flustered, she spun away from Matt and went to stare into the fire.

After a long moment, Matt came to stand behind her. "I would to God I could take you to bed and show you all the joys of being a wife. But I cannot. I will not. Lacy . . ." He smoothed her shoulders.

She curled away from him. Tears welled in her eyes at this latest declaration of his intention to reject her.

A gentle knock upon the door froze their actions.

"You may enter," Matt called over his shoulder.

"My lord," Bess sounded uneasy, "I brought you a potion for your toothache."

"Thank you, Bess. Take it to the guest chamber."

"But, sir!"

"You did prepare the room as I requested, did you not?"

"Aye, my lord. I did."

Lacy shut her eyes at the honorable resolve of her husband. Why had she hoped for other? Matt may hold her in his arms, kiss her senseless, and thrill her body to ripe satisfaction, but he had not changed his mind. He still did not intend to make her his wife.

"Do go, my lord," she told him on a doleful whisper.

"Lacy, I want to explain."

"Yes, my lord, I know you do, and I am ready to hear this explanation. But not tonight. I am weary and you are in pain. I will retire to this bed and you to your remedy. Good night, my husband. Sleep well."

She could not bear to see him go. Long after the heavy door swung into place, she stared at the fire, unthinking, unfeeling. 'Twas when she turned and saw the creamy length of lace upon the dark coverlet that tears did threaten. Resolved that she would not allow her husband's nemesis to win this night, she brushed her sorrows away and disrobed. She pulled down the coverlet and settled between the linen sheets. Well into the night did she lie awake upon the sumptuous bed she had meant to share with him.

"Here, my lady, is quite a wealth of elderflowers." Bess waved Lacy over to the patch of frothy white blossoms along the outer wall of Fletcher Castle.

"There are so many, we'll brew a strong broth for Lord Fletcher's relentless toothache and then we'll brew another to fortify us for the winter." Lacy bent to pick the herb and place it in her basket.

"Then you and Lord Fletcher will remain with us?"

Lacy continued her gathering. "I think not."

Bess sighed. "I did not, either. But I had to ask. Forgive me, madam, but I do like our lord Fletcher very much and I would see him happy for once in his life."

"I wish the same for him, Bess." Lacy bit her lower lip. "But I cannot persuade him to do things he cannot justify."

Bess struggled to her feet and ran her hand over her round belly. "He is an honorable man. Generous, too, though my David does tell me Lord Fletcher has been generous with money you sent to him."

"I have no quarrel with that, Bess."

The woman's wide mouth split in a grin. "I did not think you would." She walked toward the edge of a copse. "Will you go to live at your castle, then?"

"I will." Lacy could not bear to look at Bess as the servant turned to stare down at her.

"You mean to say Lord Fletcher will remain here without you?" She gave a hoot of outrage. "That's a sin! You two have so long been married and parted by wars not of your making. Now that those battles are done, he would not claim you? I cannot believe it!"

"Do." Lacy rose, dusting her hands and squinting back unwelcome tears. Her basket full of the frothy flowers, she turned for the main gate. "Come, Bess, we will deflower these and make our broth."

Bess plunked her hands on her hips. "My lady, when you came to us last summer, you came bearing gifts for a husband you had never seen and a house you had never been allowed to call your own."

Lacy lifted her eyes to the woman who stood in silhouette to the glaring noontime sun. "What will you of me, Bess? I was truthful with you then."

"Aye, my lady. I saw that then as I do see much else now. I know affection when I feel it and see it. I saw goodly affection the first day ever I set eyes upon my David. I did love him at age five when I watched him rescue my sister from a rushing stream gorged from a terrible storm. I do love my husband now because he is kind and noble, strong and jovial." She sidled near to peer into Lacy's eyes. "Love you this man who is your husband?"

Tears clogged Lacy's throat at the simple declarations of this woman who adored her man. "Aye, I love him dearly."

"But he has not declared like to you, has he?"

Lacy shook her head furiously.

"Nor will he, it appears, until the tail wags the dog. You come with me, my lady." She hooked her arm through Lacy's and led her toward the copse and into the cool green forest. "I hope I can receive forgiveness for this from the priest. Meddling in others' affairs is not my daily occupation, my lady. But for this, I hope my God would pardon me. You do appear to be a woman wishing to be a wife and though my lord Fletcher wishes to be a husband, much deters him."

Lacy sought to free herself from Bess's grasp. "Nay, my good woman, this story is not yours to tell. I cannot let you do this when 'tis my husband's wish to reveal all."

Bess's mouth dropped open with a jolt. "You think he will tell you the truth? Bah! I doubt it when he has not told anyone any part of it for years. The rumors do run about it, and I have only those to tell you. But armed with those, you may persuade him to the full story—and in the disarming, you may gain your own victory."

"Nay, I cannot listen, Bess."

"Very well. Then look instead."

Lacy followed Bess's sweeping arm to a clearing where one large rock bore a smooth face marked with a perfect stonecutter's cross and the name Sarah.

Lacy strode forward, a sleepwalker in a maze of uncertainties. Whoever this Sarah was, she had lived and died long ago when the wealth of weeds and ivies about her stonework budded young and innocent.

"Here lies Sarah Fletcher, our lord's mother."

"Nay! Why would she lie here?" Immediately

ashamed of her outburst, Lacy clamped a hand over her mouth. 'Twas a heinous crime to think this woman had been put to ground beyond the pale of holy church.

"We are not certain, my lady."

"You must be mistaken, Bess. My lord did love his mother and would not be so unkind as to place her here."

"He did not, my lady. His father did."

"From what my lord did tell me of his mother, she was a sweet woman. Lovely."

"Beautiful beyond words. A vision from an artist's dream of perfection. More, I remember her as sweetly dispositioned too. Generous as you, my lady, with her smiles and her care and even her dowered monies."

"Well then, you do see, this woman here must be some other one who bore the same given name as the baroness."

"Nay, my lady. Would that were so, then another woman named Sarah would grace the chapel mausoleum in the baroness's place of honor. Alas, there is a gaping hole where the last chatelaine of this castle should rest in peace. Instead, Sarah reposes in this unlikely place."

Why would Matt let his mother remain here? 'Twas not seemly when he had loved her so. His father had been dead for many years and Matt, as lord of his domain, could have had his mother's body moved if he so ordered.

"David and I have often wondered, as you now do, why our lord Fletcher has never taken his mother into the family crypt. But what David knows and what the pensioned servants do whisper in the village bear great contradiction."

Lacy's head whipped around. She could not ask for

gossip. 'Twould be a disservice to her husband even to listen. "I cannot stand here longer, Bess."

"My lady, David says Baroness Sarah loved her husband deeply for he saw evidence as a child who waited upon them both. But the pensioners say she lies here because Baron John did accuse her of adultery."

That socked the air from Lacy. "No, that cannot be!"

"Aye, my lady," came David's mournful voice as he halted in his approach among the trees. He shifted his baby daughter from one arm to the other as he said, "My wife speaks the truth of what is said."

What morass was this? Rumors, assumptions, hints of lives misspent added to the mire of Lacy's fully realized horror and her fully righteous resolve.

"David, your wife does think this controversy over the Baroness Sarah's reputation prohibits my husband from living with me in peace."

"Aye, I do agree with her, my lady. This lady in this glade rests here because her husband cast her out, and your good husband was but a boy when he saw his father do it. Think you not that makes a bad impression on one so young?"

"But there must be more logic than this insanity implies."

David nodded sadly. "Aye, but the one who knows this even now stalks the castle dungeon tearing at the stones and cursing." At Lacy's questioning frown, David stretched an arm toward the looming keep. "Lord Fletcher, muttering over his pain from his tooth, now tears at the stones from the walls of the deepest cell in the dungeon. I came to bring you back with me, my lady, for he is beside himself with an agony I would say afflicts the mind."

Lacy's basket thudded to the ground. Her eyes sought the tall gray keep that hovered over them like an avenging angel. Then, David's words drifting upon the wind, Lacy picked up her gown and ran toward her husband and the secrets he had promised long ago to tell.

CHAPTER 9

LACY FOUND MATT SITTING UPON A STRAW PALLET IN THE deepest, dankest cell of the family keep. One rush torch flaming in its socket lit his form, head in his hands, elbows braced upon his thickly muscled thighs. His dejection cut her like a knife.

She went to her knees before him and placed her hands upon his. "My darling, what torments you so?"

He raised his head slowly. His eyes, reddened from sleeplessness or weeping, devoured her features. "Though I have searched everywhere, I cannot find that which I long to give you."

She blinked. "What you give me, my husband, can never be found in a place such as this."

"Aye, aye, it can!" He gripped her wrists so hard she flinched. He stood, taking her up with him. "I know they are here. I remember—or I thought I did recall where my father had placed them, but now that I need them they are lost to me." He dropped her hands, spun about, and raked his hair. Of a sudden, he went to the farthest wall.

She went with him to watch in growing horror as he plucked at the crumbling, moldy stones.

"It was at about this height. I saw him put them in so carefully. They must be here. They *must.* You cannot leave until I find them."

At the mention that she would leave, Lacy jolted. "My lord," she said, trying hard not to sob, "I pray you, cease this gouging of the walls. I would speak with you and I—"

"Ha! *Here,* praise God Almighty. I could not let you go without you having these. They are yours. God meant them for you. I knew it the first moment I saw your eyes, years ago when you were held before the church door. I knew it. Look! Look at these!"

She fell back on her heels at the sight he revealed. Inside a hollowed brick sat three turquoise stones, one larger than the other two. Matt took them out with careful fingers and placed them in his palm for her to view. In the sepia light, she knew that in the light of day the turquoises would prove incomparable. "Matthew, they are lovely."

"Aye." He placed the brick upon the pallet and held up one stone to her temple. "But nothing to match the splendor of your eyes."

She quivered with his words. Her eyes fell shut. "My love, you torment me."

"Nay, my heart, look at me with those eyes that are no match for these poor rocks. There . . . for I would view your loveliness while I may. I am greedy, and you are . . ." He ran one feathery finger down her cheek. "You are beyond my realm in beauty of mind and body. These sad stones will have rough work to complement you. You do them the service, I dare to say."

She caught his hands. "Stop. Do not say these things to me. You do me wrong to tell me such and then expect that I can walk away from you easily, happily. Where is your heart that you could use me thus?"

He captured her close, his one hand to her waist, his other plunging into her hair and pressing her face to his throat. "I gave my heart to you long ago, my love. Now I give you what little else I can. I give you these three stones, which my forefather did wrest from an Oriental sultan after a Crusade. Never have the Fletchers had the means to put the stones in a proper setting for their wives, but I would do this for you."

"I want no presents, Matt." She wound her arms about him. "I want only—"

"You will have these! You will take them!" He pulled her away from him and bent down to peer into her eyes. "After all you have given me, how do you think I feel that I have so pitifully little to shower on you?"

"I need no presents."

"I need to give them to you, do you understand? *I* need to show you what you mean to me so that you will never forget—"

"No!" She broke from his arms. "No! Don't you see, if you send me away, I won't want to remember you." Depositing the turquoises in the brick, she wrapped her arms around herself at the agony that shook her to her soul. "Send me away with those and I will wonder every day of my life why you could honor me with only words and never the actions of love. Send me away with those and I promise you I shall never wear them. How could I? They would burn my skin like flaming pokers."

Tears glistened on his eyelashes. "If I ever hurt you again, I would cut my own heart out."

"You hurt me now, every moment, with every word that's said and those that aren't! You try to speak the words you think would send me from you. Yet you halt to kiss me, caress me, and tell me pretty things, show me loving affections with your tender hands and your melodious voice. And then when resolution falters or circumstances intervene, you bring me here." She let her hand define the cell and the gargantuan keep above them. "You must tell me now, my dearest man, before my heart does burst with pain, why I cannot—nay, why you *will* not let me be your wife."

"Lacy . . ." He strode forward to take her in his arms.

"Nay, touch me not. For that way lies more torturous delay. Tell me quick and tell me all. Then will I take your explanation with the remains of my dignity, if afterward you still insist I go."

Some frisson shuddered through his massive frame. He straightened, sobered to some sanity by her strength. Swallowing back tears, he worked the corded muscles of his throat. His eyes went round to the whites.

"'Tis fitting I do tell you here. Irony sits in that, I suppose." He laughed shortly and without mirth. "I'll tell you quick and all in a few short phrases. My father—that man so prized by the elder Tudors that they did make this advantageous match between us for his financial benefit—that man was a madman. A cruel fiend who hated women. That man, whom many valued for his military skill, was the devil's spawn. I knew it, saw it firsthand. For you see, my innocent wife, my father killed my mother."

Lacy stopped breathing.

Matt glared straight ahead at some vision from his past. "I saw him do it."

Lacy slithered down the wall to the pallet.

"Every day and many nights for years, I saw him do it. So did my sister, Marian. Poor creature, she thought it such a normal part of marriage, she did not see the same signs in her own husband and so bore a similar fate as our mother." His pale eyes sought her out. "I will not see you suffer at any man's hands, certainly not my own."

Undone to speechlessness, Lacy opened her mouth and could only shake her head.

"The amazing part was that he said he did it because he loved her. I believed him then, for he certainly conveyed the story as if it were gospel. But now, since I have known you, my sweet wife, I know fully what love is, and this . . . this compulsion he had to kiss her and then hurt her, this was not love. I *know* what love is now. With you have I seen it, felt it, sampled it in every look, every sigh, every word. What love he bore her was some figment of his imagination compared to the real design of God for men and women here on earth."

Tears refracted her view of him, and in the dimness she reached out a hand to him.

He retreated, avoiding her touch, gutting her. "There is more. It is worse." Matt spun to prowl the perimeters of the dingy room. Caged, he bared his teeth in a savagery she could feel from the roots of her hair to the nails of her toes. "He was jealous of her.

Loving her as he did—whatever the imperfections of his emotion—he knew she was a raving beauty. Who did not? Even I, her son, could gaze upon her and find her wondrous to behold. So delicate of feature and demeanor. So fair, even though the wealth of black hair did give her less a visage of an angel than one of a glowing madonna. Men, many men, *all* men I ever saw in her presence did gape or grovel the first time they saw her. After that, they would strut or cajole to gain her favor. She gave them none. I was but a boy, yet looking back on those events over the years, I know she gave them no excuse to make advances. She was not made that way. For I do remember she did look upon my father with a tender glance that now I conclude was love.

"I do wonder now how she could continue to love him, but she did. One day, after I witnessed him slap her for supposedly smiling at one of his men-at-arms, she told me when first they wed, he touched her only in gentle regard. But soon, his fears of her leaving him for another did loom larger than his reason. He thought she might leave him because she was wealthier than he. She had been an earl's daughter with a great dowry and he a penniless baron. But she had married him because he paid her great court and she had become enamored of him. Their first year was peaceful until she was for the first time with child. My father took it into his head that this child was not his. When he confronted her with the possibility and hit her, she was so appalled she slipped upon a carpet in their chambers and fell. She brought forth a stillborn daughter whose death my father said was divine punishment for her seduction of another man.

"My father, evidently, held no remorse for the

death. In fact, he continued to beat her even after my sister Marian was born and, later, me as well. He was very careful to strike her so that no one might gaze upon her beauty and suspect that beneath her gowns her flesh was black and blue. Even I did not suspect until one night I heard loud voices in their solar. When I went in, he had her across his lap and she wailed piteously. He stopped, but bold as brass, told me I was to remain quiet about this. My mother could not look me in the eye for long afterward. I never asked why she allowed him to continue. But when I asked Marian, who was eight years older than I and so much more worldly about such matters, she told me it was a woman's due." He paused to stare at Lacy. "You do not think such, do you?"

"Nay, my love."

"Good. I would not have you live that way. You are too exquisite to mar with the touch of violence." He dropped his hand as if it offended him. "But then I did not know what he did to my sister. For you see, he saw her growing into a woman and knew he could marry her off well. She resembled my mother in so many ways and when she was but fourteen, my father received the first offer for her. I remember how delighted Marian was. She was a child, but she danced about the nursery to tell me how some knight had come to beg for her hand—and her dowry, of course. Though my father did not promise Marian to that man, he did entertain many others over the next few years. And with every man who came, he was careful to temper Marian's nature with a secret beating. The night before my sister married, I discovered him whipping her. Afterward, Marian told me how he had done this for years and begged me never to reveal it to my mother. Marian by now fully believed she deserved what beatings she received."

He whirled and pounded his fist into the old wall. "I could not believe it." He rested his forehead against the stones, but when he turned, he had tears in his eyes again.

"Marian went to her husband believing she deserved to be punished. I remained here, watching what my father did to my mother. Oh, I was not actual witness to the beatings, but I did hear and I did see her grow more weary every day, every hour of his fiendish compulsion. Soon I was given out as page to a knight along the Welsh marches. A year later, I returned at the request of my father, who considered the Tudors as a good alliance for us. While I was home so was Marian and, of course, my now frail, despondent mother. One night, I awakened to the old terrors—the hideous sounds of raised voices and weepings. But this night when I left my bed to investigate, I was no longer the boy who thought this action normal in a house. I had lived with a gentle man whose only mark upon his wife and daughters was a kind hand or a tender kiss. When I heard this disorder, I burst into the solar and demanded that my father cease. He laughed at me. He simply laughed at me."

Matt flexed his jaw. "I was a green youth and ran at him. He was a big man, tall and broad as I am now, so it was easy to subdue one wailing wife with one hand and flatten me with the other. I was not so quickly downed, however. The melee brought my sister to the fray. She did not know whom to assist." Matt gave a laugh of outrage. "She stood on the sidelines, but when my father told her to summon his man-at-arms, she went to do his bidding. The man came in and saw immediately what to do." Matt dropped his eyes to Lacy's. "He took me from the solar and brought me here. He clamped irons about my wrist there on that wall." Lacy glanced to her side and shrank from the ring. "That night my father beat my mother as was his usual wont."

Long silent minutes passed.

"Sometime that night, my mother slit her wrists. My father found her in their chambers and bound her wounds, cleansed her body. He had me unchained and brought before him. He told me, with tears in his eyes, how he had so loved her and how he would miss her terribly. He said I must not ever reveal to anyone what happened that night or any of the nights before. I was so bereaved, I could do naught but cry. He took my weakness for agreement and soon sent me off to Jasper and Henry Tudor. My sister returned to her husband, but she soon was dead of birthing complications and maybe other things as well. I shall never really know. But I will tell you this, I mourn to this day the mother he killed with his brutality. She may have done the last stroke to herself, but it was his hand that did it as surely as her own did hold the knife."

"So that is why her body lies in the forest."

Matt frowned at her. "How did you know?"

"This morning Bess and I went to pick herbs to make a potion for your toothache. I . . . I saw the rock."

"Aye, he put her there beyond the reach of church. He could not lie about how she had died, he told me. The devil! He had lied to protect himself all these years, why could he not lie to the priest? Ahh, but he was too honorable. Honorable! He killed her! He made her weary of her every day, fearful of her nights.

He did that! And when she saw him even take to me, she decided to end it all and find some peace herself. I do not blame her. God in heaven, if I could resurrect her, I would."

Lacy found strength for the first time. During his diatribe, she had feared for her husband's conclusion. Had he not said he killed his mother? Now she found him guilty of nothing, save his desire to save his mother from the brute his father had become. She rose and placed a tender hand on her husband's chest. "My love, I know you would redeem her if it were in your power, because you are the kindest, sweetest man I have ever known. God in His wisdom knows you tried to rescue your mother from your father's wrath. Now I know. And honestly, I find here no reason why you should consider yourself responsible for her death."

"I am! If I had waited and perhaps spoken with him, reasoned with him, I would have gained ground. Instead, I went in as angry as he. As eager for combat and blood. If I had kept a cool head, I might have saved her."

"Oh, I see. You who know many battlefields better than most would stand here and tell me all disagreements can be settled rationally."

"No, damn it! But if I had debated him, he would not have chained me down. If he had not chained me, my mother would not have despaired so and taken her own life."

"My darling, you are not being rational now. If your mother whom he loved in his own despicable way could not deter him from his course of action, how could you? No. Your mother, by your own words to me here, grew weary of the treatment she could not escape or change. There was no way out for her except through the door of death."

"No!"

"Yes! Would her father take her back? No? Why not?"

"He was dead. Her brother, too. The estate divided."

"Well, then . . . Would she be able to escape to the Church? I doubt it. The Church returns all errant wives to their mates, does it not?"

"Aye, but I cannot bear to think she had no recourse."

Sometimes, the kindest cut was the sharpest incision. "Bear it, my love. For it is true. Your mother bore a dastardly lot for as long as she could. She bore it bravely under the worst of circumstances. And when she could no longer see herself or her son tortured, she ended it all."

Matt sank to his knees with a wail. Burying his face in her skirts, he clutched her to him and sobbed his heart out. Lacy stroked his lush hair and rocked him in his despair. Then, when his cries did dwindle to base moans, she sank to her knees before him and embraced him. She offered up the one balm she kept for last. "I love you, Matthew Fletcher. I will always love you."

His arms bound her like such tight steel bands, he lifted her to her feet along with him. His eyes ran wild. "No! You must not say that. You must not feel that."

"You have no power to make me stop loving you." She let her hand wend through his rumpled satin waves. "Neither do I."

"Do you not understand what I have told you?"

"Aye. I do now know your father was possessed of a

madness that your mother was powerless to counter. That says nothing about why I should not care for you."

"Aye! It does!"

"How so, my lord? You will stand there now and tell me you have beaten women? That you would beat me?"

"No! None of that."

"What then?" She put her hands on hips. "You would describe how you have appetites that are obscure?"

"No. But I have anger. Great anger."

"So do I, my lord, but that does not justify my staying from the man I love."

"Will—you—stop?" He grabbed her upper arms and pressed her to the cold wall. "I do not trust my anger. I feel it often, and it is a red slimy creature who makes me reel with fear that he might overtake me."

"Really? How odd. I often feel the same."

He shook her gently. "No, listen to me. He stalks me. I see his approach and I do shudder. And now, since I have met you, my darling wife, he comes with his friend, a green dragon of wild jealousy."

"How interesting." She fought back a smile of satisfaction and instead followed her trail of logic. "Why are you jealous where I am concerned, my husband?"

"Why? Good Christ in his grave! Because you are the most beautiful creature I have ever seen and the most sweet-tempered and I want you and . . . and I want no other man to gaze upon you or hold you or kiss you as I can."

Her bones began to melt beneath his searing words of desire. But lest she lose her advantage just as her goal drew near, she snapped back to her task. "And do you believe I would ever want another man?"

"Ahh, no, my love. I know you don't. You never could."

Pleased and trembling at the brink of victory, she let all her love shine in her eyes as she asked, "Why not?"

He folded her close to him, his mouth an angel's breath away. "Because you are bright and noble and so in love with me you can't see what's best for you."

"I see what's best for me, my husband." She wound her arms around his neck and stood on tiptoe. With a brush of her lips across his, she whispered, "I see him here now with me. I will ever see you and no other as my husband."

"I cannot risk it. God, if I ever hurt you . . ."

She took one of his hands and pressed it to her cheek. "You touch me and I feel only tenderness." He caressed her skin with his palm. "You speak to me and I hear only kindness." He called her name on a sob. "You kiss me and I feel only joy. Kiss me, my husband"—she feathered her lips atop his—"then tell me you wish to hurt me."

With a wild cry, he smothered her lips with his own. He took her deep into some heavenly realm where only he and she could enter. Where the press of his mouth opened the doors to paradise and the feel of his hands on her body trumpeted the joy she had prayed for all her married life.

"Lacy, Lacy," he muttered as he crushed her to him and arched her up so that he could trail hot kisses down her throat to her hardening breasts. "You rip me apart, expose all my rotting flesh and cauterize my very soul, then sew up my wounds again. How can I bear to give you up when I want nothing more than to lie down with you in fields of pleasure for the rest of our days?"

Don't give me up, she wanted to shout. She knew she needed to be rational even though his mouth on her skin drove her mad. "Your every movement declares you could give me only happiness, never pain. I know it in my heart." She struggled back in his arms and sought his passion-filled eyes. "You say you fear this red dragon of anger. Yet when you have met him on the field, the day was always yours, my love. When you met me, when you discovered who I was beneath the veils, when you learned that what I wanted was an annulment, you did not rant and rave at me. Instead, you were kind, helpful, reasonable. Far too reasonable for my taste."

"I was not kind to Gerard. The mere sight of his hands upon you engulfed my mind in turmoil."

"But ever were your anger and your jealousy contained by a gentle nature against which no dragons might prevail. Aye, I saw it. When the occasion arose in which you could have given in to ripe anger or unfounded jealousy, you gave vent to some. But it was bluster. For as you say, you knew in your heart I did not love Gerard. And as for anger, you had many occasions to become angry with me and never showed me aught but the gentler emotions. I did marvel at it, thrilled by your compliments and drugged by your sweetness." She bound him more securely to her and caressed his eyes with all the love she bore him. "My darling, you had many occasions to become angry with me and jealous of my actions, and never did you do it to such a degree that I ever feared you. Look into your soul, my husband. Don't you know this too?"

He searched for eternity in her eyes. "I know I now do battle for my one desire. But how can I single-handedly win against the two dragons who have stalked me all my life?"

"Take my hand, my lord. As you unfurl your banner against them, know I fight beside you in our mutual quest."

He quaked, and in his eyes she saw him engage his foes. Their battle raged for endless moments, until at last his sparkling lavender gaze declared the victory was his. The happiness it won her made her humble, and she pressed herself to him with tears running down her cheeks. He caught her high and began to laugh, though matching tears fell upon his own cheeks. He spun around with her as if she were no heavier than a feather. And then at once, he stopped. Inch by tempting inch, he lowered her to him. At the moment before their lips met, he whispered, "I love you beyond words, my one and only wife."

His mouth felt as warm as the sun, his hands as flowing as the seas, his words as welcome as bliss. "Come with me, my love. I wish you to be my wife by all that's holy here and above."

She kissed him back, with fingers tangling in his hair and her tongue entwining his. She could not cease her joy of him and knew not that he carried her up the stairs to their chambers until he shouldered open their door and strode toward their bed. He set her there upon her knees as he plunged his fingers into her hair and in one swoop removed the restraining crespin. Her hair fell to her waist like a waterfall. Capturing handfuls of it, he brought it to his mouth and brushed it over his lips. "I love your hair. Your curls do claim me of their own accord."

"Every part of me has belonged to you for most of my life, my love." She traced her thumb over his lower lip. "My body fair sings for want of you."

"Ahh, Lacy, my delicate wife, I hear the song. I throb with it. I vow you will not regret this."

She covered his mouth with three fingers. "Speak not to me of the past. Speak only of now and us."

He put one knee to the bed, bracing her to him. "I speak only of love." He dropped a gentle kiss upon her brow. "I speak only of how I need you." He pressed his lips to her cheek. "How I dreamed of you and the dream is but a poor substitute for the reality of you." He circled her mouth with his own open lips. "I would bring you with me to heaven. You trusted me with your life, your love. Trust me now, sweet heart of mine, with your body."

"Aye, I will." She pressed her face into his doublet and fought the demons she had met last month when one man who was not her husband had attempted to take that which was this man's. "Teach me. Tell me what to do."

Her husband smiled his lopsided roguish look of joy. "I'd say you have the drift of it. But so there is no step amiss"—his lavender eyes gleamed brightly as his arms bound her and his fingers undid her gown's laces at her back—"I will instruct you. First, as you so well know, there are the kisses. Sweet ones like this." He demonstrated deftly. "And torrid ones like this." He seized her mouth, her breath and, in one sigh, set her demons scrambling. "And then," he whispered against her lower lip, "nibbling ones and savoring ones . . . long, languid ones . . . oh, yes, my darling, you are so apt a pupil in this art."

He lifted her chin with one finger. "But the kisses of the mouth are but prelude to the kiss of reverence for the body. Lacy," he rasped as his hand slid to her hip, "I wish us to meet as Adam did his Eve. Let me take this gown away."

She gave a little jerk of her chin. "Please do. I want to be yours."

His eyes blazed with a hot new fire as his hands rose to hook inside her bodice and ease it over her shoulders down the fullness of her breasts to her waist. "Oh, Lacy, my dear love." She flushed and swallowed as he looked his fill at her naked flesh. "Your breasts are made for loving. They're high and proud. See how they fit my hand." She gazed down and shivered with the sight of his large, dark hands cupping her pale breasts. "Your nipples pout to reach my fingers. . . ." He stroked her to a peak, and she groaned. "Or perhaps, they beg for my mouth. Here, let us see. . . . Ahh, yes, this one stands firmer now. . . . Can the other want as much? . . . Ahh, my darling, you are so giving."

She arched backward in his arms as his mouth came down to be nourished at her breasts. Her hands groped for some support in a world gone spinning with delight. The gown dropped to the featherbed, and she heard his breath catch. "Sweet Jesu, you are divine. A small waist to tempt my hands. Soft hips to enfold mine and legs long enough to hold me to you all through the night. Here, love, rest you back." He gentled her upon the coverlet and swept the gown from beneath her. "My Lacy, upon the colors of my family honor, you do shine more fair than they."

She would have covered herself, but he leaned over her. "Nay, I am your husband and I would view all of you as you are due all that I am." He dropped a kiss upon her breastbone. "We will show all that we are always, so that there remain no doubts I am yours and you are mine." He stepped away, and she felt the cooler air surround her. She went up on her elbow, but her heart stopped as she watched him remove his doublet, up and over his head, and then bend to remove his boots and hose.

Flustered to gaze openly upon a naked man, she let her eyes flutter down his frame. Her survey quick, her eyes absorbed enough to make her gasp.

He was as impressive as when she had seen him that first day in the courtyard at Renwick and wished for such a colossus to protect her. He was deeply muscled, with those broad shoulders that could shield her from harm and those massive arms that could embrace her so tenderly. His chest of tufted hair tapered to a ribbed torso, leaner waist, and sharp-boned hips. She swallowed hard to quell her trembling and pass the black thatch of hair that delineated his manhood to gaze at his thighs, so thickly hewn he could bestride the world with her in his arms and never falter.

Her eyes flew to his. "The night I saw you on the road from Renwick, I did marvel at your strength of form and character. I stand in awe, my husband, that you should find me worthy of you."

He sucked in breath. "We can debate who stands in awe of whom, my wife, but I would rather demonstrate." Imperial in his nude splendor, he came to cover her with his blanketing warmth. Settling himself gently atop her torso, he placed his legs alongside her own and squeezed her tightly. He smiled, intent on his design as he spread her arms wide and laced his fingers through hers. Lowering his chest to her breasts, he rubbed his hair against her sensitive nipples until she writhed and moaned.

His eyes narrowed, his nostrils flared. She tugged her hands free to fan them over his thick-hewn arms across his strong shoulders to his marvelously sculpted chest and his throat, where she stopped in wonder.

"My lord," she breathed, her eyes traveling to his and snapping back to see the golden chain from which hung two golden rings. "These are ours."

"Aye, yours and mine. I took yours from the table whence you left it at Renwick. It dangles here between my heart and yours."

Astonished, she whispered, "You kept yours through all these years."

"Amid countless battles, you have been with me. Here, around my neck, close to my heart, closer to my dreams than I dared hope."

Tears stung her eyes. "Oh, Matt!" She fingered it and found it matched hers, not in size, for it was mammoth compared to hers, but in color and inscription. "You and No Other."

He cupped her face and placed a tender kiss upon her lips. "You, my Lacy, and no other thrill me."

She clasped him to her as if she would never let him go. "I do want to be yours, and no other man's."

"So shall it be. Beginning now." He took her hand. "Beginning now, you shall learn the nature of your husband, the man who always wanted you." He kissed her throat. "I shall ever regret that I lost all the years when I could have seen such a bud grow to full flower. I would have enjoyed that."

She breathed raggedly. "Enjoy me now. Oh, quickly, please."

"No, not quickly. Slowly. The way you will enjoy this best and first and always. My lovely Lacy"—he trailed delicate kisses down her throat to her breasts —"you weave such a spell of love about me. I am caught, enraptured by you." When he took her hands and she fought to free them, he whispered, "Nay, this is the way I will love you." He tilted his hips into her, and for the first time she felt the long, hot power of his need slide along the inferno of her own desire. "Feel how I want you. I feel how you want me, my love. Last night upon my horse, I knew you were a warm and willing wife. Now let me make you more so."

And suddenly, there were no more words. Only sighs and sensations. Trilling excitements of the body and the heart long famished for loving sustenance. He cupped her breasts, and kissed each one to blazing yearning for she knew not what. He massaged her waist and whirled his tongue into her navel, sending hot jolts of need beneath her skin. He slid lower and fanned his fingers into her hair. She clamped her eyes shut in embarrassment and tried to roll away. He brought her back with a gentle tug.

"Nay, my heart, do look at me. Yes, do. That's right."

He smiled with narrowed eyes and lush lips. His tongue licked his lower lip while he stared at her. "You were made for me to love," he said as she felt his one hand cover her mound of need. "You prepare for me because"—he slid one large finger inside her—"your body knows I am your only ecstasy. The torrent your body showers here is the way a wife readies herself for her husband, love. This is the way." He caught his breath as he slid two fingers into her and then out again. "And you need no lessons, no tutoring to make you burn, because you send me up in flames." He came up to cover her once more, but kept his hand within her to tease her with slow movements in and out. But now his talented fingers found the nubbin of her need, and at his flicking caress, she bucked, stricken from head to toe with a violent delight she craved again.

Last night when he had done this, she had never feared what would come. She knew that was because she trusted Matt, where by comparison she had had no inclination to open herself to the assaults of Charles Arnold. Now she could only marvel at how easily she gave herself to Matt's loving act of mutual need. She caught at her husband's shoulders and twined her fingers into his rich hair. This was what she had always wanted. She smiled at him.

He smiled back. "You like this. I knew you would."

"With you."

"Only with me."

He nudged her legs to allow his between. "Open for me, love. I wish you to have everything."

She did as he bid, and her reward was the feel of all his manly attributes hanging hot and hard against her woman's core. "Matt!"

"Aye, love," he said raggedly and took his fingers away. She tried to bring him back, but he had taken himself in hand and shifted so that he rubbed the tip of his manhood against her throbbing skin.

She whimpered and ran wild fingers through her own hair. This ecstasy was nothing like that other time when rough words and hands had torn at her.

He shifted to his knees and with strong hands spread her thighs apart. Feeling his heat draw near, she caught her breath. He repeated the trace of his body along the edges of her need. With the fingers of his other hand, he tested her and then placed himself at the entrance to her body. "Darling wife, this is the way your husband loves you." And then within some rapturous eternity, he made his way ever so sweetly into her passage. She felt how very big he was, how wide, how deliciously firm and blazing hot, but he went so infuriatingly, torturously slow, she trembled for more. He gave it. But he would give her only one small sample at a time and then pause, caress her waist or kiss her breast, and move once more toward her heart. Within long, luscious minutes, he had her either clutching at him or arching for sheer joy of it.

"You are so small, my love. I dare not hurt you. Yet you do stretch to hold me. How wonderful you feel when you enfold me. How soft and wet, swollen with want of me. You take my breath and my heart."

"Take all of me," she cried.

"Aye, love. But I will not tear you. Just a little more and then you are mine completely." He sank a bit further, and she watched as perspiration beaded on his handsome brow. She rubbed it away and rose to kiss him. He cradled her head. "Kiss me while I take the maiden who was meant for me." And so she offered up her mouth as he dropped into her until flesh could not yield more union. "Ahh, darling," he groaned, "now you are my woman."

She let him lower her to the bed and felt his hands drift down her body. "And this is how our love is ripened."

She had thought the possession was all there was to the joining of man and wife. But this gentle teasing of his body—this movement out and then inside her flush to the hilt—this made her thrash upon the bed. "My lord, what is this?"

He placed his open mouth on hers while his hips drove in and out in steady delight. "This is the greater joy. Move with me. *Yes,* like that."

The gentle rocking surged to a faster tempo as he taught her tenderly how to match his every thrust, his every sigh and cry of joy. Pounding through her brain, his loving brought a throbbing to her loins. Fear made her clutch at him. He kissed it all away with mindless words and artless caresses. Some fury broke upon her. From a hidden corner of her soul emerged a new desire to match him, meet him, fly with him.

"Aye," he whispered hoarsely, "this is what we seek. Come, come with me. Trust me, love me. I have need of you here with me. Lacy . . . Lacy, ever my own."

She gave herself up to him and to the rapturous abandon. Released from earthly forms, they soared. She felt such bursting and scattering to the stars, she scarce knew where the universe began or where it ceased. She knew her husband came with her, curled her close, crooned a thousand love words and stroked her trembling body back to earth's palpable peace.

For he was here within her grasp, within her body still. Her heart's desire breathing beneath her hand. She trailed her palm up his chest, her fingers catching in the gold chain whereon two wedding rings dangled in witness to the consummation of one fact. This man was her husband and she was his true wife.

CHAPTER 10

SUN SANK AGAINST THE RUBY COVERLET AND DAPPLED Lacy's skin to gold before Matt found the will to leave their bed. Their wedding bed.

He clenched his teeth and unwound her arms from his waist to leave her and collect a portion of his wits. He was to the ewer of water before a knock at the door roused his wife from her sleep. Drowsy with that and her passion, she struggled upright in the massive bed. The linen sheets fell from her flowering breasts, so rosy still with the scrape of his beard and the mark of his kisses. Her eyes discovered him gone from her, and she searched the room to find him. When she did, she beamed at him.

Another knock came at the door. "My lord, my lady? Are you in there?" It was Bess.

"Aye, Bess," Matt responded, walking to the door to put a restraining hand upon it.

"I have prepared a supper, sir. Will you dine?"

He winked at his adoring wife, so tantalizing in her nude disarray no earthly food compared. "We wish our supper here, but only if David brings it up the stairs for you. Then when he can, have him bring up hot water for a bath, will you please?"

"Aye, my lord. I will. Shall I also bring the potion for your toothache?"

"My maladies seem fewer, Bess. A curative's been effectively applied." He grinned at his charming wife's laugh. "My pain is much less." Though not conquered.

As he heard Bess walk away, he turned from the sight of Lacy still looking at him, her eyes boring into him with pleasure and desire. God, one glimpse and he wanted to run to her, seize her in his arms, and lift her to the heights of their passion yet again. But he called upon his soldier's steely strength and strode back to the basin and his ablutions. Try though he might, he knew he could not wash away his transgressions. He loved this stunning wife of his. He had taken her to bed, but what had their consummation brought them? Love—wild, fulfilling love. But what had their love remedied? Hadn't their passionate demonstrations only made matters worse? For it might be true that he did not wish to hurt her now, but what of the years to come? What if his father's madness were one he could inherit and imitate? He berated himself roundly for giving in to the desires of his body instead of listening to the lessons of his mind.

'Twas as he had water in his eyes and tears in his throat when, from the corner of his eye, he saw Lacy push the covers aside to rise, then halt and gasp.

"Oh, Matt! I'm bleeding!"

Throwing the toweling aside, he bounded to her. She sat, thighs slightly spread to show dark streaks of blood upon her skin. His heart fell, twisted, and split open. When her maiden's barrier had yielded so sweetly to his love, he, in the euphoria of his own passion, had forgotten she might display such evidence of their coupling. Swiftly, he took her in his arms and stroked her hair as she shuddered against him. "My love, you are not hurt."

"Nay, I feel no pain! Why should I now? That other time, I did not bleed. How could I when he was not as sweet or gentle as you?" Her fingernails dug into his flesh.

When he took her away from his chest, he saw terror and confusion on her face. "My love, what are you saying?"

Her turquoise eyes grew huge. "When he tried to . . . to handle me last month, he did not draw blood."

"Who are you talking about?" Matt felt disgust that another man had taken this woman in any way.

"The Arnold son. Charles. Last month he and his father crept into my castle in the dead of night, abducted me, and took me to their home."

Matt's stroking of her hair slowed to a death crawl. "And what happened, my sweet?"

"They both wanted me to sign papers that gave my lands by the stream to them. They told me I would sign or regret it. They tied me to a chair, said I could rot there until I signed, and then left me in their solar."

Matt was filled with the fury of an avenging host of angels. He knew what torture, what roiling terror and indignity it was to be chained down, helpless in the face of danger. He had promised himself to grow so big, so strong, so inviolate no one would ever attempt such outrage on him again. He had succeeded. But now to hear that the only woman he had ever loved could have been subject to the same heinous crime made him draw a breath of heartbreak. "My dearest, what did you do?"

"I did not sign. When the father returned and saw no mark upon the page, he said if I did not sign, he would find a way to make me." Lacy burrowed into his chest, moaning her regret. "He said he would have his son persuade me to be obedient. And then, he left me to him." She gulped. "He ripped my clothes and held a dagger to my throat while he . . . he put his hands on me. Everywhere. I . . . I was terrified and screamed. That made him angrier, and he tried to touch me there . . . where you . . ." She broke into a sob, and he rocked her back and forth.

But his soothing did not help for she cried harder and bit her knuckles. "He pulled up my skirts and tried to put himself inside me, and I . . ." Her head fell back, and his heart was wrenched at the sight of beauty so ravaged by pain. "I was wild and kicked and scratched and bit at him. He cursed at me and then, suddenly, he was off me. And I saw his mother with a knife to his throat. She warned him if he pursued his rape of me it would be his last act on earth. He did remove himself, and I"—she licked her lips and turned away from him—"I wondered if he had ruined me for my proper wedding night."

"Nay, my love, you were a virgin until scarce an hour ago. The blood is proof of it. You did not know this?"

Lacy shook her head rapidly. "Lady Margery was an unmarried woman and told me she knew little. She said I would have to rely on my husband to teach me." Tears dribbled down her cheeks as she gazed up at him. "And I did. You are so sweet a teacher, my husband, I did not know that the act of love could bring blood."

"Only the first time does it do that. Ever after there is only pleasure, darling. That man who touched you did not take your body's virtue with him, though I do warrant he frightened you so that he did rob you of your innocence. This blood you shed is that from the natural barrier of your virginity. As any maiden who had never felt the touch of a man's hand before her husband's, you came to me as a bride, as pure and tender as any husband could ever desire. I am thrilled you trusted me with your body and that in the first act of our loving you felt no pain from my intrusion. I willed it to be so."

"And there will never be blood again?"

"Nay, never." He thumbed her tears away and smiled into her eyes. "You are my treasure. My one and only love. What fool destroys that which he adores?"

She smiled with trembling lips. "You are not angry with me then that the Arnold son touched me?"

"No! What logic is there in that? I . . ." He stumbled on his words at the look in her eyes. "I see the point you make, my love. Another victory for you. My jealous anger focuses on him who is responsible, not on you."

"After he did that, I feared he would come again to abduct me."

"That's why you reacted so fiercely to him at Southborne Castle yesterday."

"It is also the reason I came to seek out Henry after he won at Bosworth. I feared these Arnolds would try again soon. I wanted to be married, protected by a real husband."

He kissed her forehead and cuddled her close. "Aye,

I see your reasoning now. 'Tis wondrous good you are not a man, my love, for you would make a formidable foe."

"I am your friend."

He ran his hands down her delicate back to cup her bottom cheeks and press her to his steely desire. "Friendship is wonderful, but I count many friends already. I require something different from you, my singular wife. Something more like the taste of this." He swirled his mouth over hers to hear her moan.

But another knock came at the door.

Matt sagged.

David called that he had a supper tray and hot water.

"Thank you, David. Leave the buckets there and the tray as well. I'll fetch them."

When he rose from the bed, so did Lacy. "Nay, my love. I will do this service for you. Wait there."

She did as he required and sank back to the copious pillows, looking for all the world like a pagan princess receiving in her bed. In modesty, she pulled the sheet up to her chin, but his mouth watered to see it down again to bare those round breasts he could kiss to hard crests in a moment. He tore his gaze from her to perform the tasks he set. Naked, he accomplished each one deliberately. His husbandly intent was to familiarize her with the sight of his body—and how the temptation of her own made him walk slowly with turgid, persistent need. Her eyes upon his every muscle's move showed him that she learned quickly. Her indrawn breaths told him she admired and desired that which he could provide. The way she flexed her shoulders and rubbed her legs together beneath the sheets made him smile with a satisfaction that ignited a holocaust in his blood. So when the tub, sloshing full of good warm water, sat upon thick sheets and a fire blazed beyond the hearth, he strode to his wife's side and scooped her into his arms. Her delicate hands flew across his shoulders to caress him, and her soft mouth found a hollow behind his ear to kiss the lobe.

He sank her into the water with dextrous care to hear her sigh and watch her settle her head back upon the rim. With a finger twining in his golden chain, she drew him to her for a lazy kiss. He reached for the sponge and fat Spanish soap to begin a delicate wash of the long column of her throat, her buoyant breasts, her slim waist, and elegant legs. Purposely circling that which he yearned to touch, he felt his body stretch to unbearable heights. He argued with his body to peruse that which he would savor, but time and again found new wonders in cleansing her arms or her belly or her legs. When his eyes burned from the restraint, he groaned in misery. With a purposeful move, he opened her legs with one hand and washed her tenderly along the insides of her thighs where her maiden's blood had proclaimed that she was his alone. He set the sponge adrift and bent to her.

"I have to have more of you," he told her on a growl. He kissed her until he was senseless, knowing only he'd bury himself deep within her spellbinding body again or die of suffocation. His hand found her, and she arched while her arms stole around his neck. She was liquid and boiling, more from want of him than the ministrations of the water. With gentle fingers he teased her, slipped inside, and showed her the ancient rhythm he would follow.

Of a sudden, she made to rise, but her knees buckled and he caught her with a towel. Drying her, he slid her along him so that his bursting manhood slipped between her melting lips. Her head fell forward, her hands clutched him.

"Oh, Matt, I have never felt so wicked before," she rasped as she kissed his shoulder.

"I need to be inside you now. Here—"

"But the bed—"

"Here." He lowered her to the carpet, wondering how he might show her a sweeter joy than what they had so recently shared. Never could he take her without offering more of himself to this woman who had given all to him. He spread her amber hair upon the carpet's plush ivory nap and traced her fine brows, her thick lashes, her nose, lips. "My water nymph, I drowned in your beauty. What can I ever give you to compare to what you've done for me?"

"Come here." She led him down to swirl her mouth on his in joyous abandon, taking him in and under with her sighing ardor. "You can teach me how to make you happy."

He knew he could have uttered something noble, but for the life of him, he wanted to give her what she desired—and what he craved. He took her hand and let her surround him. She gasped at the feel of him and stroked him tremulously, repeatedly, reverently. "My lord, you are so long, so wide . . . so very hard, yet soft. . . . Did all of you take . . . ?"

He cuddled her to him in her embarrassment. "Aye, all of me took all of you. You are so willing, wife, we are an easy fit." His hand dipped between them to ease into her wet femininity. "And from the flowing depths of you, I feel you want me again as I want you. This time, my lovely scholar, I'll teach you more."

This second time, no fears of hurting her held him or her captive. He felt the freedom shoot through his blood like a geyser. He felt her equal surrender to his wishes with her every breath, her every sigh and kiss. Wanting this second union to be as gentle as the first, he laid her back upon the sumptuous carpet and watched the fire's flames reflect as a desirous dance in her eyes.

He drew her hands to his chest and pressed her long fingers into his mat of hair. "I want your hands on me. To learn me as I have you."

He saw her war between modesty and the desire to please him. "What should I do?"

He arched both brows high. "What do you want to do?"

Her turquoise eyes widened in expectation. "I want to learn if your body speaks like mine." To demonstrate, she sent her hands across his chest to his nipples. At her delicate brush of his skin, he jumped. She rose, a heated smile upon her lips, and kissed first one and then the other. His fingers tangled in her hair. His head fell back. She wended across his torso to his heart and stopped. He knew what she required, so he took her hand and led her to his rigid length again. He felt her shudder along with him as he taught her once more how to stroke him. Her lips nestled into his throat, her silent words pleading with him for nameless ecstasies.

He let her experiment to discover a few delights with her hand when her literary—and graphic—artistry left him tottering to the edge of his control. He rasped near her ear, "With such parlance, my body says it wants yours, my love. Just as you declare with flowing rhetoric how you want me, so does mine." He took her thumb to rise across the tip and feel his first emissions of his need. He fought for sanity to continue the lesson. "Though you may not hear it just yet, your body responds to mine even as mine stammers for want of you." He reached down to trace the folds of her swollen satin flesh and send his fingers inside her hotly articulate little body. His fluency made her gasp and open herself to his eloquent discourse.

He settled her back and pressed himself against her, delivering a graceful prologue. "My body whispers tales of what romance it would impart. How in the body of the play, the act of love demands everything you are."

She captured his face, putting her mouth to his. "No more words."

"Nay. For this"—he sank into her with poetic ease—"is the dialogue of love."

With speechless passion, he taught her to perfect their play. To deliberate, to entreaty, to spar and improvise. To enjoin any further delay of their bodies' coupling and to moan at the moment's separation that rocked them back for more. And when the climax of their play came, it arrived with his breathless joy and his silent affirmation that this romance was a love affair that deserved a happy ending.

He enfolded his wife to him as one glowing word of epilogue filled his mind and heart. "Mine," he murmured to her and all the world most wondrously.

How had he ever denied her?

What could he do now to keep her safe, keep her happy, keep her his?

At sun's rise, he left her reluctantly once more. She slept deeply, exhausted from the night's repeated recitals of their love's expression. She never heard him wash, dress, or close the door. Within two hours, he had his message to Henry set to parchment and David off to hire a man to take it to the king. That done, he returned to his chamber, where joy slumbered, awaiting his touch to resound once more through the old castle he never thought could hold it.

He gently opened the door, set down his tray, and climbed upon the absurdly broad bed whose every delectable inch they had baptized with their passion.

Capturing one blond curl that twined about his finger, he brushed his lips with it and then her own. "Wake up, you slugabed. 'Tis past good time for a wife to be up and about her duties."

Without opening her eyes, she gave a dreamy smile and stretched like a tawny, lazy lioness. He swallowed hard, marveling that she could so easily forge his body into full plate armor surpassing the best Augsburg steel.

She wended one hand down his doublet, her eyes following her caress. "What duty would you have of me, my taskmaster husband?"

His breath came harshly through his nostrils as he chuckled. "I thought I had a chore for you, but now I think I change my mind." He drifted down to sip at her lips.

"Tsk, tsk." She wound her arms about him, kissing him back and winding her fingers in his hair. The linen sheets shifted, allowing his hands to claim her global breasts. "If this is woman's work, I like being a wife."

"I brought some sustenance for this work you perform so well, my sweet. But it seems I fight a losing battle between offering you food and keeping my body from supplying other dishes full of nourishment."

"Mmmm, I know on which side I fight," she said, trailing kisses across his jaw.

He hooted. "You undo me, madam. I beg you, keep your forces well hidden while you listen to me." He took her back with him to lean against the headboard.

Tucking the sheets up about her so that he might not succumb to temptation until his course was set with her, he lifted her smiling face to him with gentle fingers. "Now, I must know more about these Arnolds. Ah, ah, I know the subject does not please you, but you must stay here in my arms and tell me all you know. I would protect you and the best element of a good strategy is a superb understanding of your enemy."

"I want no more blood shed."

"God with us, I would not see it so, either. I hate war and fighting. To kill or maim another requires such ferocity. I hate the savagery for it does remind me of my father's, and I would escape that if I could. Shedding blood was not ever what I wanted. But I made it my life's occupation because I thought I had no choices. Today"—he traced her nose and lips with a fingertip—"I have made one choice."

For long, tremulous moments, her brilliant, tearing eyes adored him. He brushed her hair away, contesting the wisdom of voicing more than that. To tell her how he had asked Henry to consider allowing him to remain married to her, to plead for no annulment, and to sound out Gerard on the issue might offer more hope than he could at this point in good conscience substantiate.

Certainly, in the marrow of his bones, he felt Henry would not object to Matt taking his bride to wife—and keeping her. Else, why had Henry prevaricated, making them dance upon him as he made his way south to London? Why ensure Lacy's presence, her proximity, to her husband night and day? Why put her close at hand but tantalizingly out of reach, until . . . until his pain at hiding his family secret fell before the power of his need to put his hands upon her and never let her go? Aye, Henry had found it beneficial to play the politician while Harry played the matchmaker.

Now numerous questions remained. The most important was would—could—Henry permit his best friend to leave his side, retire to the country, and take with him the only objectivity upon which Harry had ever relied? Henry faced a new reign, fraught with complex problems and unexpected pitfalls. As England's newest monarch after a bloody civil war, Henry would need as many friends as he could gather to him. If Harry lost Matt, whom could he trust to . . . ?

Heartened, Matt hugged his wife and considered the striking possibility that Gerard—aye, Gerard might become the friend Harry needed. Wasn't the relationship he'd seen flower between Henry and Gerard one born of honesty and mutual respect? Matt smiled into his wife's curls. The young scholar who had come to court to claim a bride had won the friendship of a king instead. God knew, Matt would not trade one for the other for he needed his wife like air and water to survive, but could he keep his wife close to his heart and maintain an old friendship from afar?

Only Harry could say. Only Henry decree. And as the king's pledged vassal, Matt could only wait upon his liege's pleasure. In the meantime, he could not bear to explain and deny his wife any joy in these days they did share. But he could deal with today's realities. "Tell me of these neighbors, love."

She nestled to him, her hand upon his chest. "The Arnolds are wealthy cloth merchants who, as I told you, bought the Fitzhugh estate when that family grew penniless from their support of the Yorkist cause. Originally from Leicester, they have storehouses for their woolens along the eastern coasts. They grow rich, perhaps not quite as rich as we are, my husband . . . ah, ah, yes, I say as rich as *we* are, but they do save much from the fact that the Fitzhugh lands offer plenty of streams to help them wash their wool before its combing and carding, or perhaps even afterward."

"How much of the year do they reside at the Fitzhugh estate?"

"More and more since they first acquired it. Either the father or his son goes to market the goods, while the family residence does operate the year through."

"When one Arnold goes, do they take men-at-arms?"

"My villeins say they have hired five from London. None of the former Fitzhugh villeins would accept money to serve the man. In fact, two strong men ran off rather than serve the family. Their wives are terribly saddened. None of the other villeins have offered to help the Arnolds, either. They make their living from the land, and so far the Arnolds leave them to their tilling."

"What of the family itself? Are there other sons, nephews, what?"

"None, I am sure. Only the wife of the elder Arnold, the woman who put the dagger to her own son Charles to save my honor. As for that man Charles, he has no wife yet."

"Pray God, he never has. What household servants are there? Do you know?"

"A steward, a cook, and two maids. They are the same household servants who worked for the Fitzhughs. Unlike the farmers, these poor few have no other livelihood except their serving ways. Though my villeins say those people remember their former masters with fondness."

"The Fitzhughs shall never return to them. The last of the Fitzhugh sons died at Bosworth."

"No!" Lacy clutched his doublet. "I knew him well. He was a year younger than I. I would see him whenever Lady Margery took me for a visit or at the Maypole dances. 'Tis a pity. Oh, my love, so many have given much in these civil wars."

"Aye, many families, noble and not, have been decimated in numbers and in wealth. Henry assumes control over a land ravaged. Without faithful men to follow him and administer these vacant lands, I wonder if he can keep control or will lose his crown to more brigands." He hugged Lacy to him. "But fear not, my heart, this brutality of the Arnolds will not go unpunished. I give you my pledge."

"What will you do?"

"I have this morn, while you did idle for hours in this cavern you call a bed, sent to Henry a message telling him of the perversity of the Arnolds. I beg him to not see them or do anything in their regard until he has had one of his councillors investigate the Crown's land records. He and you need to know to whom this land by the stream does belong."

"But has Henry the means to gain those records? Would not King Richard or his supporters have taken them, hidden them, even perhaps destroyed them?"

"Bosworth was a rout. Many thought Richard would win. I doubt Richard hid his records or that his supporters would run off with papers when their skin was what they needed to save first. Nay, I do believe the Privy records would be in Westminster, where Richard would have left them. In any case"—he brushed a finger along her exquisite brow—"Henry will proceed with this investigation. You see, Henry Tudor likes no half-baked thoughts or whims. The reason he and I have done so well together over the years is because I am as attentive to details as he is. We miss nothing, because we require knowledge of everything before we create a new plan. And you see, my love, I had to write to him soon for I promised my king you and I would return to his train by last night or this noontide. But since Henry did give me leave to stay as long as I desire"—he grinned at her—"and since you and I have had so many tasks to accomplish"—he traced a hand down her curvaceous hip and leg—"returning to Henry shines with less promise than I anticipated. I find instead I would rather view the way your eyes do facet into turquoise stars when I kiss you . . ." He demonstrated artfully. "Or when I press you beneath me . . ." He slid them both down into the rumpled splendor of their bed. "Or when your lovely body opens to me so quickly—*aye, so hotly*—and I am once more lost in your intricate web of love."

CHAPTER 11

"GOOD-BYE, DEAREST." MATT PECKED LACY ON THE cheek and swung himself up into his saddle. His eyes already traveled the road to the village. "If I have not returned for dinner, wait not for me."

Lacy placed a smile upon her lips, but in her heart she suffered that once more he left her. This time he left her physically and would stay away for hours. She knew not which was worse—to have him near and worrying the Chinese carpet with his silent ruminations or to see him go and know that this was the first of many such occasions.

Over the past week or more, she had become so accustomed to his presence in her every waking moment—and her every sleeping one—she lamented his loss. He had become so much a part of her that she could but shut her eyes a moment to relive how he felt when he undulated deep inside her, caressing her with hallowed words and erotic acts of love. Each time he came to her, he sated her in unique and startling ways. Providing her and himself with the tender intimacies for which they had often yearned, he showed her the astral planes of sensual pleasures and the boundless expanse of their mutual affection. Yet at the very same time, over these same days, he drifted from her. Preoccupied with private troubles he would not share, he journeyed from the jubilant lover of their first night to the fretful husband of this morning. He had become a man who pondered issues that she, for all her humor and insistence, could not pry from him. Exactly as she could not pry her wedding ring from the golden chain about his throat.

With a growing sense of helplessness, she waved him off, then turned for the castle and her promise to Bess to help with the dinner preparations. She picked up her skirts and sighed. Lacy knew one thing that ailed her husband. The knowledge made her ill as well. Henry Tudor had sent no response to Matt's message of more than a week ago.

"Milady, what say you to this lovely morn?" Bess greeted Lacy with her usual grin. "No clouds today," she proclaimed as she aimed a giant cleaver for one limp capon's scrawny neck. "Except, of course, upon your brow."

Lacy chucked baby Ruth under her pudgy chin as she gurgled in the rushes, then donned a leather butchering apron and shook her head. "Bess, you see everything."

"Aye, milady. 'Tis so easy. Lord Fletcher has made you a happy woman—but now a sad one, too." She sighed and stretched her back, bent with the bulk of the unborn baby. "I understand your turn of mind, milady. I remember what torment it is to see newly wedded rapture curve about the necessities of everyday's cares."

Lacy nodded, unsure if she should discuss so personal a matter with another, especially before talking about it with her husband. She felt Bess's eyes upon her as she reached for one fat plucked capon and splayed it for the gutting. But tears pooled in her eyes, and the knife lay still upon the block.

"Here, drink this." Bess held out a Venetian rose goblet filled to the brim with ale. "Aye. We drink with the best of the Fletcher treasures, even before noon, else what's all the money for, eh?"

Lacy laughed through her sorrows and sipped her ale.

Bess returned to her capons. "A husband—a *new* husband—often keeps his concerns unto himself. As a new wife must learn to share her body, so must her mate learn to confide his troubles."

"I have told him I wish to share his burdens."

"But hearing and doing are two different acts, milady."

Lacy considered the facets of the goblet. "I do not need to hear his thoughts spoken to know what they are."

"A good sign of two hearts in tune. But"—Bess whacked off another capon's neck—"such knowledge brings you no respite. Talk, true communion, is the only cure."

"He wonders if Henry has deserted him."

Bess halted, her knife in midair. "Think you that?"

"Nay. But the messenger David hired to run to Henry has not returned. So I do conjecture about all the possibilities. I wonder if the man was waylaid by roadside thieves or if he cannot find Henry's train because the king took a route to London that Matt did not anticipate."

"Much can happen between here and London. Henry Tudor may have won the day at Bosworth, but the kingdom is not his unless he wins the capital and the right to sit upon the throne in Westminster. Still, it seems to me, a man strong enough to wrest a crown from another does not falter over one of his retainers wishing to make a bride a wife."

"If I were to conclude anything, Bess, I would venture that Henry knows my husband better than even he surmises. Henry wanted Matt to have the opportunity to choose the nature of his future. Henry loved my husband. I could see it, feel it, through the veils of rank and official courtesies. It seemed Henry and Matt understood each other implicitly and trusted each other absolutely so that no one might ever find a breach in such a fortified wall of friendship."

"The same understanding and trust a husband and wife bear each other . . . yet circumstances do intrude and, without benefit of discussion, appear to make the impossible possible."

Lacy rolled her eyes. "A point well taken, Bess."

"Thank you, milady." Bess reached inside one capon to extract the vitals. "I hope you take the point home with your husband, too. Such deeds make a marriage warmer in many ways."

"I shall attempt to remember it with cool reason."

Lacy's reason grew as cold as the capon dinner when Matt did not return even unto suppertime. Fearing that her husband may have thrown up his hands and raced south himself to find his friend

Henry, Lacy began to wear her own holes into the priceless Chinese carpet.

"My lady?" 'Twas David knocking at the bedroom door. "I bid you come to greet a messenger."

She tore open the door to question him with wide eyes.

"No, milady, this messenger comes not from Henry but from De Vere Castle."

De Vere? "Why De Vere?" she asked but knew instantly the answer. It socked the wind from her. De Vere was at risk. De Vere, which she loved and had left for her husband. De Vere, which she had forgotten in the haze of her desire for him. De Vere . . . her home, her friends, her villagers. *Please, let nothing have happened at De Vere.*

She sailed the stairs like one possessed. Before the great hall's vacant hearth stood a man she knew well, from her own village.

"Simon!" She wanted to hug him but knew the gangly, youthful carpenter would blush and stammer. Instead, she offered him her hand, upon which he placed a tender kiss. "How came you here to me?"

"My good lady, a friend of your husband, a Lord Thomas Norwich, drew me a map, gave me a good horse, and set me off. I have ridden all night and day. He told me to, this Lord Norwich. He said I must come to get you and your husband." Simon Forest's blue eyes traversed the hall and found only David and Bess with baby Ruth in arms. "Lord Norwich said you would be happy if I got here soon. I rode fast as I could because I knew you'd want to hear firsthand about what happened."

Lacy's heart did a mummer's somersault. "What happened, Simon?"

Simon's tall body seemed to shrivel. "Milady, Jim the tailor and Nicholas Dyer are dead. Both of 'em killed in a raid by the river. 'Twas the two Arnold men again, milady. They and their villeins crossed the stream they've worried us so to gain. Crossed it three nights ago at the crux of midnight. Stole some of our sheep, they did. When Jim and Nick heard the crying of the animals, they ran out and sounded the church bells. It was no use." Simon shook his long bald head. "The Arnolds came with many men-at-arms, mayhaps five or six, though none could tell in the melee. At the end, Jim and Nick were dead of accurate arrows. Jim's wife weeps endlessly in your chapel, milady. Nick's mother sits in her cottage, rocking. Meanwhile, the Arnolds keep our side of the stream firmly in their control with their men and weapons and their rough words."

"And Tom—Lord Norwich—where is he?"

"Gathering up a watch among the villagers so that the Arnolds take no more land or animals until reinforcements can be brought."

"And rightly so."

Lacy and the other three turned to the sight of Matt astride the doorway, four burly men behind him. She warmed to the words of her husband as he came to circle her waist with his strong arm.

"David, set a fire here for us. Bess, please bring us a cold supper with good drink. This night we shall prepare to meet the Arnolds at their own game." Matt's pale lavender eyes touched Lacy's as his fingers smoothed her anguish from her brow. "I feared something like this would happen when I had no word from Henry. I could tarry no longer. My love, these men are mine, pledged to me today for temporary duty wher-e'er I need them."

Lacy, terror-stricken at Simon's revelations, sank to her husband's care, her face to his throat. "I love you," she mouthed against his skin and felt him shiver, then squeeze her close.

Matt swept out a hand to indicate the place of honor at the table. "Tell us all, Simon. We must know every detail before we leave for De Vere."

Two hours later, with a September moon creeping high, Lacy rode beside her husband as they led their little band of five men from Fletcher Castle for a northwest route. Sad to leave her husband's home, she hungered for her own castle and hurt for her villeins who had suffered while she became a true wife in her husband's arms.

From past midnight until the dawn yellowed the horizon, Lacy twined within Matt's sweet embrace at the White Swan Inn, where once, weeks ago, in another lifetime, she had slept alone and dreamed of becoming some man's beloved. Though then she had not fantasized she could be this man's, the fact consoled her in her grief over what she could not change. Her villeins had died because she languished in her bridal bed. The sorrow brought to her eyes tears that Matt's solicitude could not diminish.

"My love," he crooned into her hair, "you must not castigate yourself so. You could not know the two Arnolds would be so angered by Henry's treatment that they would ride to do such ill. I am the one who should berate himself. I know such jackals come to dine whenever the shepherd sleeps. But I have not the excuse of sleep—only my passion for you. I took you to my bed and kept you there. This fault is not yours but mine."

She ran her fingertips over his lips. "Nay, my love. There is no fault in our loving. I pray you simply stay with me and hold me through the terrors of all our years."

For answer, she had only his ragged swallows and his convulsive embrace. For the first time since he took her as his true wife, she wondered if he truly meant to keep her. If he did, would he not surrender her ring along with his heart? If he did not, why remain with her and torture her anew each time she gazed upon his silently worried form?

She received no answers and, fearing them, could not ask. Not that morn as they dressed to mount their horses for the day's long ride north. Nor that noon, when they paused for refreshing dinner at a domain whose lord was a friend of Matt's. Not even by night, as once more the moon rose to glare down on them. Lacy admitted to herself that she was as saddle sore as heartsick that her husband loved her enough to take her to his bed, to his heart, but not to his eternal keeping. Terrified that she could as easily lose the love she had fought so long and hard to win, she recalled Bess's words and looked for a proper time and space to approach her husband and their problem coolly.

No opportunity presented itself, what with five men as stalwart companions. As they rode closer to her home, the September air seemed oddly balmy, but often one or two of the group would stop to pause, smell the air, and listen for what some said were others abroad in the forest. When Matt took up the same attitude, Lacy asked him if robbers roamed the woods. He shook his head and said whoever walked among them had an odd reason to be about so deep into the night. Yet they spied no one. Only felt their shadowy presence.

Soon the eight towers of De Vere Castle shown black against the glow of an ivory moon. Lacy's heart leaped in a joy she recognized as that singular affection she felt for her home. Four times the size of Fletcher in circumference, De Vere Castle comprised a compound, within which stood a keep four floors tall to the battlements and two dungeons deep. Those lower dungeon cells, she knew, had not been used for decades, but she wished she could now incarcerate those two Arnolds who stalked her people and her land with criminal intent.

At the sight of the wide moat and the outer curtain wall, Matt sucked in his breath and sat forward on his horse. "De Vere never fails to move me."

"You have seen De Vere before?" she asked, awed.

"Aye. Two years ago, soon after Richard took the throne and killed the little princes in the Tower, I came one day. I stood here among the trees and sallied forth so often I ceased to count. I wanted to meet you, test our marriage vows, but knew I had nothing to give you, as ever."

"Your person is all I ever wanted, my husband."

"Aye, sweet. 'Tis good to say and to hear you say it, but it does little for my pride. Little for my need to give equally to you."

"Does love take measurements, my lord?"

He stared at the moon. "It shouldn't. But I love you so, I would hate it if years from now you came to look on me with disrespect because I gave you less than you gave me."

"You match me in love and fulfilling passion. You freely offer affection, companionship, and witty words to pass the days. I see no lack in any of these things with you. Nor could I purchase them without suspecting counterfeit." She saw him bite back the one word that denoted the nub of his objection. Instead she supplied it, venturing into the realm of verbal communion Bess had so praised. "Wealth. My wealth intimidates you. Your currency of love and honor comes with no exchange value—I thank my God for you and that—but this shows you hold yourself beyond my means. Very well, I see I make no sale unless I give all my money away. Tell me, husband, would you still want me, poor and naked?"

He hooted, then choked. "I'll not grace that with an answer."

"Please lay down your pride as I lay down my money. This marriage we create means more to me than shillings. As example, I wish to wear those turquoise stones you gave me, and I have brought them here to have my goldsmith string them properly. Your stones with my setting. Is that not true coupling, my husband? Will you deter me?"

"Nay, my love." He lifted her chin with gentle fingers to view her eyes with his mellow ones. "I wish to help him design the means to bring the rocks to life. Ahh, Lacy"—he swallowed—"your money raises—*raised*—but one wall between us. To scale it with talk is easy compared to other barriers I have no ability to gauge." He lowered his voice so that the others who came abreast of them could not hear his confession. "I may be powerless in the face of such forces. I may not be able to become the man you need beside you through the years."

Lacy seized his hand, bringing it to her cheek. "I will help you. Ever I am your champion, as I was in the first battle you fought in objection to our union."

The five horsemen plodded past with a slow pace that drained Lacy of hope. Matt worked at words.

He let the last man pass. "My love, I am an animal of war, not a domesticated man. I—ah, let me finish—I will protect you from these Arnolds. I swear

I will or die trying. But my first objection to our union does bear much similarity to many others I cannot control. Before I was your man, my darling, I was Henry's. I cannot change that. And though I have tried to help him stride England with a crown upon his head, I cannot guarantee it him. In like manner, I cannot guarantee you he will keep it and make this land a peaceful one."

"Surely, what we have seen so far bodes well for this."

"Aye. But much can happen between Bosworth and London—or even afterward—which neither you nor I can predict. Through whatever occurs, my vow of homage to Henry cannot go untended."

Lacy knew that Henry Tudor could alter in a moment whatever dreams she and Matt might have for a long, quiet future together. And though Lacy knew Henry had Matt's happiness at heart, she also knew the king would require his Sure Arrow's help if he thought he needed it. Matt would bow to that reason of state. He must, not simply as Henry's personal retainer but as the new king's pledged man. Else, Matt could hang for treason. And that she would never allow. She'd give him up first, forever, rather than see him die.

She blinked away scalding tears. "I would not have you negate a vow."

Matt's eyes bored into hers tenderly. "I know," he whispered. "None of them."

She smiled bravely at her husband, determined to enjoy him while she could. "Come, darling, I have much to show you of your new home."

He wiggled his brows. "If there are half the surprises here as at Fletcher, madam, I will be so astonished I may not sleep well."

She chuckled. "I dare to say you won't for many reasons, my lord."

As Lacy knew he would, her elderly steward, Franklin Cooper, provided those solid reasons. True to his practice, he had stood the castle to readiness for her and her husband for over two weeks. Thanks to Thomas Norwich, who had returned Anna to De Vere at Matt's orders, Franklin had enjoyed much time to polish the brass and silver, bring out a goodly supply of heavily scented Paris candles to line the stairs and the great hall. He had had much ease to set out the best pewter plate and ivory-handled forks and knives for the cold supper the cook and Anna laid of pork and potato pudding, spiced apple dumplings, gingered breads, thick black ale, and red beer.

While the five men who traveled with the Fletchers sat themselves to the linen-covered dining table in the plushly appointed great hall, white-haired Franklin Cooper trained his sad green eyes on his new lord and master, Matthew Fletcher. Anna stood beside the steward, her eyes probing Lacy's and Matt's for answers to a thousand questions.

Matt met her gaze. "I trust Lord Norwich and you had a safe journey here."

"Aye, my lord Norwich provided well for me. He does your bidding skillfully, including rousing many means to protect a castle. He worried when you did not come."

Lacy nodded. "My husband's plans and mine did change, Anna."

Anna seemed only slightly relieved to hear that. "Tom said he will return as soon as he can get help."

"I'm certain he will." Lacy smiled a little and glanced at Franklin. "You are well provisioned?"

"Aye, milady. In food and weapons. We need only

good strong men"—his green gaze shot to Matt's—"as we have always." He cleared his throat at Matt's intransigence. "Shall I show you to your rooms? Well, then, this way."

As Franklin led Lacy and her husband through the hall and solar up the winding staircase to her apartments, she suppressed a grin at Matt's barely restrained surprise. For everywhere those lavender eyes landed, they popped with some novel finding. At her two golden-haired sheepdogs, who greeted her with wagging tails and tamed but panting joy. At the lack of rushes upon the floors. At the Arras tapestries, more glass and crystal, candlesticks of every height, books upon every trestle table, lace circlets underneath to protect the waxed woods. Embroidered pillows in each wooden chair. Portraits of her beringed father and her golden, angel-faced mother. Innumerable silk escutcheons flung down the ornately carved oak walls and Ottoman rugs upon stone stairs and across gleaming wooden floors.

"My lady love," Matt whispered to her ear when fastidious Franklin turned the long hall corner and commenced to describe some other beauteous asset, "what do you *not* possess?"

Your ring and your vow to stay with me, she wanted to cry, but she kept her tongue and her fear for another conversation. Instead, Lacy teased her husband with pursed lips and wide eyes. Then, with a flounce of her skirts, she pressed her back to a broad doorway and, as Franklin opened it, curled around to the room she wished her husband to see more than any other of De Vere's glories.

The wait was worth all the lonely years.

Matthew Fletcher stood agape.

Lacy chortled.

Franklin, awash in his devotion to relating every amenity he could recall to the new lord of the manor, missed the novel spectacle of Henry Tudor's Sure Arrow overwhelmed by the sumptuous splendor of stained-glass windows, pargeted walls, folding chairs and long chairs done in red satins and golden silks, sapphire velvets and silver brocades, posed among enameled screens and ivories from the Silk Road, books of every age and size, plus one huge writing table with a tall pile of delicate watermarked French papers. At one end stood the tools of Lacy's solitude, her embroidery needles and spindles, the lacing cushions, her board for carding, and spools of threads in every color in a rainbow.

"My lord," Franklin urged, "if you wish a bath, I have good Castile soap awaiting you and my lady in the room next to the garderobe. This way, sir."

Lacy grinned to see Matt raise both black brows at her and follow the steward with curiosity prancing in his eyes. In a moment he returned to lounge against the door frame and cross his arms to contemplate the centerpiece of the room—the bed that matched his own new one at Fletcher.

When Franklin bowed himself from their presence and closed the door upon them, Matt pointed one long finger at the bed. "You had two made."

"Aye, my lord." She sailed to the twelve-foot-square twin of the bed they'd christened in Fletcher Castle. Though this one bore the same dimensions, its similarities ended there. She ran her hands down the gossamer transparent blue silk and let her hands capture a wealth of the fabric, which ran the spectrum from De Vere blue to the bolder Fletcher ruby. "I thought when you have discovered something you adore, you should make all effort to enjoy it everywhere."

He nodded. "Sounds so sensible." Then his eyes ran past her up to the high wall above the enormous bed. Here his eyes stuck on the silk and embroidered satin declaration of her total devotion to a husband she had never met and only lately had come to love. "The shield is a master herald's work. But most certainly" —he sauntered toward her, eyes yet upon the wall— "in this case, a loving wife did craft its every stitch."

Her breath snagged on his look of delight. "You really like it."

"Oh. There really *are* no words." She watched his eyes caress the upper quarterings of golden Fletcher arrows upon the red field and then descend to find the De Vere glass bottle and white De Lacy knot upon a field of blue.

Suddenly, his eyes snapped lavender flames as he trained them on her. "My lady Fletcher, I like your taste in beds and so too their decor." He sent one hand up into her hair, scattering crespin and curls. "They speak of *blends* I never thought to sample e'er this." He pressed his torso to her so that she became pinned between the massive post and his body's commanding brush of her lips, her breasts, her belly, and her thighs.

"Then you must taste to your satisfaction, my dear lord." She caught at her breath as he slid her cloak and then her gown from her body in one agile stroke, leaving her naked to his branding kisses. "For this bed has been waiting—*Oh, Matt!*—waiting for only you to test its worth." She ran her hands along his waist down to his taut buttocks while he suckled her breasts and worked at his hose.

When he had stripped himself of his doublet, he caught her around the waist and secured her naked body to his torrid one. "I could push together all the beds from Xanadu past Araby on to De Vere, but, end to end, they could not contain all the emotion I bear you, my beloved." He pressed his steely aroused length against her flesh, which ached for his fulfillment. "Allow me to display some small evidence. *Aye,* take it in hand." He swirled his tongue inside her ear to make her tremble with want.

She stroked the length of his impressive lance, her need ripping her sanity to shreds. "As evidence, my lord, 'tis *hardly* small."

He choked on laughter. "You play at word games with me, my talented pupil?" He stripped the bed to the azure silk sheets, lifted her, and laid her to it, chuckles rumbling from his chest.

She snuggled closer to fondle his rigid manhood with firm delicacy. "Perhaps I need tutoring in some new language."

He grunted, then spread her legs apart with his own. "I vow I'll render you speechless, madam. What say you to this discourse?"

Holding her hands, he slid lower and, without preliminary, delivered a swirling, open-mouthed kiss into her nest of curls.

"Ohh, no!" She arched up in ecstasy and wild fright.

"You must not fear, for I love you." He nuzzled her hair, dropping hot homage to her burning skin. When she lolled her head upon the bed, he raised his face, laved her palms, then let her hands go to cup her derriere and bring her body up to his seeking mouth. "Open for me, darling. Let me teach you how to speak this new tongue." He glided his lips along her folds, making a lazy foray into her moist secrets. The diplomatic command of his probe made her buck and spread her thighs in terrible abandon. He growled, then whispered in heated glee, "You know already how to reply, I see. You give up a mute response which foretells great pleasure with musky poetry." He pressed her even wider with tender fingers, inserted two to test her ardor while she contorted in abject want and trepidation. "No, there is no call to run, my sweet, wanton wife, for you . . ." He found the center of her, sucked her leisurely into his mouth, and sent her catapulting among stars. *"Aye,* you like this new communication."

"Matt," she panted, twisting the sheets, "you can't—"

"Look at me, darling."

Drugged with her own shameless desire for more of this from him, she gazed down at him, his heavenly lavender eyes half-lidded with want and pride of her.

"Have I taught you anything yet in any other language than love? No. Never would I do that. Then give me all of you I crave. I promise you no less, my heart."

"My love, I do want all of you."

"Eternally."

"Eternally," she whimpered, racked by her need of him now and always.

"I am yours, my love. Come, be mine."

At her sigh, he smiled with conquest in his eyes and sank to her core of desire. Now there were no words, no speech, no sounds of coherence, save those of need and ripe expectation. He put his searing lips to her flesh and pulled her into a new world of molten, savage caresses. Time and again, he kissed her, parted her, petted her, praised her, explored her, laved her, spread her wider, and groaned for more. When she felt the first fire burn her to the bone, she thrashed in surrender and marveled at the power of his clever tongue and lips and teeth. But when he continued his soliloquy, she gasped, ranted her outrageous need of more of him, and heard him moan in satisfaction. This second blaze he tended with deft darts that loved her longer, faster, harder until she grabbed his satin hair and melted to the marrow. With a growl, he clamped her closer to give her everything and nothing like she'd ever had before. Weightless pulsing, pounding travel into a universe of chaotic delight. Divine sensation brought by his mouth exploring her secret places. The throbbing knowledge that this was sharing to its earthly ultimate and that there could be no more saving grace than to give him the same succor he offered.

Within the love-drenched daze he made, she rose to tug him to her. Still, he would not fill her, but stroked her with the rod she craved to give her surcease. When he would not comply, she rose up on her knees and pushed him back. Surprise lit his eyes, but as she knelt over him, she told him that his monologue must end so that now she might provide some new translation of her own.

As she pressed him upon the pillows, she set her mouth around his firm manhood and praised the milky, salty taste of him. He called upon nameless hosts of heaven to save him from her effusiveness. But when no such panoply dared to intervene, Lacy smiled her own satisfaction. Her husband thanked all heaven's angels. Then with one giant arm about her waist, he rolled her beneath him.

Brushing the hair from her face, he delved into her eyes with a satyr's expression and a saint's words.

"You feed my soul with every fond desire so that I cannot live without you."

"Nor I without you, my husband. Fill me now, for I cannot go into love's enchanted land alone."

His slow glide elicited a guttural cry of joy from both. Lacy paused at the brink of her known universe, then leapt the boundary with him, vowing that whatever life brought them, somehow she would help him find a way they might embrace it together.

CHAPTER 12

LACY WAS ON HER KNEES IN HER CHAPEL AT MORNING prayers when Matt strode in alone. Early this morning he had left her in their bed when she could not rise but complained of dizziness. She had not seen him until now. Crossing himself, he sank beside her to the ruby brocade cushion she had years ago placed there for him. But he did not pray nor take the host as offered. He merely stared. When mass was ended and her priest left them, Matt contemplated the richly appointed altar with a stoic expression.

It tore last night's serenity from her.

He turned, his tired eyes bleakly meeting hers. "My heart, I hate to tell you this. Two more men died this morn at the Arnolds' hands. Franklin's younger brother and the Cowpers' crippled son. The Arnolds crossed the river before dawn, took ten sheep, and killed the men who stood watch. I arrived at dawn just as the villagers awoke and discovered the bodies." He put his hands to her shaking shoulders. "I will stop them. In this holy place, I make you a vow to stop them."

"Have we any advantages?"

Her question popped his eyes, at first in surprise, then in admiration. "Aye, my strategist, a few. If we throw up a barricade of hay along the village perimeter, move a few carts from behind which to take a marksman's post, I think we can hold the village or mayhaps take back the bend of the stream they took days ago."

"Have we enough men?"

"I know a means to make it appear we do. We can fill some villagers' clothes with hay and stand these fake men at readiness, half-hidden from the Arnolds' vantage point atop their knoll. I have checked the armory as well. You were wise to keep all those bows I had Robert Morris purchase. I wish we had one hundred men to use each one, but we shall do well for we have more than enough arrows to fell half of Christendom. Our four men in the village plus my four from Fletcher should hold us for a while. In the meantime, Tom Norwich should return with aid."

"Think you Henry will allow Tom to return?"

"Aye. Henry would not leave us to such crows as these, no matter that he met the Four Horsemen of the Apocalypse on the road to London. Henry and I have too much good between us. And you have given him the same true homage all these years. Fear not, my Harry returns honor and friendship in kind." He stood, his fingers digging into her elbow in a tension that contrasted with the confidence she found upon his face. He looked around the chapel with no pleasure. "Come. Let us leave this place."

"You are uncomfortable in church?"

His eyes ran over her face as she lifted both brows. "My heart, if you had killed as many men as I and known you deprived their wives and children of their men's succor, you would not find solace in any godly place, either."

"You told me once you chose not this path of service but that it was chosen for you. Surely, that offers you some solace and permits salvation."

"Perhaps." He tugged at her elbow, but she stood her ground. "I will not discuss it." He dropped his hand and would have left without her had she not caught his sleeve.

"My heart." She turned his endearment on him and brought him around to see bright tears line his lush lashes. She would coax from him more dialogue and in the letting, draw from him those ill humors that could disease him and their love. "We will discuss this. Why will you not perform the rituals of religion? It might ease your pain."

"I doubt it. I have tried. I feel unworthy even to confess my sins, they are so many."

"Ahh, so many." She flowed near him and twined her fingers in his black satin hair. "Tell me what you have done in addition to slaying your liege's enemies in battles you did not ordain?"

"I have taught others how to kill. How to thread a bow, sight a target, aim with deadly precision. You think that not enough, eh? Well, I tell you, I have *lied.* Warped the truth to get money and support for the Tudors. I have cajoled the mighty rulers of Europe into supporting my prince." He gripped her arms painfully and searched her eyes with racked fury. "Still not enough? What say you to me then when I admit I have lain with other women?"

She stared him down. "How recently?"

"Years and years ago, and the women were countless!"

"Any one you'd say you loved?"

"No one! Ah, Christ, Lacy!" He dragged her to him. He avoided her eyes. "Don't you see I hate to stand here in this holy place planning more battles—even for justified reasons, then say I adore you, when I have never even honored the marriage vows I bore you, until now when . . ." He halted, a horrified expression dawning on his face.

She covered his mouth with two fingers. "Until now when it might be too late . . . or too soon . . . or simply was never meant to be?"

He closed his eyes. "How can you see inside me to speak such truths when you have known me only days?"

"How? 'Tis so simple, really. My heart knows yours. All your secrets are mine to share. Now or later, it matters not *when* you tell me, nor *how,* but you will tell me. And I, like a true mate, will tell you mine. One by one, like a good accountant, I will impart them, beginning now with my first and fondest secret. It is one I should tell only in this appropriate place. She brushed a fat tear from his cheek. "Aye, I'll tell you now, love. For years, in this chapel with Lady Margery or without, with my villeins or alone, have I prayed since I was a little child to kneel with you in church as we did now. And sometimes, when I was a growing girl full of ideas of romance, did I pray upon my knees for my husband's health and welfare. Then, when I knew he could not come to me in flesh, I prayed he appear to me in spirit. And suddenly, faceless, formless, you would sit beside me, take my hand, and make to me those marriage vows I was too young to remember hearing you declare to me. Through so many trials has that one vision sustained me."

"God above, Lacy, how you trust me."

"Sight unseen."

"And now seen, through flesh to rotting core, you think me salvageable?"

"Your sins are small, my heart. Confess them soon, will you? The priest will absolve you, I believe. But do forgive yourself your transgressions. For I seek to live with you in peace and joy and nothing less."

"I seek to give you that which you desire."

She beamed at him and placed a kiss above his heart. "So have you said and so have you done and so shall you always."

That night for the first time in nearly two weeks, Lacy retired to her bed alone. Without Matt, the bed seemed endless, lifeless, loveless, cold. She shivered, though the warm breezes through the new casement still spoke of summer's delights. She felt them not. For hard and heavy upon her heart lay the fear that tonight the Arnolds might come again with yet a stronger force than last night. That they might creep upon them as they had that horrid night in July or in March.

Though she trusted her Sure Arrow's military prowess as thoroughly as Henry Tudor, she feared that the Arnolds would perform any unchivalrous deed to gain their unprincipled ends. When Lacy rose before dawn from a much misused and tangled bed, she washed and dressed hurriedly. The rush made her head spin and stomach swirl so much she had to seek a chair for a few moments to steady her reeling world. With slower movements, she descended the stairs to the great hall where Anna arranged plate and cutlery for the first meal of the day.

The maid halted in her tracks and let her eyes roam over her cousin. "You did not sleep well either, my lady."

"Have you been awake all night, too?"

"Aye. I wonder about the village and what detains Tom. Wait! Where are you going?"

Lacy spun her cloak to her shoulders. "To see how Matt and the others fare."

"You shouldn't."

"But I will. I'll take good bread and ale and whatever else I can find without waking the cook this early."

"Won't you eat first?"

"No." Lacy felt repulsed by the very idea of food. She wanted only the companionship of her husband —and her friend. "Will you come with me?"

Anna smiled slowly, conspiracy lighting her eyes. "Your wish is ever my command."

As they left the walls of De Vere to take the winding road to the village, Anna wondered aloud if they should have taken horses. "All the better to fly from the Arnolds."

"Here, well inside our land? No, Anna. If they did attack last night to penetrate our line, we would have known. Matt would have gotten word to us."

"You trust this husband of yours."

"Completely. So should you."

"I wish I trusted Henry Tudor as much." Anna glanced about at the deserted road, wrapping her blue woolsy about her more closely in the beaming yellow sunrise and juggling the weighty basket of food. "Why, oh, why does Tom not return?"

"'Twas a full two days' ride from Southbourne

Castle here. You must add two or more days to London. That's four to five days each way . . . plus deliberation time."

"What is there to deliberate? If Henry wishes to show his gratitude to you for all your years of loyalty and to repay his captain of the guard with like kindness, there seems to me to be no issue to ponder."

"The matter is whether Henry will allow the Arnolds to forcefully take the land by the stream when the ownership has ever been in dispute. Such resolutions take research."

"While research progresses, we could all be dead . . . or worse."

Lacy squeezed Anna's hand in comfort. She knew the maid did ever ridicule herself as the one responsible for Lacy's captivity in July. Lacy had long since ceased trying to douse the fire of Anna's guilt with words that never seemed to absolve her. Only time, Lacy felt, would tamp that blaze or perhaps some other's affirmation that Anna's assumed sin of omission was not as severe as she thought.

In silence, she and Anna approached the thatched cottages where beyond a wall of hay, numerous villagers paced back and forth. The eight men had bows slung to their backs. Striding among them was the ninth—Matt, tall, congenial, even jovial in his conversation. Lacy halted at the sight of him. Her husband. Her helper. Her strong assurance against the vagaries of life and circumstance.

He paused at the sight of her, his eyes running to the basket, to Anna, and back to her. With long strides of his powerful legs he approached her. As he caught her in his arms, he asked her if her dizziness recurred this morning.

"'Twas slight. You must not worry. I have always been very healthy. Whatever it is, it is temporary."

"I do agree." He smiled tenderly, then brushed one thumb beneath her eye. "You did not sleep," he murmured for her ears alone. "You should have. All is well here."

"All is well wherever you are."

He hugged her and turned a comforting gaze on Anna. "I thank you for coming so early. We have need of such succor. An army is a fiendish menace without food."

Anna's sad eyes outlined the four able-bodied villagers and the four other men who hailed from Fletcher. "Should we not feed them, then, to assure us they will stay fiendish?"

Matt frowned at Anna. "You do not trust easily, do you, Anna?"

"Nay, my lord. I have seen what these Arnolds will do." Her eyes cut to Lacy. "They are devious, blustering, demanding, and when that fails, abducting . . ." She hung her head, then pivoted away. "I give you my apologies."

Matt checked Lacy and, at her nod of assurance, he trained his eyes on the maid. "You need give me none, Anna."

"I do! 'Twas my fault—" She spun, her gaze frightened and mortified. "Much is my fault."

"If you mean that you are to blame for the incident in July when Lacy was taken from the castle to the Arnolds' home, I must tell you I do not hold you responsible."

"Well, I do! I slept like a baby through their entrance to the castle and their wicked abduction of Lacy. Since Lady Margery died, Lacy has been my responsibility—to see she never wanted for anything, to see to it she always had a friend."

"Aye," he said softly. "That she did. And I am immensely grateful, as I know she is." He strode closer to Anna. "What must I do to show you how you may lay down your guilt—and your charge to me?"

Anna stared at him. "Win this day for us. Settle this affair."

"I promise you I will do my best."

"Not that you will win?"

"I will use every talent I possess to make it so, but I would be a mummer of fiction to tell you more than truth."

"Which is?"

"Our position is not the best here. But it is tenable —for a while. Unless or until the Arnolds bring in a greater force of men who are better marksmen than we possess. Or until Tom Norwich returns with men from Henry."

Anna blinked back tears and considered her basket of goods. "Forgive me, my lord. I am afraid for us and for my lady, whom they would take and hurt if they could."

Matt covered Anna's hand with his own. "No one will ever take my wife from me, Anna. That I can promise you without any earthly reservation."

But the sun reigned high into the afternoon and still they had no sign of Tom and no relief from the constant appearances of the older Arnold or his son atop the knoll they commanded by the stream. Lacy wondered if the Arnolds, looking down on the village, could differentiate the men who were flesh and blood from the men who were hay and sticks. Matt said the

Arnolds could not decide and that was what deterred them from progressing.

"Is that the only reason they wait?" she asked him as she kneaded Matt's shoulders while he sat upon a boulder at the edge of the village.

"I am no soothsayer, my love. Aye, rub there. That's good. Nay, I would say these Arnolds are stymied. They cannot get close enough to see if we are as well fortified as we appear, and they dare not move until they know for certain."

"You do not think they await more men?"

"That is a possibility."

She sighed. "But we have not the means to attack."

"You are shrewd."

"And correct?"

"Aye, though I wish it were other. These men we call our army are dedicated, God knows, but they are loathe to loose an arrow. The most they've ever killed is a bird from the dovecote. I understand their reluctance." He stilled beneath her hands and inhaled deeply. "It takes much hatred to kill a man."

"Aye," Lacy breathed and wound her arms around his neck to kiss his hair. "I imagine you feigned such hatred with regret."

"Pretending to hate takes such a hellish toll."

"Praise heaven, your days of warring are almost over."

Matt turned to bring her down into his lap. His pale, tired eyes roamed hers in trepidation. "My heart, I cannot promise you what is not in my power to give."

She swallowed hard, her chin falling to her chest. "I know."

He lifted her face with two hands to her cheeks.

"What else do you know about me without my telling?"

"That you wish to see all wars end."

He nodded.

"That you wish to see Henry rule without benefit of military might."

"I wish to see him use his great intelligence to bring the English just rule and hardy prosperity."

She smiled, trailing a hand through his lustrous, thick hair. "You would fight for that."

He grinned. "Without my lance or dagger." He kissed her sweetly. "With you—may it please God and Henry—by my side."

"Can Henry live without you?"

"Henry can, for he has means to find many good councillors and to keep happy my second in command of the guard, who is a skilled commander. But *Harry* may wish to see me often at his side for the fellowship only boyhood friends can give each other. If Harry lets me go to another life and he called me to him for spells, would you mind?"

She shook her head. "Never. For now, having had you so totally these last weeks, I feel a greater serenity than I have ever known. Though I can be parted from you on occasion, I heartily doubt that I can live without you entirely, my husband."

He drew her close, his one hand caressing her stomach, the other in her hair. "Nor can I draw a happy breath without my wife."

She melted to him, offering her mouth and raging abandon with such abject need she did not know he carried her to the privacy of the forest until he propped her against a tree whose jagged bark caught at her hair.

Freeing her, he chuckled. "Lord above, I must fight

even the earth to keep my wife mine. What will take you next?"

She gave him a glorious grin and seized his hand. "Ahh, but I would show you what can take us both. Come with me. I have a cure for tired warriors and harried husbands." She tugged him through the woods toward the place which few used as freely or as often as she did.

"Where are we going?" Matt cut through underbrush and bent low to avoid huge hanging branches.

"Here." She stood at the edge of a hillock and parted lush foliage that he might view her round, secluded lake. She turned, bright expectation on her face, when suddenly she felt her breath whoosh from her as he scooped her up and tucked her over his shoulder. One hand across her calves, his other hand made tight work of holding her bottom as he jogged down the hill.

"Matthew!" she called between gales of laughter. "This was not what I foresaw!"

"No? Why not, my lady Fletcher? I understand you like lakes." Amid the cover of tall grasses and low hanging bows, he righted her, stripped away his hose and doublet, then reached for her gown. "I know you like swimming naked. So now"—he kissed her lavishly—"you'll swim naked with me." He took her clothes from her easily and skimmed the backs of his gentle fingers down her arms to make her close her eyes and sigh. "I really do not want to swim at all. But oh, I do want you naked . . . with my hands running over you in the water. The way I wanted the first time I really saw you, the first time I held you to me, skin to skin." He captured her flush to him, sending up sizzling currents all along her nerves. "Don't you think there is a certain justice in that?" he asked as he seared her throat and both breasts with the brazier-hot trail of his tongue.

She could barely draw air, let alone answer.

"Don't you?" he urged on a rasp and sank to his knees to trail kisses across her belly to both hipbones and down to her very center.

She couldn't think. Her knees turned to tallow as his mouth did maddening things to make her open her legs.

"Don't you?" he whispered and her eyes glazed as she tried—oh, she really did attempt—to focus on something more than the blinding sensations of having him taste her so exquisitely slowly in the sight of all the creatures of the wild.

"I . . . can't . . . imagine," she panted as her body screamed for the fulfillment only he could provide.

"I can," he said and stood with her in his arms.

Seconds later, he submerged them both in the cool water that made her skin prickle and her body melt to his with more need than she had ever known. He spread his legs, found firm footing, and put his palms to her inner thighs to guide her to circle his hips. Then, with the skill for which he was famed at home and abroad, he impaled her with his own sure arrow. She reveled in the glide, the angle, the girth, the tip. The heady speed.

"My darling husband," she said, forcing herself down as he gently tilted his hips up, "your abilities . . . as an archer . . . astound me."

He circled rhythmically to string her tighter. "Mmmm. You are a worthy target."

She leaned back in a bowman's arc that allowed her to take more of him to reach their mutual mark. "I welcome your accuracy."

He snorted. "I will always give you more than a sure

shot, madam. I give you now and always my own surrender . . . Oh, God, sweetheart . . . to everything we can create together."

She clamped her eyes shut as he stroked her for an eternity, driving her to clutching, clawing distraction but maintaining some steadied—almost premeditated—course to drive her unerringly mad with longing for the final consummation.

"Matt, do this," she begged him as they churned in the water. "Do this . . . or else you'll snap my mind."

"Snap," he moaned, and swirled his tongue atop both her yearning nipples. "Loose, soar. Wherever you go, I follow."

"Nay," she sobbed in rapturous need of release, "come with me."

He twisted himself up higher into her and set her teeth to grinding. "Always."

"Now," she whispered on the first pulse of her delight.

"Now," he confirmed, and gave her another potent physical display of how far he could travel up into her heart and mind and soul. The sure slide of him, the powerful thrust of him unraveled all her sensibilities. She sank back farther into the lake and felt the unceasing flows of her delight throb through her and around him. In the next second, he let fly into her the essence of his care, and she returned the substance of her own.

The lake was still a turbulent affair when she opened her eyes, her head upon his massive shoulder. The setting sun refracted, making her remember how different this lake appeared from the last one in which she'd swum, when Matt had rescued her.

"Hold to me," he whispered as he headed toward the shore, his body slipping from inside hers and making her moan for his loss. "I know," he growled, shifting her. "But there will be endless lovings in this lake." He dropped a quick kiss to her brow and nudged her hair away from her burning face. "Or anyplace at all I stride the world with you always near my heart."

He tenderly stood her against a tree as he bent to retrieve her clothes. She had her hands in the air as he pulled her summery gown down along her arms, when she heard a rustling in the trees, the clanking of armor, and the whistle of daggers unsheathed.

"How intriguing," came a voice that made Lacy shudder and yank at her gown to continue to pull it over her head when Matt, for some reason, had stopped. "Two Fletchers for the effort of seizing one."

Lacy stared at Matt, who stood naked, eyes blazing hatred, teeth clenched—two daggers held to his throat by two huge men-at-arms.

The man sneering into her own face was no other than Charles Arnold.

CHAPTER 13

Ropes bound Matt's wrists.

Lacy saw them as chains. Knew he considered them to be none other. And she writhed against the restraining arms of Charles Arnold.

But to maintain her sanity and Matt's pride, she did not gaze into her husband's eyes. She dared not. Instead, she trained her sight on the glassy lake and walked backward, away from the menace who had weeks ago assailed her in his mother's solar.

Charles Arnold yanked her toward a clearing, holding fast to the hemp that circled her own wrists. Vivid memories of that awful night Charles had come to her and unbound her from similar ropes made her strain savagely at this one. He hauled her forward with ease. Smugness suffused his florid face as he pushed her ahead of him toward his horse, away from Matt. "I saw you both in the water. 'Twas an education."

She blew hair from her eyes and deftly found his toes with her heel.

He whimpered. "You witch." Hopping two steps, he curled the ropes around his wrist and clamped her to him, back to front, and spoke in her ear. "I knew you'd brew a hot-blooded broth. When this is over, we'll see how well you like another to stir your pot."

"You're disgusting."

"Don't be hasty. I have proof now that you not only have been well initiated to the arts of love but also that you like a lusty man to do it. So I shall see you have all the lust your lush body can hold." He laughed and stopped before a horse. "Mount."

"Go to hell."

"Nasty."

She gave him an elbow in the side.

He retaliated with a cinch that socked the breath from her. "Is that what the Sure Arrow teaches with his archery lessons? Bad manners and vocabulary for his once polite but noble little wife? Certainly, the man has ridden too long in the saddle." He grinned at her with overlong white teeth. "I shall have to put you in *my* saddle. We'll see then how powerful the fabled Sure Arrow is—and how fine a teacher of the . . . domestic pleasures." He lifted her like a sack of wheat and thumped her across the horse, sideways.

She winced at the blow to her tender flesh, so recently caressed by Matt's gentle strokes of ecstasy.

Her husband, who had evidently seen, cursed the man who'd thrown her to the horse. Arnold muttered an obscenity, then climbed up behind her as she sought to throw herself from the animal. But with a meaty hand, Charles restrained her by clutching her about the waist. Not as big or as strong as Matt, this

Arnold nonetheless could quell her insignificant efforts to avoid him.

She whimpered.

From the corner of her eye, she saw Matt tussle against his ropes and heard his violent outrage, soon muffled by the fist of one man-at-arms. Matt staggered but rebounded with an agility born of years of strife. He snarled at Arnold.

"You son of a bitch, she can't be manhandled!"

Charles chuckled. "I am the man who will handle her any way I wish."

"She's delicate and—"

"She's a hellion." He lifted the rope that tied her to him. "I won't make the mistake I did last time and set her free to bite and scratch."

"I'll kill you!" Matt seethed, as Arnold's horse pawed the earth, jostling Lacy and sending up sour signals of distress from her stomach.

"No you won't. If Henry wouldn't give an interview to two wool merchants whose methods are suspect, do you think your precious Harry would allow a murderer into his court? 'Twould set a bad example. Besides, none of us wants blood shed, do we, Lacy, love? We just desire the simple pleasures of life. Land, water, and a good soft bed." His mouth shot to one side as he threw back his head to hoot, then he waved casually at Matt and kneed his horse. Lacy knew where he headed—a segment of the stream where few usually crossed because of the sharp rocks along both banks. That area was probably where they had crossed to get to the lake. They would have been able to view Matt and Lacy from their knoll and set off to gain the advantage of divide and conquer. For conquest over the Sure Arrow had eluded them until . . . until they saw him leave with his wife.

The prospect of separation from Matt eroded her resolve, and she curled about Charles to see what the others did to Matt. She gasped, unable to bear the sight of him being mauled by two men as he fought in vain to free himself of rope and despair.

Eyes squeezed shut, she cast her face to the sky. Terrified. Fighting anguished tears.

Still, as they rode away from him, she could hear him. She was certain all the angels of heaven and those condemned to Satan's halls could hear him. With the voice she adored, he boomed so high she felt his resonance petrify the forest with his rabid oath that Arnold should cower in a hole somewhere. For he'd come for Arnold, for all the Arnolds, and though it might take him years or eternities, he'd gut him, cut him limb from limb, and call the blunt work blessed.

She shivered as her tears began to fall.

Her husband's bellows blended with the wind and broke with what she felt sure were the blows of more fists to his handsome face and form.

"You must not hurt him." She turned, wiping tears from her cheeks. "What has he done to you?"

Charles lifted red brows. "Oh, you mean aside from bringing men here from his home to fight us? You did not think we knew that, eh? We did. We had people along the roads to spot you as you entered De Vere Castle two nights ago. That failure to anticipate our move was one mistake, my lady Fletcher. Your other —or your husband's—was asking Henry not to see us. *Aye,* we did learn that from rumors among those in the train. We went to Henry with a good offer, but he would not even allow us a moment to listen. For that, your husband will pay a price. He'll sit in our dungeon until we have the whole of what we need. With you in my possession—and now him as well—my men will make short shrift of taking all the stream."

"But then you'll have to hold it," she said, feeling queasy at the mere possibility. For as they crossed the stream, she could see south toward De Vere village, where a force of eight stood in surrender to a force of ten or more. Her heart crashed to her rolling stomach. "I see how you have won the village."

"Aye, we waited until your famous husband took his notable hide from their presence. Without him, they crumbled like old bread. The stream is ours."

"Aye, for now, mayhaps. But how will you hold it permanently? For you cannot afford to spend your days and years fortifying streams nor pursuing Henry Tudor."

"How right you are, my sharp-witted marchioness. The answer to your question is simple." He grinned, sardonic fire in his umber eyes. "This time, I do believe you'll sign those papers my father did prepare last month. And afterward"—he smoothed a curl around his finger—"you and I will seal the bargain in ways I now know you'll savor."

"I'd rather die."

As they rode through the ancient wooden gate of the Fitzhugh estate, Lacy saw immediately how influential these Arnolds had become. Here, behind the curtain wall so thick and so similar in Norman viability to her own outer wall at De Vere, she saw that the Arnolds had not only the two who subdued Matt by the lake. They had hired at least twenty more strong men. And each one stood here, making some preparation for a battle. Testing bows, sharpening rondels, or polishing armor plate, each man had a task. Each man had an eye, too, for the younger Arnold and her perched before him. Some of the mercenaries were rough men, perhaps even former soldiers from the Yorkist camps, if she were to take their livery markings as a good indication. Some were weary men, dirty, travel-worn. Some were coarse of looks and tongue. She recoiled.

Then a worse thought hit her. If these men stood here, unencumbered, the ten or more she had seen holding her villeins as captives were additional. She doubted Tom Norwich would have anticipated this number from the Arnolds. Nor would Henry send great numbers, for he needed his own mercenaries to do his bidding in London more than he needed to save his vassal's wife's lands from the greedy grasp of a merchant o'erreaching his bounds.

Hope flew from her, like wind from a sail. She sagged, almost breaking into tears again. She thought to plead for Matt. For what would strong, hungry free lances do with a specimen like Matthew Fletcher?

Lacy recoiled at the thought.

To plead for mercy was no recourse. These Arnolds wanted more than silence. They desired land and water. *This* Arnold coveted a soft bed. Hers.

Her stomach curdled with the thought.

What would she give to gain her husband's freedom and her own?

Everything.

Money. Castles. Titles. Land.

But what then of her villeins? How would they fare at the hands of such unscrupulous men as the Arnolds?

Poorly. Worse, not at all.

Lady Margery and Robert Morris had oft declared that compromise was ever possible in any matter. But what compromise could she find in this matter? Abducted as she was once more in her life and subject to another's whim? What compromise would she ever wish to find if these Arnolds took it into their heads to hurt her husband?

Nay, like her loving Matthew, she would vow vengeance to him who hurt her mate. For then, reason would have long fled and ripe necessity o'ertaken whatever hold she had on this life. Matt was her life. And instinct screamed that there had to be a way to free him. Her husband's fate, perhaps her own, and the future of her people depended on her finding some way to tame these beasts.

But what was reason in the face of those who wished to use an expeditious cruelty?

Like Matt, she had seen cruelty before. She'd seen a few village boys begin to taunt the Cowpers' son, the boy who had died night before last during the Arnolds' raid. She'd seen them dog his footsteps daily, harass him with catcalls about his "differences." Then one day, in a fit she likened to that of mad dogs, they had tied him to a tree and tormented him, then beat him. He was lame before the attack, slow-witted afterward. At her leet court, she had given out harsh punishments to those who had hurt him. She'd banished them all from her lands—and no one had ever abused another in her domain since.

But that memory summoned the one of Matt's similar torment at the hands of his father. This one of all the hideous parallels made her buckle and gag.

"Here, now!" Charles clutched at her, alarmed as they arrived before the stone steps of his home. "What's the matter? God, stop fighting me and let me hold you so you don't fall, will you?" He supported her as she retched repeatedly. Frightened, the horse danced and left Lacy dangling and gasping for air, her heart pounding a frantic tattoo.

"Charles, take your hands from her!" Frail but strong fingers lifted Lacy's head when her trembling had ceased. "What have you done to her?"

"Nothing, Mother. She sickens of her own accord."

The woman reached up to smooth Lacy's brow. "You will come with me, my lady Fletcher." Her blue eyes nailed her son like icy daggers. "Help her down, you cur."

"Watch your tongue, madam, or I shall have to send you to a convent." He pulled at Lacy's thin wool dress. She fell into his arms like a rag. Nonetheless, he tried to stand her on her feet upon the cobbled courtyard. Lacy wobbled.

"Try it, Charles." The Arnold woman wrapped an arm about Lacy and led her up the steps into the great hall. "Ignore him, my lady. He is a profligate. You come with me. I cannot do much, but I will see you to some comfort."

Unsure if she could trust the woman beyond what she was already providing, Lacy plodded beside her without argument. She saved Lacy from her son now, just as in July she had saved her from him. But would she, could she do more?

Lacy dare not conjecture. For to hope without logic was folly. And Matt's life depended on what she did here.

In her growing delirium she missed a step and wondered foggily if she could count upon her brain to show her logic. The woman led her up the stairs to the room Lacy remembered with dark horror—the family solar. Here had the senior Arnold bound her to a chair and insisted she sign papers. Here had the younger untied her legs and forced himself between them—only to have his own mother point a knife to his throat and threaten an end to his life if he took Lacy's innocence.

"Here, my lady, sit you down. I will get you a cool cloth and—" She caught Lacy as she began to swoon. "Dear God, what ails you? If he did anything to you, I shall—"

"Nay, Mistress Arnold." Lacy put out a beseeching hand but closed her eyes against the dizziness that assailed her, head to toe. "Your son was correct . . . when he said he did not make me ill . . . at least not directly. I beg you . . . oh, God, the room revolves. May I seek a bed?"

"Aye, my lady. You shall have mine. Come. Hook your arm about my waist and lean on me. We shall see you to some quiet."

But quiet was all Lacy had.

Alone in Mistress Arnold's chamber, Lacy lay upon the well-hung bed and slept fitfully between bouts of fear or further illness. The woman came repeatedly to stroke Lacy's brow with a cool cloth, to offer food or drink, to be rejected and to depart again, dejected.

Lacy flailed upon the foreign bed. Occasionally, she would come to her senses, ponder her circumstances, and soon succumb to another period of disease. She would then sleep, awake refreshed for a few moments only to contemplate her physical state.

Hardly ever in her life had she suffered illness. Yet she knew how quickly one could die of seemingly insignificant maladies. An aching ear, an inflamed cut, a violent sweat could fell a hardy man. So too, whatever this affliction, she knew she could depart this earth in summary fashion with no one to know of her demise for days—or, in this hellish circumstance, for weeks. For all she knew, it could be months until the Arnolds did decide to open their gates and give out the news that the De Veres and the Fletchers had gone down in the contest over a tiny stream.

The prospect of defeat made her stomach churn, and she rushed to the garderobe for the countless time in expectation of another surge. After an awful session, she stumbled back to the bed to crawl between the linen sheets.

The candle by her bed had burned low by the time Mistress Arnold appeared again. The crack of dawn filtered through the glass window. The room was cold for the fire had long since gone out. Lacy slitted her heavy eyelids at the woman who held, as before, a tray of bread, fruit, and ale.

"Won't you try to eat, my lady Fletcher?" she pleaded. "I know this is a terrible circumstance for you, but I assure you my husband and my son, though they appear devilish, never meant to see you ill or—or *dead.*"

Lacy clamped her eyes shut at the possibility. She had proclaimed such a preference to Charles, and death did seem more alluring at the moment to the swirling urgings of her body. She could barely breathe but made herself whisper, "That may be so, Mistress. But then, how do you explain my continued presence here?"

"Oh, my lady, my husband is sore upset with our son that he did bring you here."

Lacy rolled to her side to view the comely white-haired lady who wrung her hands in honest concern.

"Where is my husband, Mistress Arnold?"

"I am not certain."

Lacy gulped back bile and whimpered in pain for her husband. "Where is *your* husband?"

"Out in the courtyard."

"With the mercenaries he hired?"

"Aye."

"Bring him to me."

"He will not come while you are ill."

"I must talk with him."

"He will not come, I say. His whole family did die of plague when he was a boy. He goes near no one who is ill."

Lacy shut her eyes in frustration and weakness. "Tell him . . . tell him . . ." She was losing her way through gray corridors of her bedraggled mind. "I want to . . . negotiate."

But the man did not come.

Not when Lacy demanded—and his wife set down her latest tray of food to demur.

Not when Lacy asked—and his wife offered cool water and juice and sobbed into her handkerchief.

When Lacy asked his wife why she cried, the woman reiterated how Alphonse was truly afraid of Lacy's illness. But the woman herself was more afraid for him whom she thought lost his mind with too much interest in money.

As day sped to night, no papers appeared for Lacy to sign. No ravisher, either.

Time wended by—amid her trips to the garderobe—and Lacy felt a greater peace descend. She knew it was not reasonable. Nor did she have anything other than a feeling. But, oh, she did begin to drift into a timeless void where her retchings subsided and she took a little food—and her mind intervened in her sorrow to show her only bright things.

Her husband's enthralling lavender eyes. His roguish one-dimpled smile. His luscious sculpted form as he embraced her, entranced her, enchanted her willing body and mind to open to him to create warm, wonderful sensations . . .

She flung off the coverlet and made her way once more to the garderobe.

'Twas as she shivered her way back to her lonely, cold bed, she remembered how this same unease was one her mother had once suffered. The De Vere villeins oft spoke of it. Her steward Franklin, too. The marchioness De Vere had taken famously and gloriously ill after being married to her lord only a brief period. A few weeks, in fact.

Lacy mused anew on this local story, which now presented such a novel prospect as she sank to her pillows like a stone.

Her door opened.

"Marchioness," said the lady of the house once more, "won't you please eat to keep up your strength?"

CHAPTER 14

ETERNAL DARKNESS BROUGHT ENDLESS AGONY. TIME ceased to wend in any order. So long secluded in this dungeon of his mind, Matt sat on his pallet or paced. Visions of his wife in his arms, in his bed, in his heart—and ripped from him—tore his sanity. In the void, he could detect only two companions in the vague torch light. He stopped to gape at those two dragons he thought his wife had banished with her love. But for that love, he instinctively knew they came now to argue their new cause before him. To parley with each other and whisper in his ear. *Come forth, break these chains. Take the man and any other who dares to touch that which is yours alone.*

Matt yanked at the infernal links that lashed him to the moldy wall. They clattered vacuously against the stones. Resounding in the caverns of his memory, they called forth memories of the night so many years ago when he was pinned to Fletcher Castle's cell after his defense of another dear woman . . . who later died. By her own hand.

He dropped his head to his palms and rocked, convulsed by this, his life's recurring ordeal.

But Lacy would never take her own life.

She was not downtrodden but brave and strong. Bounteous of heart and mellow of soul. Aye, his complex Lacy was fragile and, God love her, probably with child. His baby. Their creation. He'd seen the signs—the dizziness, the nausea. But at so early a stage, he could not be certain, and he had left the subject as a lesson for another day. A day when this strife with the Arnolds was finished, decided by his own strategy in the village or by Henry's show of might or royal decree.

But that day had not arrived before the one when Charles Arnold again abducted Lacy and mistreated her.

Matt clamped his eyes shut at the hated scene of Charles yanking Lacy to him with a rope and throwing her over his saddle. The man had hurt her. Matt had seen her wince, watched her struggle against retching. If she lost this baby or died from mistreatment or neglect while he himself sat here, chained to his misery, he'd do as he had vowed. He would. He would. He'd kill this Arnold and any other who bore the unfortunate name. And if they killed him first, he would entreat his God to employ His assertion that vengeance was His alone.

For what other recourse had he?

Only Henry . . .

Where was Henry? And Tom?

Matt knew the exigencies of war and peace. First-hand had he experienced them from Brittany to Saxony and beyond to Venice and finally at Bosworth.

He knew armies took days or months or years to supply, train, and march. He knew they moved as much by hope as plan. But of this interim between war and peace he now acknowledged he knew little. And such a lack fell as despair about him like a freshly tailored shroud.

Will you allow her to sicken and succumb?

Matt's head shot up to see the green and red monsters thrash their tails in punctuation of their mutual question.

He raised his wrists to display the substance of his response.

They sneered, conspiring to send up flames of hatred and jealousy that seared his soul to ashes.

You will do naught? asked the red.

Ah, Christ! He rose, shaking his shackles with his violent helplessness.

The green one inhaled. *This reaction is not the one you claimed would have won the contest the night your mother was abused. What ails you that your memory is so vague?*

Love chains his mind, mourned the red to his brother.

Matt frowned.

For how many years had he denied the power of these beasts in favor of a more righteous might he called reason?

Since the morn that he learned his mother had ended her sojourn here on earth, he had promised himself to honor reason more from that day forward. And in the intervening years, though he hated war and the virulent emotions battle brought to the fore, he had endured them in the name of necessity. But today—as he had told his loving wife not long ago—he had choices.

Rational choices.

Now from the black hole of his heart walked a new apparition, resembling in many luminous ways his wife. She stood before him, resplendent in her possibilities, and he knew he could call her by no other name than Hope.

At that moment, he saw two scaly dragons link forelimbs and cavort as Matt turned to bellow to the rooftop for these two Arnolds who numbered now his only foes.

"My lord Fletcher," pleaded the white-haired woman before him with a full tray of food and drink, "I beg you to cease this infernal yelling. You have driven my steward and my two maids outside to seek peace."

He narrowed his eyes at her in the dim light from the torches on the dungeon walls. "My actions brought me you."

"But I am afraid I am all you'll get." She set down the tray upon his straw pallet. Though she was within his reach, she quickly retreated, outside his sphere. "Besides, you do not want to trouble your wife."

His chest expanded with this success at leading her to the only subject that soothed him. "Where is she?"

"Upstairs. In my chambers."

He detected a hint of remorse there. Hate and jealousy prodded him to gain information. "Is your son with her?"

"Nay. She is alone."

"Has he done—?"

"Nay, my lord. I would not let him even if . . . I simply would not let him. He is really a good lad—or was—until his father imbued him with ideas of riches and estates." She waved a hand about the cell. "Such glories are heady temptations for a poor man who has done well in business."

Matt flared his nostrils. "This *business* he engages in may see him at the most a pauper and at the least a dead man."

"Aye, my lord. I do agree."

"But you cannot persuade him thus?"

"Nay. Can your wife persuade you to her reasoning?"

Matt smiled and heard his two dragons scoff over his shoulder at the woman. "Aye, always."

"Then you have a fortunate alliance, sir. I wish I could claim such myself."

"You say you have tried to stop him from this course. But with what reasoning?"

"That Henry Tudor's victory at Bosworth is no mere battle in the civil war for the crown. That Henry, who was your lady's royal protector, would not see her hurt or relieved of her domain without a great conflict."

"And your husband did not agree. How sad."

"Aye," she whispered raggedly, and spun on her heel.

"What if I said it is not too late to save your husband?"

"Your words fall on deaf ears with me, sir."

"You are not deaf. Nor are you helpless. You simply have not found a way to make others heed the warnings sounded."

"I beg you, sir. I am a merchant's wife, and your courtly riddles do not string out to good sense with me." She stepped past the rusty iron bars and would have clanged them shut behind her had he not stopped her with a palm out.

"Please, hear me. What will it cost you? Your husband and your son are not here, I do presume."

"Aye. They see to the defense of the stream. But to consort with you would not go well for me if they ever knew."

"I will not tell them."

"Still, I am afraid."

He nodded. He of all men knew how women could be intimidated by the threat of violence, verbal or physical, from males. "I think there is a way to ensure that Henry Tudor would not fix your husband with the worst judgment of death."

"Is there also a way to ensure that the land by the stream becomes his? For you see, if not, then death is preferable for Alphonse to failure."

"I am not certain of that. But I can tell you that the land may not be either my wife's or your husband's to contest."

She drifted closer. "What do you mean?"

"There is reason to speculate that it might well belong to the Crown."

"No! Who told you that?"

"My wife."

"Well, of course. Why wouldn't she?"

"Why would she lie to me that way? Why not simply say that the land belongs to the De Veres and always had?"

That made her stumble and cast her eyes about the cell. "How would Henry Tudor look with mercy upon a man and his son who had taken what was not theirs?"

"I know him well. He would grant clemency if there were ameliorating circumstances that came to light."

"Such as?"

Matt strode as far toward her as his chains allowed.

His eyes nailed hers in compassion. "Let me take my wife home."

"I cannot do that, my lord, for when my husband found you both gone, with his bare hands would he kill me."

Matt ate the bread and drank the wine, cheered on by two dragons who claimed he'd won a tactical victory with Mistress Arnold. As for him, total victory could not come soon enough.

Hours passed, and he wondered how Lacy fared. He had not taken the opportunity to ask that question of Mistress Arnold. He wondered, too, if the woman had the tenacity and strength to stand watch every hour of the day against the intrusion of her son to Lacy's chamber. For that he had no answer, only comfort in the form of hope.

Hope also led him to believe that Lacy was as well fed as he. And not too despairing, he prayed. For he had promised Lacy so many things, including safety, and until he himself walked through death's portal, he would give every ounce of strength to see that she was not only safe but happy and dearly loved.

The reaffirmation let him doze.

But the pallet was thin and scratchy. He tossed, dreaming of gossamer-soft arms and twinkling turquoise stars. He turned, fantasizing that two lush lips kissed his ear . . . then finite sounds upon the dungeon stairs made him struggle to a sitting position.

Rats?

Aye. Two large ones.

He drifted silently to the farthest, darkest corner of his cell. From this vantage he could spy who or what descended the torchlit steps.

He focused and blinked at the sight of the steward

who had escorted him into this place days ago. The steward, a young man of his own steward David's age, had said little but had been extremely polite as he took the care of Matt from the two mercenaries who had brought him from the lake. Ever after, as the man brought food or drink, did he seem distant but friendly. This was the steward whose family Lacy had told him once served the former lords of the manor, the Fitzhughs. And though Matt constantly looked for an opening to conversation by which to sound out the steward's loyalties, the man offered none.

Now this silent steward came accompanied by a younger woman. She, from her attire, could be none other than one of the maids.

Why came they now to him? At their master's requests or their mistress's?

"My lord," breathed the towheaded steward as he hoisted a rush torch to help find Matt inside the cell, "fear not. Ah, there you are, sir." He inserted the huge key and twisted it in the lock of the grated cell door. The maid hung back, her ear attuned to the stairs. "Come, sir. I do not free you to hurt you. Nay. The opposite. Right, Nancy?"

"Aye, aye. Hurry."

Matt sat down on the pallet, his entire body wary of betrayal. "Why are you here?"

"To let you go, my lord." The man set his torch in a wall socket and knelt at Matt's feet.

Matt braced himself as the steward bent to work this miracle come true. The scrape of the chain's lock dug beneath the frayed fabric of Matt's hose and into his ankle. The prick of pain made Matt circumspect amid his burgeoning rejoicing. "That I see, but why, man?"

The steward raised his round face with innocent

eyes. "My lord, I have lived here since my birth and known your lady wife since hers. She and her guardian, Lady Margery, were very kind and generous to us when the Fitzhughs owned this estate. Never would I see Lacy De Vere mistreated. Neither would Nancy. Don't you want to be free, my lord?"

"Aye. More than anything. But—" he groaned as the steward worked at the rusty lock and key of the second chain around his raw ankle. "Aren't you afraid of what the Arnolds might do to you?"

The steward stopped to search Matt's eyes. "Aren't you?"

"Aye, but I must live my life with hope that my wife will be by my side."

"And Nancy and I must live with hope that we can do the same—in peace—for people who deserve good service."

With a lump in his throat, Matt began to smile. "I promise you, if my wife and I escape this, we can assure that to you. What is your name, sir?"

"Gabriel, my lord."

"Fitting, that the man who leads me out of here bears the same name as the archangel who blows the trumpet on Judgment Day. Gabriel"—Matt held out his wrists with a smile bursting through him—"tell me where my wife is and how I can find her and take her from here."

Gabriel, working like a fiend, bit his lower lip. "That will be a problem, my lord."

Matt turned to ice. "Why? Where is she? What's happened?"

"Nothing, my lord. Nothing that hasn't already happened."

With his one free hand, he gripped the steward's wrist. "What do you mean? Gabriel, where's Lacy?"

"Where she has been since she entered the castle, my lord. In my mistress's chambers above the great hall at the top of the main stairs."

"What *else?"*

"She is not well, my lord."

Nancy made a small sound of fear. "She is very pale and vomits often. I fear they've fed her poison."

Matt's mouth dropped open in an outrage that was a silent scream to the heavens. *"Nooo.* No, they wouldn't. Would they?" He twisted Gabriel's doublet. *"Who* would feed it to her? Who? *Tell me."*

"Not I," said Gabriel.

"Nor me," offered Nancy. "But why else is she sick? Day in and day out? Only Mistress Arnold takes her food and drink. I clean the room and see your lady has eaten little. I swear I never thought my mistress could do such a thing, but your lady is so ill . . ."

Matt could barely find breath to summon hope. "Show me where she is, for God's sake, Gabriel. Now, before I lose my mind."

"Aye, my lord. But I do ask you to be quiet."

Matt jerked his head, horrors of Lacy dead of insidious poison before he could hold her in his arms blotting out all other thoughts.

"Nay, my lord, stop a minute, listen." Gabriel grabbed Matt's doublet to restrain him and turn him in the dim light. "We are at risk here. I know this castle well because I was born in it. I do know of a secret passage, long used by those who needed such. But to get to it, we must traverse the main stairs and great hall. When Nancy and I came down to you, no one was inside the castle save Mistress Arnold. She paces in her solar, which is next to the room where your lady lies."

"Where is everyone else, then?"

"That is what I wanted to tell you, my lord. They have all gone to the outer curtain wall to gaze from the walk to the valley."

A shock scaled Matt's spine. Hope rose, then turned once more to fear and sorrow. "Why, Gabriel?"

"A hundred men or more assemble there this morning for a vast attack, my lord. They unfurl the green-and-white standard of Henry Tudor."

Matt could barely keep from flying up the stone steps, but reason backed by the cold hand of Gabriel kept him on course. Up to the main floor garrison quarters, past the great hall, and beyond the main stairs to the chambers where Lacy reclined unto death.

Death.

Matt trembled at the mere idea.

But before the door of her chamber, he had no moment to prepare himself for such a sight. Gabriel, swift and sure as his namesake, thrust open the door, let Matt in, and shut it silently behind them.

The sight of Lacy upon the bed hit him like the blow of a battle-ax.

She was a frail heap under the voluminous coverlet. Barely breathing. Alone.

But no more.

He bounded across the room and bent to her. Her face, as infinitely lovely as ever, was thinner. Her skin was the smoothest cream and ripest peaches and—by some jester's trick—what he would call luminous. Her lips were chapped. Her eyes, at first closed, now opened into his. She recognized him with a blink of glowing serenity.

"My heart," he whispered and stifled the quaver that came to his throat by reaching for her delicate hand and kissing her fingertips.

"I knew you would come," she said without voice.

That cleft him in two. "Aye, darling. Didn't I promise you?"

In response, she smiled like an angel.

"My lord," Gabriel urged vehemently, "I beg you, come now. Take her. Let us go before anyone returns."

"Wind your arms around me, love. I'll take a blanket so you won't get cold." But as he lifted her heartbreakingly lighter body, he felt how chilled she was. Was she already at death's door and had he no time to savor her, detain her, or barter for her with his God? He very nearly crushed her to him at the thought. Then he remembered himself and, fighting away tears, he nodded at Gabriel. "We're ready. Let's go."

"Tread quietly, my lord. No sound, my lady. I do not know who might be about." From the folds of his doublet, Gabriel extracted a long butcher knife.

He opened the door, checked the stairs, and motioned for Matt to follow. They were both down a few steps when a woman gasped, and the two men turned to see Mistress Arnold at the top of the stairs.

"What are you doing? Gabriel? How could you turn traitor?"

"Aye, madam," said the servant implacably. "I can and will. Do you try to stop us?"

Her sad eyes ran from Matt to the sight of Lacy, limp in his arms.

Below, angry voices drifted up from the garrison.

Matt knew they had to go now or never leave. He'd have barely enough time to kill her before whoever was downstairs heard a scuffle and came up to slay him, Gabriel, and Lacy. "Madam, how say you?"

"Nay." She threw her head high. "I will be instead your bulwark."

In a fog of fear, Matt took the stairs with his precious burden in his arms. At the great hall's entrance, Gabriel spun to Matt, a finger to his lips. Waving Mistress Arnold on to intercept whomever came up from the garrison, Gabriel scurried through the hall with Matt taking one step to his three. At the other end of the hall, Gabriel opened a door into a minor room, the buttery. Leaning against a portion of the far wall, the steward grunted as he pushed. Matt watched as the whole thing gave, groaned, and creaked to offer an aperture.

"Here, my lord. 'Tis a long, straight hall with occasional steps down, so do be careful. It is musty, filled with cobwebs, but"—he smiled compassionately—"it will lead you beyond the outer wall to the west, where you may walk easily to De Vere land."

"I will not forget this, Gabriel."

"Thank you, my lord. But I did not do it for reward."

"I know."

"Take this." Gabriel pressed the butcher knife to Matt's hand.

"What defense will you have?"

"I'll take another. You need something. Get you gone now. I will pray for you."

Matt shouldered his way into the passage. "And I for you."

Gabriel closed the stone wall with a resounding thud.

The world grew pitch black, but with his wife in his

arms, Matt swore he could walk through hell and never falter. For if there was a way to save her from these beasts, he would. Today. Any day. He stepped into the unknown, hurrying to save this day and give her some peace before she . . . left him. . . .

Hope stumbled.

Matt paused and pressed his face into his wife's thick hair, finding resolution. And firmer footing. He would save her from these Arnolds and from any torment these last hours of her days on earth. He would take her to her home, make her comfortable and happy. There in the place she loved best, he would commend her to her God, who he was certain would love her and cherish her until Matt himself was called to join her in heaven.

"Hold fast to me, my love. We're going home to De Vere."

The passage seemed so fluid, Matt marveled at the ease with which they arrived at the end. Fearing some element that might surprise and undo him, he slid open the armored wooden door with great trepidation and care. But the door, so half-sized it was hardly worthy of the name, made him bend in a contortionist's mode to squeeze Lacy out along with himself. And then he discovered that they sat in a nest of berry bushes with sharp thorns.

"No wonder few have discovered this escape," he murmured.

Lacy acknowledged with a loll of her head against his shoulder. Her eyes, in the daylight, seemed as absurdly beautiful as before.

He pushed her hair away from her cheeks, then settled her against the wall. "Rest here a moment until

I examine what we face." She nodded. He rose to a crouch.

Within moments, he returned, took her up into his arms, and strode from their prison with the ease of a condemned man freed.

The force that Henry had sent stood at the south main entrance to the Arnolds' castle. From his vantage point, Matt had seen them begin the assault with two catapults and a trebuchet. Two contingents of his own archers stood at the ready to follow the initial blows with a rain of arrows. He saw Tom Norwich at their head, prancing on his gray destrier. The Arnolds would pay for their thievery.

Let them suffer. Let them.

He recited it like an incantation for the dead. It gave him strength. Took him home. Guided his purpose and resolved his need to hate and condemn those who had so brutally hurt his Lacy.

He made the walls of De Vere within the hour. A few of the women from the village who had taken refuge there saw him coming and ran to see their marchioness.

Though Lacy opened her eyes and blinked in greeting, Matt knew she could do little else. Her weak fingers clutched his doublet, and she muttered into his chest.

"My lord," asked one frightened village woman, "what ails my lady? Did they hurt her?"

"She looks nigh unto death!" exclaimed another. "Already with the heavenly host. What did they do?"

Matt swallowed hard. "They took her from me. But we will make her better." He buried his lips in her hair. "I promise you, darling, we'll make you better."

But he knew he lied. In misery, he strode not for the

keep but for her chapel, where once she had told him the tale of a little girl who wished for a knight to come and love her. Now, before she departed this world, he would see her have everything he could give her. Himself. His heart. His troth, forevermore.

Shouldering open the chapel door, he strode to the altar. There, upon the first step, he knelt with her in his arms and laid her tenderly along the second step. Avoiding her eyes, he arranged her hands across her waist and with a violent throbbing pain in his heart, left her for a moment to return with the ruby and turquoise cushions from their pew. The ruby he placed beneath her head and the turquoise he knelt upon.

Her eyes fastened on him in question.

With a rending sound that reverberated in the empty church, he tore his doublet from the neck. The woolsy hung in tatters as he curled two fists about the golden chain he'd worn for fifteen years. It ripped with a pop. Two rings slithered from it to his hand.

"My heart," he whispered, his voice cracking, his vision refracting at the sight of the shimmering rings, "until late I have been a soldier. A rough man bent on killing. But since I have come home to you and love, I find I wish I were a poet. Today I wish I knew the words of a priest. For the substance of what we were made to do when you were four and I was fifteen has long been denied us. I do assert that what was done then in God's and man's wisdom was never valid because you were too young to know your will, and I—I mouthed the words but meant none of them.

"And now, lest when you meet your God in Heaven He does say you never were truly married to any man, I give you this once more. The way it was meant to have been given. By a man who loves you dearly, my Lacy." He took her hand and, with his shaking fingers, held the golden circle to the tip of her wedding finger.

"My heart, in the sight of God, I tell you now in complete truth as I did not that day before the door of the church, I . . ." He sought for memory of the words he had heard others repeat countless times. "I will have you to my wedded wife. You will find in me the will to love you and to hold you." He slid the ring to her finger. "Aye, just as the band is inscribed, my love—'you and no other'—will I cherish until this life ends. I, Matthew Michael Fletcher, take you, Catherine Lacy De Vere"—his eyes lifted to her glowing ones—"in . . . in this holy church, to . . . to my wedded wife. Oh, Lacy, I don't know the rest, love."

His head fell to his chest and tears obscured his vision.

Her fingers laced into the hair at his nape. "My heart," she rasped, "say 'forsaking all others'—"

He gasped out the words. "Forsaking all others . . ."

"Holding me in sickness and in health . . ."

He seized her hand to bury his lips in her palm. "In sickness and in health . . ."

"In riches and in poverty . . ."

"Aye, darling! It's only you I want—"

"In happiness and sorrow—"

He was sobbing against her chest as she wended her fingers from his hair along his back. "Lacy, you are my happiness."

"'Til death us depart."

"No!" He clutched at her, lifting her off the step and rocking with her in his arms. "You can't leave me. Not now. Not when I have only found I can't live without

you." He twined his fingers in her hair, adored her eyes.

"And thereto," she whispered, a beatific look dawning on her features, "I plight you my troth."

He shattered into a thousand pieces. Broken by his impending loss of her, he clamped her to him while she stroked his back, then pushed him away to take his own ring between her fingers. In a solemn voice, with her incomparable eyes in his, she repeated the words of the sacred service that at age four she never said but that today made him truly her husband.

He trailed gentle fingers over her features. She seemed so calm . . . too calm.

"Thank you," she breathed at last, content. "I always did want a real exchange of vows."

His heart paused.

Lacy beamed. "And I think it's so typically sweet of you to marry me truly before the baby comes."

"Baby?" he wondered, stupefied by this element, which beckoned hope return . . . and stay.

"Aye, love of mine. It seems we have created one. But that, I think you knew."

"How do *you* know?" he asked, stretched upon a rack between hope and death's despair.

"My mother's family—the De Lacy women—always become terribly sick . . ."

His fingers dug into her arms. "Mistress Arnold didn't try to kill you? Poison you?"

Lacy gazed at him with wide turquoise eyes of incredulity. "Kill me? Sweetheart, she was the soul of succor. I would have preferred you with me, though. You are my favored companion through any trial, and—"

He hauled her to him. Sanity stood at bay. Hope sat down to play with joy.

The shout he gave made his wife smile.

It made his throat sore for days. But his rapidly recovering wife soothed his every lingering horror with a honey mixture of hot potions and endless ecstatic remedies within her loving arms.

EPILOGUE

HER FIRST PAIN STRUCK IN SOME UMBER HOUR BEFORE THE world awoke. It was a small pain, no more than the prick of a needle, and so easy to bear. She had known much more potent ones. Much more fearful ones. Hence, she called no one to her. For this challenge to her courage and her physical stamina she took the joyous opportunity to rally all her internal forces. She welcomed them. Alone. For now.

Soon, she knew in her soul, her husband would come home to her. He had promised. And he had never failed her.

He *was* her heart, her other self. The complementary half of her she had prayed for, longed for, found, and now adored. He was her love, eternal.

And soon she would bring forth the living proof.

She smiled, blissful, amid her gathering unease.

For that was all this was, this drawing down within her loins. This push of her womb to bring forth that full expression of what Matthew Fletcher and Lacy De Vere meant to each other.

She placed her palms on her hard belly and marveled at this gift God granted her and her husband. One glorious gift among so very many.

The sun streaked through their mullioned chamber window, promising a radiant June day for the birth of their first child. Roses bloomed in their garden and birds sang, mated, and tended their own young chicks in their forests. People in De Vere and Fletcher went about their days in orderly rounds. Others in innumerable English villages did the same. Peace, pierced now and then by small annoyances to Henry the Seventh's pervasive power, flourished in England.

Lacy inhaled the fragrance of this ripe tranquility. She burst with pride that her husband had helped to make it so. For though he had gladly given up his post as captain of the yeoman guard, her Matthew was a man to reckon with in Henry Tudor's kingdom. For he was Harry Tudor's friend, called now three times to his court since the siege that had confirmed that friendship for the understanding of the thieving Arnolds and all others within this kingdom.

Harry had certainly smiled upon his lifelong friend. He had sent Tom Norwich to head the royal force of one hundred to quell the challenge of the Arnolds. The siege of Henry's troops lasted less than twenty minutes. For when the trebuchet and catapults sent missiles inside the walls, the mercenaries hired by the Arnolds folded like old parchment. So long at war here in England, these weary men wished more to go home than to earn a few shillings from a merchant who had overestimated his abilities. They sent out a white surrender flag to Henry's men and within the hour the foes mingled to quaff the Arnolds' best beer.

Tom Norwich had orders, though, that with the easy taking of the merchant's estate, he was to bind both Arnolds by chains and cart them down to London to view King Henry's violent displeasure. To this day, the two remained at Henry's beck and call, trussed up in the Tower of London as suited the young king with heavier concerns than two brash merchants who set in motion great trouble over rights to a stream.

Lacy winced, a sharper pain striking her, pulling at her body. She panted, as the midwife had oft instructed she must do. Soon the distress subsided. Lacy sank into her pillow and focused on the positive blessings she could barely count for all their wealth and endless promise.

Though certainly, it had not seemed that way to Matt the day he carried her from the Arnolds' clutches home to De Vere. Nay. He had thought her virtually dead. Dear heart that he was, he took the maid Nancy's conclusion to be truth. For he had no means to judge the total complexity of Mistress Arnold's humanity nor her loyalty to her husband. Matt, pressed as he was to pluck Lacy from the castle before anyone would discover him gone from his cell, did not take the time to argue with himself over the viability of Nancy's logic.

"How could I know if Mistress Arnold truly had poisoned you?" he had bellowed, then crooned into Lacy's hair as he rocked her in the chapel. "I thought the woman kind but afraid of her husband. And I know so well how helpless one can be at the hands of a merciless aggressor. Ah, Lacy, how could you deduce you were with child?"

She grinned now as she had then.

"I thought at first my illness came from fright at Charles's seizure of me. But then, as I did recapitulate, I began to realize I felt ill before he took me. And though for a while I thought it might be some disease, I began to remember much of what Lady Margery told me about ladies' maladies when they conceive."

Matt pulled her away to peer at her with confused lavender eyes. "You mean to say this lady—this maidenly woman who knew nothing of men's and women's relationships—knew about such things?"

"Aye, and told me, too. She was a dear, our Margery. She had learned so much of the world, and all of it did she impart. Except of course those two subjects which she could not know—the part of life about physical communion between man and wife—and the subject she never told me of, your reason for never coming to me." Lacy snuggled into his arms. "But now that you are here, I can tell you the virulence of my illness is nothing to be dismayed about. You see, the midwife in the village did often tell me about my mother. It seems she too conceived me instantly upon merely gazing at my father. The speed of it became a local legend, which told of her physical distress so great it drove her to the garderobe too often. And much like you, my father did fear for her life at first. But then, she settled into motherhood with ease and brought forth her baby with little commotion."

"I pray it must be so for you, my heart."

And so had she willed it to be.

Another pain hit with more strength.

Grimacing, Lacy stretched herself into another position on their huge bed and prayed for her husband to return from London before their baby drew first breath.

Dusk rouged a brilliance across the gleaming stones of De Vere Castle as Matt and his cohort Gabriel rounded the last crest. Living here as Matt had for most of the past nine months, he had come to treasure it as did his wife. Her wealth coupled with her tender care of the old place made it a haven amid the storm of daily life. The home he'd never found but always craved was now wherever she was. For within these walls, his wife embraced him and took him to the tranquility that was her hallmark—and his saving grace.

He kneed his horse, who he knew grew weary of such urgings from him. For four days he had hastened here with news and expectation of their baby's birth. London held no charms compared to the bliss his Lacy held forth here for him.

"Think you can race me to the inner courtyard steps?" he asked his companion.

The towheaded man who had once served the Fitzhughs and the Arnolds gave a lopsided grin to the new master he served as chamberlain. "Aye, my lord. I think I can control this beast well enough. But will I win?"

"Will you wager?"

"Nay, sir. I am quick-witted but no fool." He inclined his head toward the rosy compound. "In there awaits a lady longing for your assistance. When my Nancy's time comes, I'll leave you, too, to give her comfort. For now, I hope you do not mind if I advance more slowly, as befits my more unaccustomed seat." He sat forward, implying by his grimace the discomfort brought on him by his lord's hard riding these past days.

Matt's black destrier snorted and pawed the earth. With Matt's croon and command, the animal took off. Sentries had already dropped the drawbridge and cheered as they saw him cross the plain and moat. He never stopped or slowed until he passed the second curtain wall, when the stallion headed for the keep in understanding of the bold requirement to leave his master near the door.

From years of training to this skill, Matt easily unseated himself and slid to the stones. His horse continued, cantering off to the stables. Divesting himself of dagger, sword, and gauntlets, Matt dropped to the dust those elements he never needed here. He smiled and greeted those about him but kept on for the object of his quest.

Franklin appeared with a goblet in his hand. Nancy came to grin at him from the table in the great hall. He acknowledged them both, but saw them not.

"Where is she?"

"In your chambers," offered Franklin.

He and Nancy moved forth to stop him, tell him something, but he had no desire to listen. He had other more important words to say and hear.

At the top of the stairs, he flung open the door. And halted.

"Lacy?"

His whisper stilled the elderly gray-haired woman whom he knew from the village as the midwife.

With a sheet draping her torso, Lacy had her eyes closed, her knees up, her back cushioned against the huge headboard. She was pale, perspiring, and panting for air.

"What's the matter with her?" He slammed the massive door and took the room in two strides to grasp Lacy's clenched hand.

"Naught, my lord, save that which is natural."

"You're certain?"

"Aye, very sure. Our lady is quite strong, and her travail is almost finished."

"And the baby?"

"Comes into the world headfirst and steadily, my lord. We should see his face soon."

He licked his lips and tried to straighten out his wife's fingers to soothe her. He could not. Her steely strength defied him.

He gazed at her anew.

This delicate lace, his tender-hearted wife, had acquired while he was gone to court the robust vigor of ten men. He smiled and bent to bring her fist to his lips. "My heart, how may I help you?"

She gave some throaty animal sound. "Tell me a story. Anything." She thrashed her head back and forth on the pillows. Her fist curled tighter, defining the elegant bones of her hand.

His eyes shot to the midwife's.

"Tell her, milord."

He reached behind him to draw a chair near. With her fist cupped to his mouth, he began to babble of his latest trip to London.

"I suppose it is good I went now, even though I did not wish to leave you. Now that I am home in good time for this, my leaving is a moot point, I do suppose."

Lacy inhaled a huge draft of air and sank to her cushions. For the first time since he entered, she opened her eyes on him and smiled in peace.

"What's the matter? Are you finished? Where's the baby?"

"My lord," chuckled the midwife as she raised the sheet over Lacy's knees and nodded at her inspection, "your lady rests between the pangs of birth. I pray you, go on, keep your lady's mind on you, please."

He gulped.

Lacy shot a grateful look to the midwife, then

grinned at him before her eyes closed. "Harry? What of him?"

"He sends you greetings and fond wishes that this labor of yours will be short."

"Mmmm. It will be sweet, too."

"Aye. He tells me his Elizabeth will soon find herself in a similar bed." His joy stumbled on fear as he saw her smile descend to pain once more.

"He likes her then?"

"Aye. Very much."

"Even though—*ugh*—she came to him for politics more than—oh, Mary, here's the next one—than for . . . for love?"

"Aye!" he shot back virulently, watching in dawning horror the look of torment as it stole away his wife's peace. "He says—he says she is not only beautiful of face but heart. A boon companion to the troubles of his days."

"Like you to me," she moaned.

"And you for me."

She arched, her fist opened, and she snatched at his hand. The force with which she held him could have crushed a stone. His eyes popped.

"Tell me"—she drew air loudly—"tell me . . ." She was whimpering.

Terrified, he rushed to do her bidding. "I saw Tom and Anna. Tom is well. Anna, too. They—they like to be in London. Tom builds a house and thinks Anna too may be pregnant. So it took her only three months to conceive. Not as fast as you, of course, but that is naught. No one is as fast as you. And Henry . . . Henry says my former second-in-command of the yeoman does a good job in my place. And I . . ." He scoured his mind for things to reveal to her as she began to pant. "I think he likes his new power. I spent the last evening I was there with Gerard. He's fine. Asked after your health and wishes you well. He says he likes his role as adviser to the King and holds no grudge against you or me for renewing our marriage vows. He says he began to see, even at Renwick, how much we cared for each other." Matt grinned. "Gerard also declares he is fond of Harry. Aye, aye, that is what he called him, though I wonder if he does it to his face. Henry does not care for such familiarity unless he invites it and the friend has proven his worth."

"Like you did." Lacy loosed her grip of his hand and settled into her pillows once more.

"Aye. Can I give you water, love? Or . . . or . . ." He waved a useless hand.

Her eyes drifted closed in answer. Her fingers squeezed his.

"Gerard likes his new post on the council then?"

Matt nodded, his eyes watchful for her next bout. "Henry reaps many rewards from picking Gerard's rich brain. His one idea of reclaiming former Crown lands lines Henry's coffers with so much money, the king says he may one day be as rich as you."

"As we."

"For what you give me, I am the richest man on earth."

She presented him with a gorgeous smile.

"My love," he whispered, "both Henry and Gerard bless the day you brought them each other."

That made her chuckle, then groan and writhe. She laughed more lightly. "I had no intention of any such thing. *They* found each other."

He gave a crack of delight. "And left *us* to each other."

"Together."

"And, soon, not entirely alone," he pointed out.

Her answer came with a taut draw of her back as if a master archer strung her to his purpose.

"My lord," shouted the midwife, "don't let her do that! She cannot push well at that angle."

"Lacy, sweetheart." He rose, hands to her shoulders, mad to have her back against the headboard. "I beg you."

Her head fell to his chest. She let him settle her as she gritted her teeth and seethed through them.

The pain left as swiftly as it came.

"My lady, one or two more and we should have our heir."

Matt heard the midwife rustle with her preparations. He had eyes only for Lacy.

"And so . . . what of the Arnolds? You have not said."

"Nay, they are well. Well as can be expected what with Henry hot because of their challenge. After their endless pleas, he has released them from the Tower to 'wait' upon him each day at court. And wait they do." Matt could not help the chuckle that escaped him at the memory of Alphonse and Charles cooling their heels each day at the end of a long table—at the end of Henry's string. "They are escorted each day from a nearby house to sit in Henry's presence all the day long in one corner and learn obedience. They know if they loose the chains that bind their tongues, they could lose their heads completely."

"Have Henry and Gerard found the land records?"

"Aye. Finally, Gerard has translated and confirmed the authorship of all of them. That is why Henry called me to London this time. You were right about the disputed ownership. Four centuries ago, William of Normandy did divide land between the Fitzhughs and the De Veres, settling the conflict only by declaring that the land along the stream was the Crown's. In your father's time, Henry the Sixth did declare it again officially his, as much to thwart the Yorkist-leaning Fitzhughs as to keep the peace between the two families."

"Ah, so the land by the stream is not theirs or ours."

"Nay, not exactly." He smiled, the joy of what he had to tell her making his lips quirk.

But she bucked, groaned, and would have bowed once more in that peculiar way that made the midwife yell. With tender hands and thumping heart, he cajoled and entreated Lacy to comply and push, for God's sake, push. Not bend. Not arch. Push. Aye, that way.

In two more pushes, the midwife cooed as the sound of moisture parting gave forth a child who sighed and burbled with content.

Matt cuddled his wife close and sank her to her pillows. He thanked his God she had survived this pain, which emboldened her but rent his heart in two.

"My lady and my lord," said the midwife as she wrapped the bundle in a sheet, "you have a daughter."

Matt grinned at his wife.

But suddenly, Lacy's eyes went wide. "Why does she not cry, Mary?"

"Because, my lady, I am certain she sees nothing here on earth to cry about. She is perfect, madam. Here, look."

Mary came to the other side of the bed and leaned across to place the baby in Lacy's arms. She took her, swallowing against tears that dribbled down her cheeks.

Matt caught a fat drop with a thumb. "My heart, through all this you did not cry. Do not now, of all times!"

She lifted her face to his. He cupped her cheek in his palm and placed a kiss upon her soft skin. Then, with tears he could not suppress himself, he viewed his child whom he had conceived in utter love with her mother.

She was perfect. Tiny. Red-faced. Blond. Heart-stoppingly lovely as she gurgled and snuggled to her mother's breast. He traced a finger down her tiny cheek. Her skin was as delicate as Lacy's.

"What shall we name her?" asked his wife.

He and she had debated names for months and come to no conclusions. Today Matt had a new suggestion, backed by new logic. "I'd say we name her after you."

"Lacy? Nay, that came to me because my mother wished not for her De Lacy family heritage to die among us. Besides, there'd be confusion in the household."

"We'll call her Catherine, then."

"Not Sarah? Nor Marian?"

"Thank you, love, but I think it appropriate we save those family names for our other daughters." He kissed his wife on her smiling lips. "You bring children to this world with such ease—from divine inspiration to delivery—that I have no doubts we'll have many, both girls and boys. But our first child will be the next marchioness De Vere. She deserves your name along with your title."

Lacy took on that stalwart look that told him he had better settle in for a long siege. "I thought we decided this before you went to London. Did we or did we not agree that the title of marquess would go to our son?"

"Aye, we did. But, my heart, we have a daughter."

"You have changed your mind?"

"Aye."

The midwife hooted in laughter. "I bid you both to argue after I am done and gone. We have more work to do, *Marchioness.* You must deliver now the birthing organs."

Within minutes the work was accomplished, the midwife temporarily waved off to the kitchen, and the three were alone.

As their daughter rooted for her first taste of milk, Matt poured his wife and himself some juice from a cool ewer. He gave his wife her glass and drank her and their baby's health.

Lacy grinned and downed the drink. "Now—" she began.

"Ah, ah. I know what you are going to say. I know the arguments. I have heard them—nay, I can recite them in my sleep. Such blending of assets is what God intended of man and woman. Such combination means that the accountings for two separate and distinctly different estates are easier. The administration is simpler. Only the heraldry is the complicated draw, for the wife's sign always combines with the superior husband's." Matt drew closer to the bed and his wife's charming nod. "But I am not your superior husband."

"You are."

"I am your mate."

Her turquoise eyes faceted in glee. "Aye, I know."

"What if I told you I am other things?" He pursed his lips to contain the smile that curved his mouth. He could not and had to move away to refill his goblet.

She sighed. "I seem to remember a conversation in which you told me you were many dastardly things.

All of them were false, too. My heart, I know who you are. And what. I would know you in heaven or in hell. By sight or touch and, barring those, by mere instinct."

He turned, swirling the juice in his glass. "Gerard has done wonders with this reclamation of the Crown's lands."

Lacy blinked. "Aye, but what has that . . . ? Such abrupt transitions are not usual for you, my eloquent man."

"Quick to all inferences, aren't you, my marchioness?"

"With the Sure Arrow as master archer here, I hasten to catch his points as he darts by me."

He strode forward, inches from her beautiful motherly body and her unending love for him shining in her sweet eyes. "Henry and Gerard have presented the Crown with an enormous source of regular income. Lands lost by the Crown over the past decades of civil war have been numerous and costly to the Privy Purse and the Exchequer. Now, with Gerard's good translations of older English documents, he examines all the Crown's land records for the past four centuries."

"Ah, I see. Since William conquered England and—"

"And the De Veres and the Fitzhughs gained their domains at his pleasure. Aye." Matt knelt to his wife and their baby. "Gerard's findings require administration. And collection of taxes from those who over the years came to till it or settle on it without knowledge that it was the possession of the kings and queens of England." He reached out one finger to stroke his Catherine's tiny hand as it rested against her mother's full breast. His eyes drifted to his wife's. "Henry has asked me to administer the changes in the

Midlands. I am also to judge the lands' worthiness, set the rents fairly according to their good yield, and collect them for the Crown. I account for them and take them to London twice yearly. The rest of the year I will travel about in the service of their administration and as judge in the courts I hold. When they can, my wife and children can come with me so that we are always a loving family, never far from each other's hearts."

Tears were falling down Lacy's cheeks. This time he knew it no help to plead that she contain them.

He took her hand and stroked her fingers with his thumb. Her golden wedding ring flickered at him. "For this service unto Henry the Seventh of England, my liege has given me much." He met her adoring eyes. "He gave me you long ago . . . long ago when none of us knew how much I would need you for the rest of my days. He gave me leave to form a family and now count two cherished ones I live to love and would die to protect. A few days ago, he gave me more." He bit his lip and fought bright tears of his own. "Before the Arnolds and Tom and Gerard, Henry did name me Earl Fletcher. I am his liege man as I have never been before. But I am yours and Catherine's more than I could ever be last week or last year. For now I bring you not merely a poor barony but an earldom built not on land but on loyal service."

"Oh, my love"—she leaned forward to kiss his cheek—"ever have you been a king to me."

"Lacy, I was a man of war."

"Now you have become a man of peace. My heart, I know of no man who deserves entitlement more. You are so just, kind to the marrow of your bones."

He thought on that a moment, the first test of his justice on his lips. But his wife had suffered so at the

Arnolds' hands, he needed to find at what point her fear might meet or even entangle her sense of righteousness. For without her leave, he would do nothing in regard to the Arnolds and the disputed land. He would never see her frightened again—or unprotected. Not for Henry or England or all the titles in the world.

He cleared his throat. "I have seen the purchase papers from the Fitzhughs to the Arnolds. The papers are in order, and the price paid by the Arnolds was more than fair. These Arnolds do rightly own the Fitzhugh lands that William the Conqueror did gift the old Fitzhugh family. Therefore, I judge that the Arnolds deserve to return to the land that is rightfully theirs." His eyes searched hers. "What say you?"

She did not blink. "I say you are right."

He wanted to smile at his forgiving wife but—straight-faced—pursued his second point. "Furthermore, to ensure that I stay the hands of the two Arnold men from taking that which could never be theirs, I say Mistress Arnold should hold the land in trust for her husband and, if he dies before her, for their son. She should do the financial reckoning on the land they manage nearest the stream. She should pay the Crown rents. What say you?"

"I say you do the lady justice for her kind assistance to a man and his wife when once they stood within her walls in desperate need of her mercy."

He let his breath escape. He took her hand to kiss her ring. "My heart, you are so sweet a wife and sound a person, I do thank God for you every day."

"So, this means . . ." Lacy settled with a dreamy smile to her pillow. "If you are an earl, you are almost a marquess. So now perhaps you will cease fretting over your barony's inequality with De Vere's."

"I may be your mate, madam. I may also be an earl. But I am still not your equal. You walk before me in any court procession to Henry."

The courage that characterized his wife in brigandine and horned hats or alone in a bed giving birth blazed from her turquoise eyes. "Hear me well, husband, I will walk nowhere without you ever again." Before he raised his finger to argue that such adamance might earn her a reprimand from Henry, she arched two brows at him. "And now I see the thread of your decision about Catherine taking the title of the marchioness De Vere."

He viewed her euphoria and smiled indulgently. "Catherine will take the lands as well. Though, as her father, I would advise her never to give them to anyone, save her firstborn daughter. I believe a woman has as much right to hold land as any man."

Lacy beamed. "I know." She wrinkled her brow. "And our first son will then inherit the barony of Fletcher and his father's earldom."

Matt chuckled. "Aye. If his father can administer his earldom's charge correctly to pass the glory on."

"Never fear. I understand Earl Fletcher has resources to make that an easy task. After all, have you not heard, his wife can do the accounting with the agility of Henry Tudor's master of the exchequer?"

"Aye. I have heard. Better, I have seen this remarkable woman you speak of." He let his lips skim her cheek and her throat. "She came to me in copious garments and a very funny hat. Beneath all that, to my delight, I found she was a wife divine."

"Oh, heavens!" She jumped as she had that first day he'd seen her and fleas bit her.

"What's the matter? Are you ill? In pain? I'll call—"

"No. No. It just occurs to me . . ."

"What?"

"Why, my lord husband, I am not only the marchioness De Vere, I am the baroness Fletcher, and now—in addition—your countess!"

He caught her to him in relief and joy. "My heart, you are my *countless* everything! You, forever you"—he brought her golden wedding ring with its apt inscription to his lips—"and no other."

AUTHOR'S NOTES

"You and No Other" really were words inscribed on medieval wedding rings. Sometimes seen in England engraved with the French version, *"Vous et nul autre,"* these rings found their way to many hands clasped in hasty ceremonies of the type Lacy and Matthew Fletcher heard performed. The marriage vows, as Matt and Lacy recite them at the end of their travail, are—with a few minor modernizations by me for clarity's sake—as they were then. And *aye,* they do include the words "you and no other" as Matt repeats them to his wife.

I heartily hope you enjoyed this, my first Pocket Books historical romance. I enjoyed writing a story that has teased the edges of my writer's imagination for years. As my wonderful writing friends would say, this was a story I felt compelled to write.

Please write to me to tell me how *you* liked it. My address is: 13017 Wisteria Drive, #384, Germantown, MD 20874.

I will respond with news of my next release for Pocket Books, titled *Angel of Midnight,* due out in the summer of 1995. Lady Angelica Forrester is a widow, twice over, who wishes never to wed another man and so abducts the Midnight Devil, who lives like a brigand destroying her villeins' peace of mind. As she barters with him to play the part of her husband and deter those relatives who would wed her to yet another man, Angel finds the Devil wears a dangerous disguise. Not only is he a divinely devious man to fear, he becomes a sinfully luscious man to love.

Happy Reading!

Jo-Ann Power